PRIME DIRECTIVE

Also by Davis Bunn

Speculative fiction *

TRIAL RUN
FLASH POINT
FAULT LINES
EMISSARY
MERCHANT OF ALYSS
THE GOLDEN VIAL
RECRUITS
RENEGADES
ENCLAVE

Novels

THE GREAT DIVIDE
WINNER TAKE ALL
HEARTLAND
LION OF BABYLON
UNSCRIPTED
BURDEN OF PROOF

Miramar Bay series

MIRAMAR BAY
FIREFLY COVE
MOONDUST LAKE
TRANQUILITY FALLS
THE COTTAGE ON LIGHTHOUSE LANE

* *Published under the pen name Thomas Locke*

PRIME DIRECTIVE

Davis Bunn

SEVERN
HOUSE

First world edition published in Great Britain and the USA in 2021
by Severn House, an imprint of Canongate Books Ltd,
14 High Street, Edinburgh EH1 1TE.

Trade paperback edition first published in Great Britain and the USA in 2022
by Severn House, an imprint of Canongate Books Ltd.

severnhouse.com

British Library Cataloguing-in-Publication Data
A CIP catalogue record for this title is available from the British Library.

ISBN-13: 978-0-7278-5026-3 (cased)
ISBN-13: 978-1-78029-785-9 (trade paper)
ISBN-13: 978-1-4483-0524-7 (e-book)

This is a work of fiction. Names, characters, places and incidents
are either the product of the author's imagination or are used fictitiously.
Except where actual historical events and characters are being described
for the storyline of this novel, all situations in this publication are
fictitious and any resemblance to actual persons, living or dead,
business establishments, events or locales is purely coincidental.

All Severn House titles are printed on acid-free paper.

Typeset by Palimpsest Book Production Ltd.,
Falkirk, Stirlingshire, Scotland.
Printed and bound in Great Britain by
TJ Books, Padstow, Cornwall.

ONE

Lieutenant Amanda Bostick completed her presentation in six minutes and fifty-two seconds. Eight seconds under the limit was neither bad nor good. She had been aiming for five minutes flat, but the sector commandant had asked a question. The query should have been held for when Amanda was done, but she did not have the rank to make a point of order. And the commander seemed genuinely interested in having an answer to the question, so Amanda had responded in detail. And still finished in time.

'Let me get this straight.' The Galactic Space Arm's commandant was an iron-hard woman named Rickets. She was spare in the manner of a long-distance runner, so lean as to appear famished. Her reputation was fearsome, her expression as cold as her voice. 'In the past ninety days, sixteen colonists have been murdered, and nobody thought to report it until now?'

Amanda resumed her seat next to her superior and waited. She was good at it. She should be. She had been doing little else for two and a half years. Waiting. For this. Her chance in the limelight.

Commander Rickets hated wasted seconds. She treated every meeting as though it was battleground preparation, where an extra word might cost lives. '*Well?*'

Amanda's superior was the reason she had been straitjacketed for twenty-nine months. She hated the man. She loathed his very shadow. But he held both her future and any hope she might hold for advancement. Amanda had learned silence the hard way.

Her superior was unprepared. He did not consider Amanda's system worth notice. Which was why Amanda had been assigned to oversee the system's lone human outpost.

Silence had never come sweeter than now.

'I am *waiting.*'

Her superior had no choice but to say, 'I will allow the system coordinator to respond, Commander.'

Amanda was instantly on her feet. 'There are four issues,

Commander. First, the Lorian system is officially part of the Arab Protectorate. They agreed to this initial settlement and its limited number of scientists. Until now, the GSA has seen no reason to request the settlement's status be upgraded. Officially, the settlement on Loria is not a colony at all. It remains classed as a scientific outpost.'

'But your report stated we first settled there . . .'

'Sixty-seven years ago.'

'Why is that, I wonder?'

'Land mass is limited on Loria to one hundred and nine islands. The largest is barely a hundred square kilometers. Every island is occupied by sentient Lorians. Our scientists are reluctantly accepted, but their numbers are restricted. One hundred and sixty scientists and support staff were the maximum allowed. The only reason they reported the deaths at all was in order to request replacements so as to return to full strength. In short, until the deaths began, there was no reason to upgrade the system, and every reason to limit our numbers to a small group of analysts.'

The commander eyed her with unblinking intensity. 'You're saying that has changed?'

'That is the second issue. The manner of these deaths has completely shifted our assumptions of the sentient race. We assumed the Lorians were without technology. Instead, we discover they are potentially far ahead of us.'

'Specifics,' the officer rapped.

'There are no metals on Loria, and yet they have managed to create a method of transport based exclusively upon silicates. Apparently, they control these devices through a joining of their collective mental powers. And the devices move by some form of gravity negation. According to the scientific report, there is no evidence of the machine's passage. Not a blade of grass out of place, not a ripple on the sea's surface. That is how the scientists described it.'

'Except for these murders,' the commander corrected.

Amanda decided the comment did not require a response and remained silent.

Rickets said, 'Four issues.'

'The third factor is that there is no military contingent. There was originally. But the chief scientist barraged GSA headquarters with requests for their removal, to be replaced by more scientists. And the Arab Protectorate resented this military encroachment into a system it claimed as its own. After eleven rotations without incident, the troops were removed.' Amanda hesitated, then added, 'The last military officer described her assignment on Loria as boring in the extreme.'

Rickets made a note on her tablet. 'And finally?'

'The scientists did not report them as murders.'

Rickets planted elbows on the table between them. 'Their chief is seeking to *hide* sixteen deaths?'

'Not at all. The deaths were included in the standard quarterly report. As incidents.'

'Sixteen scientists killed by the sentient race do not make an "incident."'

Amanda stood and waited.

Commander Rickets took her silence as the rebuttal Amanda meant it to be, and barked, 'Explain, Lieutenant.'

'The scientists have apparently been accepted as full members of the race. But this means abiding by rules they did not know existed. Rules that are neither written down nor ever expressed out loud.'

'That is *unacceptable.*'

Amanda nodded. She totally agreed.

'They're scientists, not idiots. Why didn't they take precautions?'

'After the first three, the scientists attempted to equip the . . . the word they used was "condemned." They equipped the condemned with portable shields. The machine simply picked up the shielded individual—'

'That is not possible,' Rickets declared. 'Shields *anchor* the wearer.'

'The machine scooped up an entire segment of the island, carried it out to sea, and sank it to the bottom. It held the shield there until the wearer ran out of air.'

Rickets exchanged a look with her subaltern. 'And then?'

'Apparently, the bodies are transmuted into ferns of some sort and hung from a special grove of trees. The scientists suggest that this is an honor accorded to full members—'

'Enough.' Rickets aimed a finger. 'You are to go, you are to assess the situation, and you are to prepare a full field report.'

Amanda's superior rose to his feet. He was so portly his belt dragged against the table's edge. 'Commander, I must protest.'

'Is that so?'

'The subaltern is untrained for fieldwork. There are any number of seasoned officers—'

'Who know nothing of the planet's current status. Is that not so, Colonel?' She thumbed her tablet. 'I have read your efficiency reports of this officer, and I must say I am concerned.'

'Lieutenant Bostick holds some small potential, Commander. Possibly. In a few more years—'

'In fact, Colonel, it is *you* that concerns me. Are you aware that she graduated second in her Academy class? Or that she was considered outstanding by every superior other than you?' She halted his protest by turning to Amanda and saying, 'You are dismissed, Lieutenant.'

'Aye, ma'am.'

'Alert the Lorian outpost and prepare yourself for immediate departure. Clear?'

It required all her self-control not to break into song. 'Crystal, Commander.'

'You will travel with two armed Guardians.'

'Actually, General, the original treaty forbids—'

'Forbids the murder of innocent scientists. I quite agree. Two Guardians that I will personally assign. And a fully armed probe as backup. Whether or not their chief scientist agrees is immaterial. You will meet your non-com officer on the observation deck. I want you outbound with the next available transport, and a full report in ten standard days.' Rickets leaned forward, her voice as hard as her gaze. 'Ten days, Lieutenant. Not an hour more. Your future career depends upon your being on time.'

TWO

Amanda Bostick had learned early and well to hide in plain sight.

She was not by any means unattractive. Instead, she

was a specialist at camouflage. She had learned to accent her most average components. She was slender and used this to mask her speed and tensile strength. She seldom wore make-up, which kept many people from noticing the fullness of her lips and the refined balance to her features. She was by nature both quiet and still, which the more aggressive or competitive members of her corps assumed meant either shyness or lack of ambition. Her raven-dark hair was trimmed to military brevity, forming a soft helmet that drew attention from her burning determination and intelligent gaze.

Amanda had been born twelve miles from Canaveral Spaceport's western boundary. Her family had farmed the land and fished the Atlantic waters for generations. They were simple folk, and proud of their rooted lives. They raised scrawny Florida cattle on nine hundred acres of stumpy marsh and scrubland. They also grew palms on their driest forty acres, supplying the gardeners who tended oceanfront estates. Amanda had often traveled with her brothers to deliver their trees. She loved observing these rich folk who had no idea of the timeless lives and Florida culture that existed a few miles inland.

The lone high school in Titusville had graduated Amanda and her brothers just as they had her forebears, knowing that most of the education they required came beneath the blazing Florida sun. The teachers focused upon the hardcore subjects that made sense to people like Amanda's kin – mechanics and book-keeping and letters. Her family had never found a need for more than a community college education. They were prosperous, set in their ways, and content to stand at the boundary fence and watch other people fly off into the wild blue yonder.

Her childhood friends grew into lovely young women whose aims never went beyond beachside parties and choosing mates from among the local crop. Life was easy and good. Money and jobs were there for the asking. Florida had the best weather control on Earth, thanks to the spaceport's need to maintain its allegiance to the clock. Amanda's grandparents spoke of the state's last hurricane with a fondness that was almost comic.

With the help of several teachers and a sympathetic principal, Amanda hid her ambitions from almost everyone, especially her family. The first they knew of her application to the Georgetown

School of Interplanetary Studies came with the letter announcing she had received a full scholarship. Amanda hid her true aims even then, claiming she merely wanted a government job and this required a full four-year degree. Which was at least partly true, and it satisfied her parents. They did not know she had been accepted into the Galactic Space Arm until the day she arrived home in her sky-blue cadet's uniform, there to say her farewells before shipping out.

For the Academy. On orbit around Ganymede.

It took nine months before her mother would even speak to Amanda by vid-phone. Still now, their monthly recorded messages often showed both of her parents leaking tears.

Amanda watched their newly arrived communication with genuine impatience. She did her best to calmly describe her new assignment, offering them no reason to worry. When she signed off, Amanda left the phone cabin with a relief so intense it felt like guilt. She hefted her valise and headed straight for the departures. Beyond the steel portal and the guards doing final security checks lay her dream. The secret ambition she feared would never be hers.

Planetary assignment. Independent observer. Full authority.

At long last.

THREE

A manda had spent countless free hours in the planetary departures terminal, leaning against the observation balcony's railing and watching the ships. GSA's sector headquarters was an island in space, orbiting the same planetary system for five years before shifting to another. The mobile structure of the empire's command centers was one reason for a political system that had remained stable for nine and a half centuries.

Sector headquarters in fact held three different cultures. The Galactic Space Arm was ruled by the Diplomats, the point at which the military arm joined with the empire's central government. Diplomats could be drawn from any profession, bureaucrat or civilian included, but more than half came from the GSA and all were then trained at the Diplomacy School on the empire's capital planet.

Since her first day at the Academy, Amanda's aim had always been focused on Diplomacy. But the constant downchecks from her current commanding officer had crushed all such hopes. Now the highest she could possibly achieve was avoiding a formal discharge from the service.

Flying home in disgrace, being deposited in the humid prison of a Florida summer, formed the basis for regular nightmares.

The sector headquarters' second population consisted of the civilians who supplied, serviced, fed, counseled, and managed the GSA's daily existence. Most of these were drawn from whatever planetary system they currently orbited. Only a select few were transferred from five-year employment contracts to permanent positions. Competition was intense, and by all accounts vicious.

The third culture was based on interplanetary tourism. One of the few places where the three groups interacted was on the observation deck. But even here distinct separations were strictly maintained.

The GSA headquarters was shaped like an old-fashioned ice-cream cone. The upper rounded top held all senior quarters, navigation, comm-links to the empire's center, and a cockpit that was employed only once every five years.

The main flight deck formed the central portion of the GSA. A thick core connected the upper decks from the lower levels of maintenance and engineering. The flight deck itself was a flat doughnut whose outer face offered a shielded view into deep space.

A vast balcony curved around the central core, a good nine hundred paces in circumference. Tourists were restricted to a lounge halfway around the core from where Amanda entered. She was one of the few GSAs who had ever ventured over to the far side, where a single drink cost more than her monthly paycheck. When shipmates asked what she had been doing, Amanda replied honestly. She wanted to observe the beasts at play.

The observation deck was one of the few positions from which the sector headquarters' true scale could be observed. The largest

tourist liner was dwarfed by the hold. The entire structure had
been designed with one aim in mind: to overwhelm the visitor.
Amanda had studied the strategy in great detail, as it formed one
component of the initial Diplomacy exam. Military vessels lined
the interior walls. The six ledges that opened below her could
contain a hundred and fifty battleships and twice as many fighters.
Far in the distance opened the starlit void. The sector headquarters
completed a slow rotation every sixty minutes. When Amanda
entered, the planetary system with its cloudy blue blanket and six
moons was dead center. She would have halted and breathed in
the prospect of freedom, at least for a moment, except for the
voice that greeted her.

'Major Bostick?'

An olive-skinned man with the flashing good looks of a courtier
saluted her. The gray coverall and sergeant's stripes were a lie.
Amanda knew this within an instant of turning around.

Her early days in her family's marshlands had taught her many
things. One was how to read tells. A tell was the means by which
a hunter identified both prey and danger. There were a hundred
different tells Amanda saw within the space of two breaths. All
of them told her that she faced an officer masquerading as a non-
commissioned grunt.

But all she said was, 'It's Lieutenant Bostick.'

'Not anymore, ma'am.' He offered her a file embossed with the
GSA's official seal. 'Commander's compliments, Major. Two of
Loria's residents carry the rank of captain within the GSA's scientific arm. Commander Rickets thought it best to assign you a
temporary brevet. She wanted no blowback from the locals.'

She pretended to study the file's two pages. 'And you are?'

'Sergeant Hamoud.'

He was a head taller than she was, and he carried himself with
the languid ease of a professional dancer. It suggested a wealthy
background and the clout to win himself whatever position
money could buy. Amanda shut the file and said, 'Think carefully
before you answer. Your reply will shape our entire relationship.
For the last time, tell me who you are.'

The dark eyes flashed momentarily, and the jaunty ease vanished.
He handed over his GSA ID. 'What I was before has no bearing
now, Major.'

'And yet I insist upon knowing.'

His spark of very real anger made him more handsome still. 'Flight Captain.'

Which meant Amanda faced an experienced military pilot. 'What happened?'

'I was accused of interfering in my home planet's politics.' The words were clipped now, precise enough to reveal the carefully hidden accent. 'I was stripped of my commission.'

The liquid gaze revealed a man enduring the harsh flames of regret. Amanda had a hundred more questions. But she had learned enough for the moment, and she did not wish to add to his naked distress. 'Hamoud. That is a name from the Arab Protectorate?'

'Aye, Major. The Omani system.'

More than likely his clan had been involved in interplanetary politics for generations. Hamoud did not strike her as the sort who might be easily corrupted. Which suggested he had been presented with a blood oath, one set in place by the clan elder who dominated both Hamoud's home fief and his family's fortunes. She said, 'I grew up reading the legends of your worlds. I made the Arab Protectorate the focus of my Academy thesis. I have dreamed of going there since childhood.'

The fact that she had spoken in System Arabic pushed the man back a step. He shaped several responses, but the words did not come.

Hamoud's silence was as satisfactory a reply as Amanda could have possibly hoped for. She decided it was time for a confession of her own. 'There is a grand total of one hundred and sixteen scientists and research staff currently on Loria. The fact that this remains a small-scale outpost sixty years after first contact is the only reason my superior officer assigned me as planetary observer. He was inches away from having me summarily dismissed and shipped Earthside.'

Amanda gave him a chance to respond. Which Hamoud did, in a very Arabic fashion. His dark gaze cleared from the pain of his own declaration. He seemed to see her clearly for the very first time.

Amanda went on, 'I assume you have participated in crisis interventions?'

'Eleven times, Major.'

'Which is why Commander Rickets assigned you. I am grateful

for her choice. And here is what I propose. To the outside world, we are major and sergeant. Between us, we are student and teacher. Do you find that acceptable?'

'Very.'

'The commander ordered us off-world in an hour.' Amanda hefted her single case. 'Let's go resurrect our two careers.'

FOUR

The GSA transport *Invictus* was a medium-sized star cruiser, minus all military markings since its destinations included worlds in outlying protectorates. Once shipboard, Amanda saw little of Hamoud. He and the third member of their little band, a Corporal Nasim, bunked in general quarters with the other non-coms. Amanda's temporary rank afforded her a private cabin. She could reach out and touch both side walls at the same time. The steel deck was scarred, the small desk was battered, and the screen on her comm-link was cracked. But it was the first time since leaving Earth that she could shut a door and close out the universe.

Amanda shared her mess quarters with eleven scientists from Interplanetary Disease Control, on their way to monitor an outbreak of some unknown sickness on Jubble. Because of the mission's urgency, Jubble was to be their first stopover.

They arrived two days later ship's-time and remained in close orbit, taking on nothing, not even water. Jubble had officially been quarantined while they were underway; the message was waiting when they emerged from n-space. The chief IDC scientist complained loudly as they were stuffed into a single lander. But the shuttle would remain on Jubble until quarantine was lifted, and the *Invictus* skipper refused to sacrifice a second. Amanda watched the scientists fret over which of their treasured equipment would be left behind, then helped them load. When they sealed the portal, the vessel was so jam-packed that most of the scientists could not even sit down. Amanda stood by the hold's single window long after the lander was no longer visible. Two and a half years starside and she had never been on a single planet outside Earth's system.

A few hours after leaving Jubble's orbit, Amanda walked the central passage leading to the ship's meager library. She had read through all her files on Loria and wanted to access whatever unofficial records might exist. For that, she needed the permission of a ship's officer. As she walked from her assigned hold to the central keep, she found a pair of non-coms on their knees, scraping points along the corridor's walls where rust had bubbled the paint. She was shocked to discover the two men were Hamoud and Nasim. The former pilot glanced up, recognized her, and flushed crimson before turning back to his work.

A ship's ensign leaned against the side wall, his tattooed arms crossed over a belly as large as a water-barrel. The ensign grinned as Amanda passed.

She gave no sign that she noticed anything at all, just another officer coolly ignoring the lesser ranks. Inwardly, however, she was mortified. The Arab Protectorate was an outlying realm loosely bonded with the empire. Their fierce independence was only matched by their pride. The ensign no doubt had recognized Hamoud as a disgraced former officer and was taking great pleasure in grinding him down.

As with most military transports, entry to the vessel's operational decks and the flight center were accessed through a broad vestibule known as the duty room. A shipboard cadet was seated at the security desk, pretending to be busy. He was a year or so older than Amanda and saw nothing in her ship's coverall that suggested a need to do more than ask, 'You lost, ma'am?'

'No. Major Bostick, requesting a moment of the duty officer's time.'

The cadet bolted to his feet. 'Sorry, Major. I didn't . . . They'll want to know what this is about.'

'I wish to study shipboard records.'

'One moment, Major.'

They left her cooling her heels for over an hour. Amanda did not mind in the least. She took up position beside the exit and did her best to disappear in plain sight. She observed the shipboard routine with the quiet relish of a famished traveler being offered a seat at the main table.

The flight deck opened directly ahead of where she stood. Every time a crew member came or went, she feasted upon glimpses of the naval world and the star-flecked void of deep space. She knew the view was computer-generated estimates of their positions, traveling as they were through n-space. She did not care in the slightest.

'Major . . . Bostick, is it?'

'Aye, sir.' She came to rigid attention before the gray-haired executive officer. 'I was wondering if I might be granted access to transport records.'

'You're outbound for . . .'

'Loria, sir.'

'Right. Our next port of call.'

'Roger that. I've been going through the official files. There have been seven supply runs in the colony's history. I was wondering if I might be allowed to study the naval records.'

The empire's transport system kept two sets of records. Those passed on to GSA sector HQ were distilled to terse bites. In most cases, a single line was enough to state that the transport landed, did its duty, and departed on schedule. But these notes were derived from much longer reports, written or dictated into the ship's own log. These transport logs were available to any skipper visiting a world for the first time. Such records contained anything the skippers found noteworthy, from the personality of planetary leaders to the finest places to eat.

'Highly irregular,' the exec responded.

'Understood, sir. But we're facing a huge question mark and we're going in blind. Ten percent of the scientific colony has been killed in the past ninety days.'

The exec's eyebrows rose a notch. 'Not another infection.'

'No, sir. They've run into difficulties with the world's sentient race.'

'What kind of trouble are we talking about?'

'That's just it, sir. We don't know. The scientists list the deaths as mere sidebars. Noted and dismissed.'

The exec was burned almost black by either genetic heritage or some distant sun. It added an intensity to his squint. 'I'll allow this, so long as it remains off the books.'

'Understood, sir.'

'You'll make no note of anything you discover in your own records.'

'Not a peep, sir. And thank you.'

He turned to the cadet on desk duty and said, 'Alert the library.'

'Aye, sir.'

Amanda saluted and started to turn away. Then she pretended to be struck by a sudden thought.

'Something else, Major?'

'Not if it means stepping out of bounds, sir. But, well . . . It's just . . .'

'Let's hear it.'

'Sir, I shared my hold with the Jubble mission.'

He nodded understanding. 'They off-loaded and we took on no passengers because of the quarantine. Must be lonely back there.'

'Like a pebble in a barrel, sir.'

'You want to shift quarters, then.'

'I could. But, sir, I'm going in with two non-coms I don't know. A team of three in potentially hostile terrain. I thought . . .'

'You want to get to know them.'

'If I'm not breaking regs. Aye, sir.'

'I suppose we could look the other way for two days.' He turned to the cadet. 'Cut orders reassigning that pair. Their names?'

'Sergeant Hamoud and Corporal Nasim.'

'Hamoud . . . Not the former pilot.'

'Aye, sir. You know him?'

'I know of his situation.' The exec started to say more, then thought better of it. 'I meant what I said about making no record of your findings, Major.'

She snapped off her finest salute. 'I won't even take notes.'

FIVE

Hamoud and Nasim were preparing a meal when Amanda returned from the ship's library. Nothing was said about their sudden shift in living conditions. Which Amanda found a thoroughly satisfactory response. Instead, they filled the hold's ready room with Arabic fragrances. A trio of places was set in as formal an arrangement as the ready room's meager supplies permitted.

The oval-shaped hold was rimmed by private chambers. The central area contained a galley and ready room with four long mess tables. A large vid-screen and comfy chairs dominated the rear section. Along the wall opposite the galley stood a scattering of exercise equipment. A larger gym was positioned directly below the ship's central hold, but on many transports this was considered off-limits to all but crew members and the most senior passengers. Hamoud waved a spoon in greeting and called, 'We eat in five minutes, Major. Join us.'

'Give me ten,' Amanda said. She showered and dressed in a clean ship's coverall and joined them in nine. The two men served her as they would an honored guest. The rice was flavored with cardamom and raisins. There were mulberry leaves, at least in appearance, wrapped around a lovely concoction of lightly pickled vegetables and mint. Even the lowly protein packs had been elevated to some lofty delicacy that resembled lamb. The two men accepted Amanda's compliments with gestures as formal as a stage play. She knew it was their way of declaring thanks without speaking a word. She had read about the Arabs for years, ever since childhood, but only met a handful, and never had the opportunity to break through their boundary walls of customs and secrecy. Until now. It was as fine a meal as she had ever known.

She told them what she had been doing, and said, 'The captain's logs aren't of any help. Of the eleven previous transport landings, two did not bother to say more than that they had come and gone. The others describe a science colony with no interest in discussing their work. The landscape is monochrome. Everything is some shade of pink. Plants, ocean, earth. Even the clouds. The scientists seemed reluctant to turn away from their work long enough to thank the transport staff for the supplies.'

Hamoud asked, 'They're hiding something?'

'The exec officers of two ships requested tours. Both were granted. The summaries make for a boring read. The planet has no known resources. The sentient race are telepaths, which has created numerous difficulties. Communication remains basic in the extreme. The scientists write articles that are of no interest to anyone except other scientists. They have made no discovery of note. The execs were both glad to return shipside.'

Nasim rose and began clearing the table. Hamoud observed, 'Something troubles you, yes?'

'Not about the planet. Our mission. Why are we going? I know what our mission statement says. What I don't understand is why the commandant is interested. Sixteen deaths are a big deal only because of the colony's size.'

'Sixteen *murders*,' Hamoud corrected.

'Sixteen incidents, according to the official reports,' Amanda replied. 'I flagged Loria's losses mostly in the hope of escaping from my superior officer.'

'You succeeded.'

'Yes, but *why*? What is there about this situation that justifies the sector commandant involving herself personally?'

Hamoud leaned back and waited. Nasim took the silence as a signal and returned to the table. Only when the corporal was seated did the sergeant speak. 'I might have heard something.'

Amanda asked, 'Are you telepaths?'

Both men smiled. Hamoud replied, 'We are from the same clan. Our families have been intertwined for generations beyond count.'

Nasim added, 'In our dialect, the word for friend and brother are the same.'

Hamoud went on, 'But no, to answer your question, we are not telepaths.'

Amanda said, 'What did you hear?'

Hamoud rose from the table. 'I need a map.'

SIX

While at the Academy, Amanda had gained her civilian pilot's license. But unlike other cadets she had never sought a place in the Fleet Arm. The requirements were extremely stiff, the competition fierce. Far more was demanded than simply being able to pilot a vessel. Among the most difficult elements, as far as Amanda was concerned, was three-dimensional map reading.

With time and intense effort, she had managed to pass the required basic exam on positioning and n-space mapping between stellar positions. But even after years of study and hours of private tutelage, she was still often worried that she had gotten something wrong. The trick, she knew, was to ignore the pretty lights and see it as interlinked sectors with specific conduits for n-passage. The lights were not stars to a pilot, unless they signified the launch point or destination. All the others were concentrations of force. But whenever Amanda was faced with the prospect of maps and positioning, what she still secretly saw was a three-dimensional array of jewels. A multitude of realms that would someday be open to her. Stellar systems filled with mystery and adventure. Beckoning.

Hamoud's map station was the one favored by most pilots, a squat cone slightly broader than his hand. He pressed the central button and the galaxy swam into being. He took one of the black rings set into the base and placed it on the middle finger of his left hand. Pilots were taught from day one to keep their right hand free to handle a ship's controls.

The ring covered his left hand in a glove of electric currents. He swung two fingers as if he were conducting a symphony of lights and colors. The map swiveled, tightened, refocused. One double-star system began softly pulsing. 'Here is the Lorian system. Two suns, one solitary planet. Very rare. It holds the lone transit-point to the Arab Protectorate.'

'Which is the only reason the system holds an interest to anyone but scientists.'

'Correct.' Hamoud changed the map's perspective so that the system shifted to one side. 'Out here in empty space lies a planet known simply as Random.'

'I've . . . I don't know that name.'

'Few do. Officially, it does not exist. Random is an unstable world. No star. We do not know its precise location. Only that it is located somewhere well outside the Lorian system. And that it holds a secret mercenary base.'

She straightened. 'Space pirates? Really?'

Nasim said, 'We have heard rumors for over a century that a miserable colony existed on this starless world. Most preferred to believe it was a myth, pirates having a secret haven in this day and age.'

'But we continued to lose ships for which there is no other explanation,' Hamoud went on. 'Then last year we were approached by an officer who confirmed the pirate world's existence and said he would spy for us. In return, he wanted gold and citizenship.'

'Who is "we"?'

'The Omani system. A preliminary payment was received. Citizenship would only be granted if he could supply us with the planet's actual location. Apparently, only a few senior officers are entrusted with that information. We offered to give him a beacon. But all returning ships and personnel are thoroughly searched.'

Nasim added, 'To be granted the right to visit the Omani moon is a sign of status among the pirates.'

Hamoud said, 'According to this officer, the pirates have grown far more powerful than anyone expected. They intended to establish a beachhead on one of Loria's uninhabited islands.'

'Uninhabited by humans,' Amanda corrected.

'Positioned halfway around the globe from the scientists' colony,' Hamoud went on. 'Safe from observation.'

'Their intent must have been to prey upon ships passing through this n-space bottleneck.'

Hamoud nodded. 'The officer was assigned duty as leader of the landing party. They were taking no chances. They sent a battlecruiser. Weapons hot.'

'A battleship to an unarmed planet,' Amanda said.

'They carried such force in case the empire had anticipated the move and prepared a surprise attack.'

'So what happened?'

'We have no idea.'

For a disgraced former pilot, Hamoud's intel was astonishing. Amanda had heard how certain protectorates maintained unofficial diplomatic ties through officers in GSA or the civilian services. She did not want to break the free flow of information by asking questions Hamoud might not wish to answer. Instead, she focused upon the one clearly identifiable issue. 'So the sixteen deaths among the science colony . . .?'

'Began at that precise moment,' Hamoud confirmed. 'To the very hour Random lost contact with their battle group.'

'This is why you were demoted, isn't it? Enemies of your protectorate within the empire's government stifled your intelligence.'

The two men exchanged a look. Nasim said, 'Now tell her the
rest.'

'There's more?'

Hamoud gave a tentative shrug. 'We are now shifting from hard
intelligence to pure conjecture.'

'She needs to know,' Nasim said.

'Tell me. Please.'

'It has to do with our assignment,' Hamoud said. 'And the time
issue.'

She said, 'Ten days.'

'You are aware that the Arab Protectorate officially controls the
Lorian system. Obviously, this lone planet is not the issue, but
rather the n-space portal. And our demand that the Protectorate
maintain its independence.'

Amanda looked from one to the other. 'They sent us to fail?'

'Not the commandant,' Hamoud replied. 'I trust Rickets with
my life.'

'As do I,' Nasim said.

'But there are others who resent the Protectorate's loose relationship, its quasi-independent status. This galls certain generals
no end. They want us brought into line. Or crushed. Either option
is fine by them.'

'Commandant Rickets disagrees,' Nasim said. 'But quietly, quietly.'

Amanda could see it now. 'Rickets' foes want to use the murders
as an excuse to invade. Plant a permanent GSA military base on
Loria. Pressure you to accept full GSA membership.'

Hamoud nodded. 'So what does the commandant do, but assign
the mission to a young untested subaltern whose superior thinks
she is barely worth keeping.'

'And two recently demoted Fleet Arm officers,' Nasim said.

'And give them no time at all to succeed.' Hamoud was smiling
now. 'Any of her opponents who check on us will assume we are a
failure in the making. They are delighted to see us go. The timeline
only confirms that Rickets has already accepted the inevitable.'

Amanda said, 'If you are successful on Loria, it would do much
to heal your rift with the GSA and restore your careers.'

'*We*,' Hamoud corrected. 'If *we* are successful.'

She wished she could share their good humor. 'Can we succeed?'

'Without question,' Hamoud replied.

'Rickets would only send us if we held a genuine chance of success,' Nasim said.

'Stop the killings,' Hamoud said. 'Solve the mystery behind these deaths. And in the process, strip away the generals' excuse for invading.'

Amanda felt overwhelmed by the pressure of time and responsibility and the need to not let the commandant down. But all she said was, 'Thank you for trusting me.'

SEVEN

After clearing up from the meal, they spread their equipment over two long mess tables and began a final inspection. The scope and thoroughness of their gear left Amanda mildly breathless. The commandant's written orders were placed where they had dined. The key question, the one they circled back to repeatedly, was the last sentence: *If a threat is deemed to be either beyond direct control or unidentifiable, you are hereby authorized to extract the colony. Direct GSA military intervention remains a final option. Good hunting.*

They parsed the orders, discussed the meaning, and tried to determine what would be registered as an official success. Amanda felt the pressure to live up to Rickets' trust mounting with every passing minute.

When she finally retreated to her cabin, Amanda did not expect to sleep. The prospect of landing on Loria was compounded by the anticipation of leading a mission with a genuine purpose. She was not merely free of her despised superior. She was doing what she had dreamed of since university. Of course she wouldn't sleep.

But her exhaustion proved a potent elixir. She was gone the instant her head hit the pillow. The next thing she knew was a soft tapping on her door.

For a moment, Amanda had no idea where she was. Then the tapping came again, metal upon metal. Soft, polite, insistent.

Amanda slipped into her coverall and hit the switch unlocking her portal. 'Yes?'

Nasim smiled apologetically and handed her a steaming cup of tea. 'You are summoned.'

'Who by?'

'You're to report to the bridge. That's all we've been told.'

She entered the fresher and finished the tea before she emerged. The same barrel-belly ensign slouched by the exit, surveying the line of gear on the mess tables. Amanda assumed the glittering eyes meant there was a shipboard black market for pilfered material.

Hamoud was checking the charges on their holstered sidearms, a chore they had done twice the previous night. He studiously avoided even glancing at the smirking ensign. Amanda said, 'Sergeant Hamoud, you are to accompany me.'

'Aye, Major.'

The ensign pushed off the wall. 'The skipper didn't say anything about that one coming along.'

She ignored him. 'Corporal, you are ordered to remain on duty here. Seal the hold upon our departure. Under no circumstances are you permitted to leave your station. If anyone tries to force entry, you are ordered to fire on them.'

'Aye, Major.'

She addressed the scowling ensign for the first time. 'Lead on, sailor.'

The transport's bridge covered two floors. The lower deck held all support-staff stations, including logistics, engineering, and maintenance. The control room was only a third its size, and ended at a railing that overlooked both the lower floor and the monitor portals dominating the ship's bow. The same cadet ushered Amanda onto the bridge and announced, 'Major Bostick reporting as ordered, sir.'

'Thanks for joining us, Major.' The *Invictus* was skippered by a man named Barrat, a lantern-jawed older man with a general's bearing. He glanced at Hamoud, and his gaze tightened. 'Do I know you?'

'Sergeant Hamoud is my second, sir.'

'Hamoud. Of course.' He returned his attention to Amanda. 'I assume you're aware of why I summoned you, Major.'

'No, sir, actually I'm not.'

'The situation on Jubble requires a change in plans. Your request for a lander is denied.'

Amanda heard every component of his unspoken message. He addressed her with the total authority of a captain underway. His tone carried years of dealing with passengers and planetary assignments. She heard the ticking clock that dictated his journey's parameters.

Not to mention the time pressure she faced.

She knew this discussion could have been carried out in Barrat's private quarters, away from the bridge staff who now pretended not to observe. But the captain had chosen to handle this here because she was young. Inexperienced. Of minor importance. Easily molded to his will. And dismissed.

Amanda responded in the same manner she had last employed with her despised superior. It was as though the years of hiding herself away had compressed her emotions into a single pulsing knot. Waiting for just such a moment as this to go on high alert and reveal her burning fury in the midst of an icy calm. 'I did not request anything, sir.'

The captain was forced to swallow his next stage of attack. 'I thought . . .' He turned to his exec. 'Hand me that order.'

'Here you go, Skipper.'

'Right.' He frowned over the portable panel, then stabbed the illuminated letters. 'Here it is in black and white. A lander—'

'Was *ordered*,' Amanda finished. 'By the *sector commander*. I have not *requested* anything.'

He flushed. 'I'm not going to parse words with you, Major. The Jubble quarantine robbed us of the lander originally assigned to your team.'

'Understood, sir.'

Her seeming agreement unsettled him. 'I'm sure we can find some adequate alternative in stores—'

'Excuse me, Captain. But that is not your decision to make.'

The executive officer shot Amanda a warning glance, which she pretended not to see. Barrat's voice took on a graveled edge. 'As skipper of his vessel, I assure you it is most *certainly* within my purview to—'

'All due respect, sir. But those orders were cut by *your* superior. The sector commandant specifically ordered—'

'Do not attempt to tell me my business!'

'—Ordered me and my team to maintain strict quarantine. No contact with the planet. Under no circumstances are we to—'

'Circumstances have changed!'

'Very good, sir. As soon as we fall from n-space I will send an urgent communiqué to HQ requesting—'

'Out of the question!'

'Then my mission is hereby canceled.' Amanda's voice remained soft, calm, utterly disconnected from the skipper's ire. 'As per your orders.'

'*I am not ordering any such thing!*'

All eyes were on her now as she replied, 'You are officially choosing to revoke a direct command from your superior. I have no choice in the matter. I cannot go against *your* commander's express wishes. I will return to base and request—'

'*Get out!*'

She snapped off her finest salute. 'Sir.'

EIGHT

Only when they were back in the hold, with the portal sealed and the ship's crew shut out, did she give in to queasy tremors. Amanda sat at the table with the commandant's orders spread out before her. And despised herself. Was this her fate? Would she create enemies wherever she went? Hiding her blade in such a velvet calm did not mean she was right. Why could she not simply go along and get along, as everyone else in the department had managed with her despised superior? Why did she seek confrontation? Which was what she knew she had just done. Again. A tactic she had used since childhood. Her father and brothers had spent her growing-up years shouting the same invectives. Stubborn. Sneaky. Loving to attack and then slink away.

Just like now.

The ship's comm system chimed with the tone assigned to the comm deck. The exec's face appeared on the wall monitor. 'Major Bostick?'

She did not bother to rise. 'Aye, sir.'

'You are assigned landing craft four, port bay, deck seven. Prepare to offload in six hours.'

She did not respond because he had already signed off.

The exec's stony features remained imprinted on her brain as she rose and headed for her cabin to gather up her personal items.

The officer's expression had said it all.

She had gained another enemy.

At Hamoud's suggestion, they held to the standard shipboard schedule and took a rest period. Before doing so, Nasim sealed the main portal and set a pair of security alarms. Amanda felt a burning shame as she entered her cabin. She was certain her argument with the captain left them vulnerable to shipboard thieves. And her two team members knew it.

She slept in snatches, fighting her way through troublesome dreams. Three hours later, the security alarm sounded. Amanda was first into the main hold. Whoever had triggered the alert had vanished, which was good because she had left her sidearm in the cabin.

It seemed the men were as restless as Amanda. Without asking, Nasim made them strong black tea, and they got busy hauling their gear to the landing craft. All of them openly wore sidearms with the power light blinking amber, signaling that they worked with their weapons' safeties off. Between trips, they kept both the lander and their hold locked and alarmed.

The shuttle was battered and ancient, and smelled of cramped quarters and hard use and farm animals and human sweat. But Hamoud checked the controls and did a slow and careful sweep of the engines, then declared himself satisfied.

The connecting corridors remained oddly empty. Their confrontation with the ship's captain had made them pariahs to the crew. The three of them were sweat-stained and exhausted by the time their craft was loaded. As they sealed the airlock and readied for departure, Amanda heard the unspoken message loud and clear.

The *Invictus* skipper was livid. Barrat would find a way to exact revenge. It was only a matter of time.

When their gear was stowed and lashed into place, Hamoud slipped into the pilot's seat, hit the comm-link, and said, 'LC Four to bridge. We are sealed and ready for departure.'

'Roger, LC. Hold for release in three minutes and counting.'

'Three minutes, roger.' He turned to Amanda and said, 'Would you care to act as co-pilot, Major?'

Now that they were a vessel underway, Amanda's rank was subservient to the ship's pilot. 'What about Nasim?'

'Unfortunately, Major, the corporal has all the piloting abilities of a groundworm.'

'It is a shame,' Nasim replied, 'that your brain-eating virus has reached such a critical level.'

'In the corporal's hands, this ship would soon be orbiting an asteroid no one but Nasim could ever locate.'

'So much potential,' Nasim responded. 'Wasted on a man whose brains belong in a goat.'

'That is Sergeant Goat to you, Corporal.'

Nasim responded with a comment in a dialect that Amanda was certain could not have been found in any book on military protocol. She also knew they were doing this for her benefit. It was unprofessional for her eyes to burn in gratitude. She slipped into the co-pilot's seat and secured her straps. 'I earned my license at the Academy. But only because the examiner was feeling extremely generous that day.'

'Never mind,' Hamoud said. 'I am an extremely good pilot.'

'For a goat,' Nasim agreed. 'Actually, compared with a wide variety of farm animals, he is not at all bad.'

Hamoud made a process of checking the monitors, and said to Amanda, 'I have served under Commander Rickets on three missions. And I know what she would say right now.'

Amanda asked, 'And that is?'

'It all comes down to results.'

'So, you're saying, nothing's changed.'

'No, Major. I'm saying, if you succeed here, if you return having identified a solution to this crisis, all your adversaries will be silenced.'

The comm-link came to life. 'Bridge to LC. Release in five, four, three, two, dropping shields.'

The lander rose from its station. When the light above the exit went green, Hamoud tapped the power-lever forward.

Space.

NINE

Flight crews operated with a greater sense of mission purpose when the bridge had a view of space. Amanda had found the windowless training vessels both oppressive and claustrophobic. The sensations vanished when she was transferred to a bridge with wall monitors. It did not matter that she knew full well these viewports showed computer-generated sequences of stellar patterns. She wanted to *see*. She wanted to *experience*.

Because their shuttle was never intended to enter n-space, there was no need for the extremely expensive systems required to determine and show positioning within the nothingness of a hyperlink. Instead, there was a real window that stretched across the space before both pilot stations, half as tall as Amanda.

The view was breathtaking.

Hamoud said, 'The situation you faced with the skipper is far more common than you may think.'

Amanda reluctantly tore her attention away from space. 'I'm sorry, what?'

'My clan has a saying for such situations,' Hamoud said.

Nasim added a comment in dialect, which Hamoud translated as 'Better to be an irritant than to be ignored. Even a flea can change a camel's direction.'

'Or a goat's,' Nasim added.

Amanda did not respond because she had no idea what to say. The men's concern was touching because it was genuine. They seemed to find nothing wrong with her silence.

The pod's main engine drummed softly as they accelerated away from the transport. The noise reminded Amanda of an unbalanced

fan they had used on her family's rear porch. Every time the fan
swept around, it rattled. The sound was so repetitive and constant
that Amanda had come to think of it as the house chattering through
humid sunsets, joining in their evening conversations in a language
all its own.

It was good to have such memories with her now, because
everything she saw was completely and utterly alien. Loria filled
more than half the viewport. The globe was a dusky pink, utterly
unlike any planet she had ever studied. Hamoud must have been
thinking the same thing, for he said, 'It looks like the face of an
angry infant.'

'Strange,' Nasim agreed. 'What makes for pink clouds?'

'They have an abundance of silicates,' Amanda said. 'And little
else.'

Hamoud said, 'Try to raise the colony again.'

'Roger.' Nasim swung his chair around to the side console and
keyed in. 'Lorian Scientific Colony, this is GSA Planetary Adviser
and team confirming our approach. Please respond.'

Hamoud gave the silence a few beats, then asked, 'You're
broadcasting on open frequency?'

'All channels,' Nasim confirmed.

Watching the globe expand before her helped Amanda concen-
trate. 'What if Rickets knew about the missing pirate
battleship?'

'She knows,' Hamoud insisted. 'Of that I am utterly certain.
Commander Rickets knows everything that happens in her sector.'

'And what if this is why she sent you two?'

'I have assumed that from the outset,' Hamoud agreed.

'So we haven't heard from the colony. Which means we have
not officially supplied them with our ETA.' She looked at both
men. 'Why don't we swing around to the planet's other side and
have a look for ourselves?'

'In case things get hot later,' Hamoud said, nodding.

'We will need to take great care,' Amanda said. 'There's no
telling how the pirates responded to a lost ship.'

'I am always careful,' Hamoud replied.

Nasim added, 'For a goat.'

TEN

They reached parking orbit above a coral globe.

The viewport was filled with a rainbow of pinkish shades, everything from a dark ocher to the lightest pastel. Amanda did not need to read the instruments to know they hovered just beyond the planet's atmospheric boundary. Directly below their station drifted a pale crimson veil.

Hamoud asked no one in particular, 'Have you ever seen the like?'

Nasim had squeezed into the space between the two pilot's chairs. 'You say this planet has no metals?'

'None whatsoever,' Amanda replied. 'That's according to both the science reports and the initial planetary surveys.'

'If I did not know that, my first thought would be sunlight seen through particles of oxidized iron crystals,' Hamoud said. 'It is iron that colors sand red. I should know. The deserts of our world have an abundance of it. We are known as humankind's second red planet.'

Nasim said, 'Perhaps they forgot to check the atmosphere for drifting molecular metals.'

Hamoud tched. 'Not for sixty years.'

'Actually, the first GSA survey was over a century ago,' Amanda said. 'The sentient race showed no interest whatsoever in making contact. The surveyors were not even sure they had the power of physical speech. In fact, they had the distinct impression most of the locals did not notice them at all.'

'A new molecular form of silicon crystal, perhaps,' Nasim said. 'One that refracts all light in the shades we observe.'

'Perhaps,' Hamoud agreed doubtfully. 'What now, Major?'

'You're seeing no sign of other vessels?'

Hamoud gestured to the instrument panel. 'Sensors indicate no activity.'

Amanda rose from her seat. 'Then we send down our probe.'

*   *   *

Landing vehicles came in three basic types. Military transports, or MLVs, were massive, intended to carry an entire squad and all their gear. The smallest pods were known as buckets among the cadets, and nowadays were normally restricted to training runs. They held four passengers with very little equipment, no fresher, and had originally been designed for quick up-and-down runs. Most starships had replaced them with a newer brand of vehicle.

Amanda's LV was primarily designed for civilian use and could hold a maximum of twelve plus equipment. The unused seats folded down into the floor. There was a fresher of sorts, very cramped. Their equipment formed a floor-to-ceiling pile down the middle of the rear hold. To either side, they had carved out two sleeping spaces, just large enough to stretch out bedrolls. The rudimentary galley was on the side where Amanda would sleep, granting the men a fraction more space. There was no mess table, no space for downtime. They unpacked the probe, tested the systems, set it in the airlock, then returned to their seats. Amanda stared out of the viewport at the pink planet and thought she would be quite content to sit here for a week. No problem whatsoever.

'Launching probe,' Hamoud said.

The airlock sighed, then recycled. The probe was their largest single piece of equipment, a spear-shaped unit as long as her outstretched arms. Amanda watched as it emerged around the LV's starboard side, drifted down to where the pink veil began, and hovered.

'Equipment check,' Hamoud said.

'Checking,' Nasim confirmed.

Amanda desperately wanted to be the hand on the controls, but she was forced by her status as crew leader to delegate. The absence of anything to do except watch the monitors was unexpectedly frustrating.

'All systems in the green,' Nasim said.

'Beginning descent,' Hamoud said.

Nasim had swiveled his chair around so as to face the navigator's station. The LV had two large monitors, one stationed between the pilots and the other at the center of Nasim's controls. They both showed an identical image of drifting pink clouds.

Hamoud asked, 'How far down do the clouds extend?'

'At this rate of descent, five minutes and counting,' Nasim replied.

Hamoud glanced over. 'You want to speed things up?'

'Let's hold to this velocity,' Amanda said. 'Any sign of our presence being registered?'

'There is nothing,' Nasim replied. 'No signals. No radar. No weapons. Not even birds.'

'Atmosphere?'

'High nitrogen content. Otherwise, within human norms.' Nasim was silent for a moment, then, 'Interesting.'

'What?'

'Instruments detect no airborne bacteria. No observable life forms of any kind.'

Planetary probes were designed to take regular air readings. Dangerous viral or bacterial infections were almost always detectable in the higher atmosphere. Airborne microscopic life reflected the genetic make-up of their planetary cousins. Amanda asked, 'Have you ever heard of such a thing?'

'Never,' Hamoud replied.

'Run another instrument check,' Amanda said.

'Hold one.' Then, 'Instruments green across the board.'

The silence held for another three minutes, then Hamoud said, 'We should be through the clouds in twenty seconds.'

The veil shifted, closed up, then shifted again, and revealed . . . Nothing whatsoever.

Below them stretched a pinkish-blue sea, utterly placid. The surface was as bland as the clouds. The soft light should have been comforting, but there was a disconcerting element to the vista. Amanda had the distinct impression of an enemy hovering just out of sight, masked beneath the pastel waters.

Amanda asked, 'Where did the Random vessel land?'

'The spy's intel was very specific.' Hamoud pointed at the empty sea. 'The island they used as a LZ is twenty-seven klicks dead ahead.'

'We should see it by now,' Amanda said.

The three of them studied the vast pink ocean. Nasim said, 'Perhaps the spy fed us false intel.'

'His full payment and citizenship depended upon him getting this right,' Hamoud said.

Amanda decided, 'Hold to this altitude and do a sweep. Maintain subsonic speed.'

'Beginning sweep now.'

It was hard to detect any motion whatsoever. After ten minutes of nothing, Amanda said, 'Accelerate the probe to Mach three.'

'Roger. Mach three.' The only shift was a minor shiver to their view as the sound barrier was broken. Below them, nothing.

They watched the probe travel over pink waters. Eighteen minutes passed, then Hamoud asked, 'You are sure there is any land mass at all?'

'One hundred and nine islands,' Amanda confirmed. 'The largest is the size of a major metropolis. The smallest—'

'Land ahead,' Nasim announced. 'Decelerating to subsonic.'

Dead center on the monitor, a darker pink blob appeared. Amanda said, 'Instruments?'

'No change. Not even heat.'

When the land mass covered half of their screen, Amanda said, 'Stop here.'

Nasim halted the probe. 'Holding steady.'

'Show infrared.'

'Roger.' The monitor shifted over. And went utterly blank.

'Go back to the visible range.' When the island reappeared, Amanda said, 'Cameras to high magnification.'

The monitors showed a rapid swoop and dive. The view shifted out of focus, then sharpened. Pink sand gave way to pink grass and pink trees. A lone pink mountain rose from the island's heart, a perfect cylinder, topped by a smooth pink cone.

Filling the beach were Lorians. Hundreds and hundreds of beings. Some appeared humanoid, others appeared to shift in shape. Or not. It was hard to focus on any one being as they blended into the pink landscape.

But one thing she could say for certain.

All of them watched the probe.

Which was impossible.

Amanda asked, 'How far away are we from the island?'

Nasim replied, 'Eleven thousand meters and holding.'

Hamoud said, 'A probe the size of a large bird, camouflaged to mirror the surrounding environment . . . What kind of eyesight do these beings possess?'

Nasim said, 'Still no heat signal.'

Hamoud murmured, 'What does that mean, exactly?'

'The beings we see are the precise temperature of their surroundings. We have some low-level species on my home planet with this trait. But this would be the first such sentient race on record.' She glanced at Nasim. 'Still no sign of airborne life?'

'Nothing.'

They sat there for another twenty minutes, staring down at a multitude of sentient beings who stared back. Unmoving.

'All right, enough,' Amanda decided. 'Retract the probe.'

ELEVEN

All planetary LVs had a level-five sterilizer built into their airlocks. But from the worried frown Hamoud showed as he drew the probe inside, Amanda knew he had neglected to check and ensure it functioned. When he hit the button, the vessel was filled with a rumbling murmur. Hamoud breathed more easily and said, 'Cycling.'

As they stowed the probe atop the pile of gear, Nasim said, 'The beings must be able to detect radio frequencies.'

'That will be my first question to the scientists,' Amanda agreed.

They strapped in and headed east, traveling into the planet's double-solar dawn. The smaller Lorian sun was positioned to the right and slightly above the larger, close enough for streamers to funnel between the two globes. The first sunrise was a pale-yellow wash, reflected in luminous pink streamers below them. Then the second sun came into view, hot and fierce. Hamoud lowered the shields and strengthened their internal lighting.

The LV remained silent until Amanda asked, 'You've served on eleven planetary crisis teams?'

'Correct,' Hamoud replied.

'How many of them would you class as failures?'

Hamoud gave a thoroughly Arab response, lifting his head with a slight jerk. To most foreigners, it would appear as merely half a nod. But Amanda's favorite professor at the Academy had been from the Arabian system. He had explained how the gesture predated Earth's written history, and was intended as a subtle gesture of pulling away. Arabs as a rule detested saying no, for fear of causing offense. So this half-nod of agreement had become their preferred means of disagreeing. The upward motion signified an absolute negation.

'Please, what failures?' Hamoud replied. 'If you are ever to succeed as a planetary adviser, this is where you must begin.'

'So the most catastrophic of outcomes . . .'

'Form the foundation of partial successes,' Hamoud finished. 'And that is all you highlight in your final report.'

'Commander Rickets does not strike me as being interested in rose-tinted reports,' Amanda pointed out.

He tched. 'The commander will ask and you will answer in full. You will hold to the hard facts unless she requests your analysis, but you will tell her everything. The reports are an entirely different matter. You write for all those unseen watchers who seek reasons to hold you back.'

She nodded understanding. 'So if the commander were to request complete honesty . . .'

'Three,' Hamoud replied. 'Three were total disasters.'

Amanda liked how they spoke in synch, like two minds dancing to music they made up as they went along. 'Three of eleven . . .'

'Is about the norm.' Hamoud seemed very comfortable completing her thoughts. 'More than that, people in authority will question your tactics. Choice assignments will begin to go elsewhere. You will be relegated to planets where the chance of success is nil.'

'Advancement becomes . . .'

'Someone else's opportunity. Or problem.'

Amanda mulled that over while Nasim tried once again to raise the science colony on the comm-link. When the response was only silence, she asked, 'What would you say was the major difference between the failures and the successes?'

'Rickets would approve of that question. And the answer for me has been the same in all three cases,' Hamoud replied. 'The crisis for which we were sent was not the *real* problem.'

'There was another hidden crisis,' Amanda said. For some reason, the direction of their conversation sent her heart into overdrive. As though she had just been whispered a foretelling of her own future.

'A bigger problem below the surface. And if you don't identify the hidden, or you can't, or you identify the wrong one . . .'

Both men were watching her intently now. Hamoud asked, 'Truly, you are on your first planetary mission?'

'The GSA station was my first assignment,' Amanda replied. 'I have not left the post in two and a half years.'

Nasim asked, 'What was your training?'

'Regional GSA Academy on Ganymede, a planet orbiting a gas giant—'

'We know Ganymede,' Hamoud said. 'And before that?'

'A cattle farm in the Florida scrublands.'

'I'm sorry, where?'

'Earth.' She waved it aside. 'Doesn't matter. The middle of nowhere.'

She was about to ask about their own backgrounds when the comm-link came alive. The sound of a stranger's voice in their isolated space was shocking.

A woman's voice cried, 'Help, oh help! They're going to murder me next!'

TWELVE

S tandard protocol for a small team's entry into a hazardous environment was part of every cadet's training. It was one thing to read about such matters in a safe classroom, tucked inside the GSA Academy, circling the gas giant of Amanda's home system. It was another thing entirely to live the event. The woman's screams still echoed in Amanda's head as she suited up and stepped into the airlock.

Even so, the most piercing emotion she felt at that moment was excitement.

The truth also made Amanda extremely guilty. A woman had pleaded with them to hurry and save her life. The panic in her shrieks had apparently been fueled by learning she was about to become yet another scientist the Lorians devoured. That was the word she used. Like an animal upon which the Lorians intended to feast. Again, her words. Dread and terror had shredded her communication. First Nasim and then Amanda had tried to have her answer the most basic of questions. How many combatants did the colony face? Were they armed? How many survivors?

The woman had screamed a final time, then the connection was cut.

There was every reason for Amanda to be terrified. Her giddy sense of anticipation had no logical basis. And yet that was how she felt as she faced the cycling airlock.

'Move out two hundred meters and hold position,' Hamoud instructed.

'Two hundred meters. Roger.'

She had only worn a next-generation spacesuit three times. Cadets and junior officers were not generally assigned to even clean such gear. The suit cost as much as an LV pod. The material was a fine-mesh alloy that could shield the wearer from a direct hit by an EV bolt or assault weapon. The gloves were so supple the wearer could feel the grooves in a coin. The helmet's visor was almost invisible.

Amanda shoved off the airlock's leading edge and floated into the dark void. Her view was in all directions and left her utterly breathless.

Hamoud said, 'Activate your PV.'

She laughed silently. Hamoud was far kinder than her instructors, who would have been barking for her to wake up and pay attention to the assignment. 'Activating.'

Her suit was nothing, not even a speck of space dust, compared to the gear in her right hand.

The newest gadget to fuel late-night sessions among cadets and techies was this baton. She pressed the button embedded in the end, and out flowed a next-gen planetary vehicle. Normally referred to as a scooter.

Old-fashioned pods, or buckets, had been superseded by these new PVs. Energy shields were now being formed into semblances of material structures. The baton in Amanda's right hand contained an energy pack, positioning equipment, and onboard computer. All the readouts were channeled through sensors in her gloves and displayed directly below her chin. She half stood, half sat on a narrow bench with her feet anchored to a platform only a hair's breadth wider than her boots. The baton now formed the acceleration and steering and braking controls.

She sat upon a scooter made from pure energy.

She said, 'This is wild.'

'We are releasing the probe,' Hamoud said.

His unspoken admonition was clear. Amanda swallowed her desire to yell with delight and replied calmly, 'I see it.'

'Nasim is cycling through.' Hamoud gave that a beat, then, 'Turn on your lights, Major.'

'I don't . . .'

'Touch the fourth finger of your left hand to the ball of your thumb.'

'Right. OK.' Everything glowed now, her suit, the PV, all emitting the same silver-blue.

'You are blue, Nasim orange, the probe is—'

'Green. Roger that.' She waved a hand at Nasim's approach. The gesture streaked space with a silver-blue ribbon. She could not completely suppress her amazement. 'Oh. Wow.'

Nasim was close enough for her to see his grin. But all the corporal said was, 'Ready to begin descent, Major.'

'OK, Hamoud. Send down the probe,' Amanda said. She could hear her racing heart create tremors in each word, like footprints on water.

The probe swept away from them and down. 'Probe is underway,' Hamoud confirmed.

'I am descending,' Amanda said. She pushed the baton forward, leaning into it as if balancing against unseen winds. The descent, however, was without any sense of motion until the pinkish outer atmosphere seemed to grip her. She asked, 'Nasim, do you feel that?'

Hamoud demanded, 'Feel what?'

Nasim answered for her. 'The outer atmosphere is unnaturally thick. It feels as though . . .'

When he hesitated, she said, 'Like we're passing through spiderwebs.'

'And those are . . .'

She searched and came up with, 'Like a sticky veil.'

Hamoud was silent a moment, then, 'Noted.'

'The probe is OK?'

'Normal atmospheric friction. Nothing else impacting its descent. Three minutes to position.'

The probe served as Hamoud's eyes and ears. It also possessed a great deal more than just scientific instruments. The spear-shaped apparatus was heavily armed. Amanda said, 'Still encountering resistance from the clouds. It almost feels like . . .'

'Hands,' Nasim said. 'Or netting. It requires a genuine effort to break through.'

Nasim held to a position five hundred meters above her, both to observe and watch her back. All this was part of standard ops. Amanda was on point, and as a result went in unarmed. The probe and Nasim served as a dual support system. Nasim was as heavily armed as the probe. Amanda had opted for point primarily because the corporal was clearly more experienced with weaponry. Amanda asked, 'Anything more from the colony?'

'I'm radioing every ninety seconds requesting an update,' Hamoud replied. 'No response.'

The clinging resistance buffeted her with increasing severity, like malleable fists now. Amanda started to draw up her shields but held back because they halved the PV's life before recharging was required. She tightened down, gripping the control lever with clenched determination.

Then she was through. The clouds parted, and the island was there in front of her. 'Target island is visible and closing.'

'Roger that.' A break, then Hamoud added, 'We are receiving from the colony.'

A breathless woman's voice said, 'I see you! I see you! *Hurry! They're about to kill . . .*'

The comm-link went dead.

THIRTEEN

Even as the woman's plea cut off in mid-scream, Amanda could not help but feel an intense thrill at the power and speed under her control. As she accelerated, the scooter's shield was automatically thrown up, protecting her body from the wind's buffeting force. She dove to within inches of the placid sea and sped toward the island, shooting a liquid streamer in her wake.

Her voice sounded impossibly shrill to her own ears. 'Five hundred meters and closing!'

Hamoud, by contrast, sounded impossibly calm. Almost bored. 'Drone and Nasim are both in position.'

'Do you have the victim's location?'

'Still hunting. Hold one, Major.'

She took that as the admonition it was, and slowed. The island was a hundred meters ahead. It appeared to be a mirror image of the one on the globe's opposite side, perhaps fifteen kilometers in diameter with the same steep-sided pink hill rising at its center. The same pink sand beach gave way to pink grass and trees. The island appeared utterly flat, less than a meter above the water's surface, except for the tall conical hill at its center.

'I am getting numerous heat images,' Hamoud said. 'All on the beach area.'

'Humans,' Nasim said. 'The scientists. Has to be.'

Amanda halted twenty meters off the shoreline. The coral beach held hundreds of the stumpy Lorians. Perhaps thousands. There were two differences from the island on the planet's opposite side. Here the Lorians paid her approach no attention whatsoever. And scattered among them were humans, all of them half as tall again as the local race. At first glance, it appeared some of the humans had pink hair. Or perhaps it was just the oddly muted daylight.

'There are seven long barracks just off the beach opposite your approach,' Hamoud said. 'Four heat images in the central structure. Make that six. Three are clustered together, perhaps either embracing or struggling.'

Amanda accelerated and swerved. 'I am circling the island.'

Nasim said, 'Holding at five hundred meters.'

'Go weapons hot,' Amanda ordered.

'Roger that,' Nasim said.

'Probe is armed,' Hamoud confirmed.

From her position at sea level, Amanda did not spot the structure until she was upon it. Seven long, low buildings bordered the shoreline and were fashioned from the same pink sand as the beach. The commotion rose from the central structure. The buildings were rimmed by broad open windows and fronted by double doors connected by a ramp to the beach. Several voices emanated from the openings. The loudest by far was a woman's pleading wail. Amanda thought it was the same voice she had heard screaming.

'No, no, I won't . . .'

'You signed on to this at the outset.' The man was tense, angry, oppressively loud. 'They are *waiting*.'

'Alert, alert,' Hamoud said. His voice held to a monotonous drone. 'The top of the island is shifting.'

And indeed it was. The peak of the lone hill lifted and drifted towards them. Silent, smooth. Shifting like a solid pink cloud, slightly smaller than the barracks.

The male voice inside the barracks grew frantic. 'They're coming. Help me shift—'

'Get your hands off me!'

When they emerged from the building, the intended victim was easily identifiable. A man held the woman by her upper arm and pulled while three other women grimly shoved her from behind. The victim was dressed in little more than rags, a scientist's cloak aged to pinkish-gray. Her bare feet scrambled for a hold as they dragged her down the ramp and onto the shore.

Amanda started to shout, then realized the locals would be unable to hear her. All suit controls were voice-activated, so she barked, 'Onboard computer! External speaker! Full volume!'

The instant the confirmation chime sounded, Amanda shouted, *'Release the woman and step away!'*

The reaction was almost comic. The scientists and support staff all jumped as if they had been electrified. Every single one of them spun about and gaped at her.

When the clutch of people kept hold of the woman, Amanda shouted, *'Release her or you will be fired upon!'*

Only the Lorians remained as they had been, intent upon the approaching hilltop. The structure was far larger than it had first appeared. The mound drifted out over the sea, swiftly circled the island, and then swooped toward the throng. The clutch of people released the woman. She spotted the approaching mound and screamed in pure terror.

The man was a scarecrow in a ratty lab coat and cut-offs. He waved scrawny arms at Amanda. 'Keep away! This is forbidden!'

Amanda swooped down and positioned herself between the wailing woman and the disembodied hilltop. '*Stop or I will fire upon you!*'

Now it was the man who wailed, '*No!*'

Amanda snapped, 'Fire on my command!'

But she gave no command. Because at that instant Amanda lost the ability to breathe.

The air within her suit solidified. There was no other way to describe the sense of being trapped inside invisible concrete. She could not move, not even blink.

She knew she was going to die.

Then a searing blade of flame creased the air overhead. The disembodied hilltop absorbed the blast and fractured. The air surrounding the mound vibrated, like waves from a stone tossed into a pond.

The weapon fired a second time. The light was blinding. Furious. Beautiful.

The mound evaporated into drifting coral dust.

Amanda was released.

Her limbs were boneless, liquid sacks that trembled with each breath. Even so, she managed to lower her vehicle down to where the woman sprawled on the beach. Amanda gasped, 'Climb on board.'

'No, no, no, no.' The male scientist approached with arms outstretched. 'It's forbidden to—'

'You are under arrest for willful participation in the murders of sixteen colonials.' Amanda did not recognize her own voice. Her words were hoarse and a full octave lower than normal. 'Take one step closer and you will be shot. Hamoud?'

'Target acquired.'

The scientist's bony arms flapped like broken wings. 'You don't understand! We are forbidden—'

'Be quiet.' Amanda reached out one gloved hand to the woman. 'Climb up behind me.'

The woman struggled to rise, clearly as weakened by the experience as Amanda. 'I couldn't breathe.'

'I know.' Amanda pulled the woman upright and then guided her onto the ledge that extended out to form a second bench. 'Let's get out of—'

The instant the woman's feet left the sand, she disintegrated.

A crimson cloud spread out from Amanda's vehicle.

One moment Amanda clutched the woman's hand, the next it was *gone*.

Amanda's vision was blurred and distorted by the mist of blood that now covered her helmet. She fought down an impulse to vomit. Then she wiped her helmet, but the glove only smeared the goop worse. She swallowed again, harder this time.

In a choked voice she said, 'I can't see to navigate.'

'Inbound in two,' Nasim said. His voice sounded hollow.

She had time for a few difficult breaths, then strong hands gripped her and said, 'Step to your left. Good. Feel the seat? Now deconstruct your PV.'

She felt the subtle whoosh of being pulled away from the island, but all she could see was the drying crust that blanketed her helmet. She asked, 'Did you see that?'

'Everything. Turn off your external speaker.'

She gave the command, then said, 'You saved my life, blasting that thing.'

'I did nothing.' Nasim's words were as low and as deep as her own. 'I was frozen solid. Dying with you.'

FOURTEEN

Amanda made them cycle her through the sterilization process twice. When she finally stepped out of the airlock, Hamoud met her with a mug of tea heavily laced with brandy. She allowed both men to help remove her suit. Then Nasim held her mug while she zipped through the too-brief shower permitted by their limited water supply. The men pretended to busy themselves in the cockpit while she changed into fresh ship's coveralls. When she joined them, Hamoud handed her a second mug and said, 'Drink.'

'I'll be a wreck with this much booze on an empty stomach.'

'What booze? This is medicine. Drink.'

In truth, the two mugs only left her feeling a touch removed from everything that had gone down. And that certainly helped. When she was done, Nasim handed her a third mug, this one containing a thick soup made from dried peas and desert sorrel. She had thought eating anything would have been impossible. But her stomach had settled and she ate with guilty appetite.

Hamoud said, 'We need to debrief.'

'I know.'

'We should record this.'

She handed Nasim the empty mug. 'That much brandy is bound to show.'

'Less than you think,' Nasim said.

'Shock does strange things to people,' Hamoud agreed. When she did not respond, he took her silence as assent and turned to the controls. The camera attached to the computerized ship's log slid up on its adjustable stem. Hamoud checked the monitor to ensure all three faces were visible, then said, 'Perhaps you should take the pilot's seat.'

Which would have meant she would be managing the proceedings. 'I can't,' Amanda replied.

'This record is bound to be viewed multiple times,' Hamoud warned.

'It's going to be hard enough just trying to remember and describe,' Amanda said. 'You handle it. Please.'

'Very well. Nasim?'

'Rolling.'

Hamoud adopted a formal air as he gave the date and time and ship's position. He then turned to Nasim and guided the corporal through his account. Amanda thought Hamoud came across as a gentle professor. He probed delicately, amplifying several points, then turned to Amanda and said, 'Ready, Major?'

'Yes.' She allowed him to break it down into segments, from the moment the first scream echoed through the LV to the point when the scientist vanished in a cloud of bodily fluids. Hamoud then turned back to Nasim and had him repeat in greater detail being threatened with death by invisible cement.

Hamoud gave it a thoughtful pause, then said, 'With respect, Major, I feel the report should include a bit more on the life-threatening events.'

'Agreed.'

'Did you notice any sign of force before being . . .'

'Gripped,' Nasim said.

'Clenched,' Amanda said.

'Clenched is better,' Nasim agreed. 'Every atom of my being just stopped.'

Hamoud asked, 'With regard to their weapon, did you observe its strike?'

'The answer is no,' she said. 'I can't say for certain that the thing was what actually attacked us, except for how the impact ceased the instant you destroyed whatever that was.'

'And you were observing closely the . . .'

'Hilltop. Mound. Weapon. Whatever,' Amanda confirmed. 'I stared straight at it the entire time. The only point at which I noticed any change was between the probe's first and second strikes.'

Hamoud said, 'You didn't mention that before.'

'There were ripples in the surrounding air, steady vibratory patterns, like waves coming off a rock thrown into still waters.'

'I saw nothing,' Nasim said.

'They only lasted a few seconds. But they were there.'

Hamoud drummed his fingers on the padded armrest. Thinking.

Amanda asked, 'Why did you fire on the mound?'

Hamoud refocused on her but did not speak.

'I couldn't issue the command. What caused you to strike?'

'Because,' Hamoud replied, tapping the screen that showed their body monitors, 'I watched you both die.'

FIFTEEN

'Your readings just froze,' Hamoud said. 'Breathing, heart, everything.'

Amanda recalled the instant and struggled to breathe. 'So . . . my heart stopped.'

'And Nasim's. Ten seconds, perhaps fifteen. So sudden I did not understand. It was good Nasim was there. One set of biometrics going flatline, I might have wasted precious seconds checking the system for a glitch. When two stopped at the very same moment, I fired.'

Nasim asked, 'I *died*?'

'You both came close to dying,' Hamoud said, his gaze steady on Amanda. 'Most certainly.'

Amanda asked, 'What does that? Stop a human heart at two hundred meters with no sign of attack or discernable force?'

Hamoud shrugged. 'Nasim is more the weapons expert.'

'Never have I heard of such a device,' Nasim replied.

'You need to enter the bio readings into the ship's log,' Amanda said.

'Excellent point.' Hamoud's hands flew over the controls. 'This brings us to the second event.'

'The exploding scientist,' Nasim said. 'Again, never have I heard of a weapon that vaporizes a human being with no evidence of force being applied.'

'We need to back up,' Amanda said.

'I agree,' Hamoud said.

'The two events are linked,' Amanda said. 'You destroyed their weapon. *Then* the woman was killed. By what?'

Hamoud did not nod so much as rock slowly in his seat. 'If they still had weapons at the ready, where were they? Nasim?'

'I saw nothing.'

'I have been over the probe's view, and I saw no movement from the Lorians. No weapon, no aggressive action, no threatening stance, no protest – nothing.'

'The only one moving was the male scientist,' Amanda said.

'Waving his arms and telling his colleague not to go,' Nasim said. 'What a clown.'

'After you destroyed their weapon, they did not retaliate,' Amanda said. 'There was no attempt to take out the probe.'

'And you were not attacked again,' Hamoud said. 'Not even when you went to the woman's aid. She was killed, but you were free to depart.'

The silence held them all for a time. Finally, Hamoud reached over, cut off the recorder, then asked, 'What now?'

'The scientist has to be arrested,' Amanda declared.

Hamoud resumed his slow rocking. 'I suppose . . . Yes. Perhaps.'

'You *suppose*? That guy might as well have pulled the trigger!'

Hamoud remained silent.

Nasim said, 'Who was he, anyway?'

'Professor Arne Sayer,' Amanda replied. 'I recognize his photo-graph from the colony files. Sayer was recently named leader of the colony.'

'When the deaths started?'

'Just after the first death – that of the former leader, a Professor Darin. The next planetary report, the one that sent us here, merely noted that Sayer had taken Darin's place. No mention at that point of the cause of death. Then at the bottom was a formal request for sixteen new academics to replace all those who had died.' Amanda kept her gaze on Hamoud throughout. She demanded, 'You can't possibly think he's innocent. Sayer dragged her out where their weapon could target her!'

Hamoud met her gaze. 'You remember what I said earlier, yes?'

She took a mental step back. 'About planetary crises.'

'About the *hidden* crisis. To me, none of this adds up.' Hamoud ticked the items off his fingers. 'A scientist classes the deaths of sixteen members of his very small workforce as routine incidents. He sends an official request for replacements. The sentient race has developed a weapon without metals, one that is capable of killing without visible force. When their weapon is destroyed, the local race does not retaliate. And immediately after their only visible armament is blasted to dust, another woman is killed. And this happens while you hold her hand. And yet you suffer no harm whatsoever.'

Amanda found herself rocking in time to the pilot's motions. She repeated softly, 'The hidden crisis.'

Hamoud dropped his hand. 'In my opinion, we are missing the true problem facing this colony. Only once we identify that will we be able to know whom to arrest.'

That was the moment when the comm-link came to life. Nasim announced, 'We have an incoming from the colony.'

'Put it on the speaker,' Amanda said. 'And record.'

Nasim hit the switch, then said, 'Comm-link one.'

Amanda waited as Hamoud hit the comm button and shifted the mike closer her way. 'This is Major Bostick.'

The man's fury and bluster were both gone. 'This is Professor Sayer. I'm, ah, I suppose you'd call me the head—'

'I know who you are.' Amanda made no attempt to disguise her loathing. 'What do you want?'

Her cold response only made him more hesitant. 'We . . . that is, our hosts – they want to speak with you.'

Amanda exchanged glances with Hamoud. 'Say again.'

'Their appointed spokesman wishes to talk with the leader of your—'

'That would be me,' Amanda said. 'What's their name?'

'They do not use names. They assign a single individual who speaks with us, whom we call the Diplomat. By this I mean, there is just one Lorian at a time who even learns how to talk.'

'OK, so put them on.'

'Ah, that's not possible. They insist on you being present.'

'Tough. Explain matters to them.'

'Explain . . . Look, Major. They don't talk unless you're grounded.'

Hamoud was even handsome when he frowned in confusion, Amanda decided. She repeated, 'Grounded?'

'Here. On Loria. It's part of what makes them special.'

Nasim huffed a humorless laugh. Amanda said, 'Special is not the word I would have chosen.'

'You don't understand *anything*. Will you come? It's the only way you'll ever get a grip on what's happening here. Why our work is *vital*. Which is why we desperately need those replacements!'

'What, so you can help the Lorians murder more scientists?'

His ire broke through once more. 'Are you certifiably insane? I didn't murder anyone!'

'No. But you were most certainly complicit in their deaths. Which would be grounds . . .' Amanda stopped. Neither man had moved. But she caught the warning from before. She took a long breath, then said, 'Can you guarantee my safety?'

'Can I . . . Our colony is not under threat!'

'Hold one.' Amanda cut off the mike, then asked the men, 'Does that exchange make any sense whatsoever to either of you?'

'This is wicked strange,' Nasim said.

'I don't see any other way to get to the bottom of this,' Amanda decided. She turned the mike back on and said, 'I am leaving now.'

SIXTEEN

Amanda fought down another wave of revulsion and forced herself to don the suit. The men remained solicitous and very patient. Once she cycled through the airlock, the probe emerged and took up position. Hamoud said, 'Ready when you are.'

'Descending,' Amanda said. This time there was no sense of exhilaration or abandon. Only grim intent.

Hamoud asked, 'What kind of operation would kill one woman, then do nothing to stop another woman's departure?'

'Perhaps it was a question of loyalty,' Nasim said. 'The scientist had declared herself part of the colony. Major Bostick is an unknown.'

'That makes sense,' Amanda said. The men's voices filled the inside of her helmet. Amanda found it very comforting to descend through the ocher sunset with them for company.

Nasim had wanted to accompany her, of course. Amanda's first-ever argument with her small crew came when she ordered him to stay on board. But the results of the confrontation had been abundantly clear. She did not want to risk two lives. Not after the Lorian weapon had frozen them both with such deadly ease.

Instead, Nasim and Hamoud had rummaged through the LV's standard equipment and come up with what they referred to as a sled. It was, in fact, an older method for hauling goods to the surface, a self-powered unit that could carry four or five wheelbarrow loads. When Amanda had said that to the men, she had needed to explain what a wheelbarrow was, and then why anyone would want to push a burden around in a metal container with just one wheel.

Now they were back on the subject of what she should expect to find down below. Hamoud piloted the probe, which traveled behind and to her left, while Nasim's improvised weapon flew on point. He had mounted a pair of field guns on the sled. The two armed devices now flew to either side of her. Amanda had to admit that they made for a comforting sight.

The smaller sun had set, and the second orb was nearing the horizon. The ribbon of flame connecting the pair streaked the surrounding clouds with a bloody pastiche. Amanda forced down yet another surge of dread over what might await her. Every thought was filtered through the mental image of a crimson mist drying on her helmet.

Nasim said, 'Perhaps they were restrained by your destroying the flying hilltop.'

'Remember the timing,' Hamoud said. 'They killed the scientist after the hilltop was blasted.'

Amanda said, 'Maybe we should send the probe to make a closer inspection of that hill.'

'We must think on that very carefully,' Hamoud said. 'We only have the one probe.'

Nasim asked, 'Major, what can you see?'

Amanda was surrounded by clouds thick enough now to cut off most light. She replied, 'To my left is the sunset. Up ahead is only darkness.'

'I can transmit control of the probe's night-sight to your suit's system,' Hamoud said.

'Let's wait and see what illumination the colony uses,' Amanda said. She reflected on this highly comforting discussion. It could have been so very different. These two Arabs could have shown sullen resentment over being led by a woman. A *young* woman. Inexperienced and totally out of her depth. She said, 'Hamoud, Nasim, I just want to say thanks.'

Her gratitude silenced them both. Which in a way was also very pleasant. A few moments passed before she realized, 'I'm encountering no resistance.'

'Say again.'

'You remember how the first time Nasim and I both passed through some form of web-like substance until I broke through the clouds? I'm traveling now with no shield, and there's no resistance, no web, nothing.'

Nasim said, 'Perhaps it is the dusk?'

'Maybe.' Then she thought of something else. 'Who is they?'

Hamoud said, 'We do not understand the question, Major.'

'We keep saying, *they* did this. They attacked. They let us go. Who is *they*? None of them moved or spoke or . . .'

'Telepaths,' Hamoud said. 'I have dealt with them once before. They are baffling. And perilous. All the normal warnings . . . poof. Gone.'

There was an astonishing abruptness to her breaking through the cloud covering. One moment she was surrounded by a blank gray void. The next . . .

She breathed, 'Oh. Wow.'

The island was rimmed by a pink lantern glow.

The beach was a broad ring of illumination. And not just the beach. The grass and trees rimming the sand were tall lamps with gemstone branches. And not just the sand. The water that lapped the beach was alight as well. The further away from the island, the dimmer grew the light, until it vanished entirely some thousand meters out.

The central hill was a brilliant beacon.

Amanda asked, 'Are you seeing this?'

'We are, yes.' Hamoud sounded almost reverential. 'Is it as beautiful as it appears?'

'Oh, no,' she replied, slowing for her approach, 'it's far more than that.'

Hamoud's voice sharpened. 'Major, please hold where you are.'

She stopped and hovered fifty meters above the gleaming waters. 'What is it?'

'Wait one.' The probe silently sped away.

'Hamoud?'

In response, the pilot asked, 'Nasim, you see it?'

'No question whatsoever.'

'Tell me,' Amanda demanded.

'The hilltop is back.'

Her veins congealed. 'Say again.'

'The portion that forms the machine, it is shaped differently from the rest of the hill. Steeper-sided with a peaked top.'

Nasim added, 'When it took off, the hill looked chopped off. Totally flat. The machine has been replaced. No question.'

Hamoud asked, 'Should we blast it?'

She was sorely tempted. But it was one thing to attack a

machine preparing to kill them. And another thing entirely to go against it where it rested. 'Nasim, shift your sled over and take up a guard position. Hamoud, keep the probe as my backup. The instant you detect any motion at all, you both fire and take out that weapon.'

'Roger that.'

Amanda nudged the controls forward. 'I'm going in.'

SEVENTEEN

As she approached the beach where the community watched and waited, Hamoud said, 'Are you familiar with your scooter, Major?'

'I have played with one while shipboard.' It was comforting to be so at ease with admitting her weaknesses. 'I've read the manuals. Four times. Other than that, the answer is absolutely not.'

'One aspect you might have missed. You can order it to form a hover platform.'

'Outstanding,' she said, and meant it. The last thing she wanted was to address the scientist while seated. And to step down to the beach meant going against the commander's express orders. 'Tell me how.'

The tiny brain packed inside the control-rod was limited to a precise set of verbal commands. Hamoud repeated them twice. When Amanda braked in front of the chief scientist, she stood and gave the command. The response was seamless. The bench and surrounding vehicle both disappeared, reshaped as a circular platform hovering inches above the glowing sand. The controls now formed a mini-rail by her right hand. 'Excellent.'

'You can still accelerate away if required,' Hamoud said. 'Only be sure to hold tight to the control stick.'

The chief scientist was almost at eye level as he approached. 'Commander, I am Professor—'

'Major.'

'Excuse me?'

'Major Bostick, GSA. And you are Professor Arne Sayer.

Correct? Good. Pleasantries concluded. Now explain to me why I shouldn't haul you back starside in manacles.'

Sayer appeared utterly confounded by her demand. 'What are you talking about?'

Through her comm-link, Nasim said, 'Do you believe this guy?'

'Scientists,' Hamoud agreed.

Sayer said, 'For one thing, Major, if you even try to take me off-planet, I'll dissolve just like my associate.'

'Explain.'

He gestured to the first building. 'Shall we go inside?'

'Out of the question.' Amanda had no intention of being anywhere alone with this man. She had a number of reservations about addressing him at all. She could still see her vision clouded by the blood of the woman Sayer had been ready to sacrifice. 'Where is the Lorian?'

'She is referred to as the Diplomat,' Sayer replied stiffly. 'She's coming. Now can you please get that *thing* out of my face?'

Amanda did not need to glance over to know Hamoud had positioned the probe a meter above and behind her right shoulder. 'Most certainly. Just as soon as you explain why you as leader of this colony are willing to be complicit in the murders of your own team.'

Sayer astonished her then. He turned to the humans that surrounded them in a broad half-moon and said, 'Can someone *please* help me get through to this woman?'

Nasim said slowly, 'What is going on?'

A female voice responded from the crowd, 'Explain it to her, Sayer.'

'It could take all night and get us nowhere!'

'You have to try. What choice do we have?'

Nasim said inside her helmet, 'I am utterly and completely lost here.'

Hamoud murmured, 'Major, my gut tells me that here before us is the hidden crisis.'

Amanda raised her voice and called to the crowd lining the beach, 'Who among you addressed Professor Sayer?'

A woman stepped forward. Amanda instantly recognized her as one of the women who had helped push the dead scientist from the building. 'Ying, exobiology.'

'Join us. Please.' When the woman stepped forward, Amanda asked, 'Why did you help this man sacrifice one of your own?'

In her own way, Ying was as impatient as the chief scientist. 'Every word you just uttered is incorrect.'

'You pushed one of your team—'

'Our tribe,' Ying countered. 'Go on.' Her tone was immensely irritating.

'Team, tribe – that holds no importance whatsoever—'

'On the contrary, Major, it has *vital* significance—'

'You pushed the woman out to where a machine could obliterate her!'

Ying nodded stiffly. 'I did. Yes.'

'Do you realize you just admitted culpability to murder?'

Another jerk of her head. 'Seventeen of them now. Yes. But they were not murders.'

Sayer added, 'Every member of our tribe signed a compact prior to landing. They agree that their eventual death is part of this experiment.'

'You . . . What?'

'We signed our own death sentence,' Ying replied. 'All of us.'

'It is required in order to participate in the greatest experiment the human race has ever known,' Sayer said. 'To join with a telepathic race.'

'We signed on for life,' Ying said. 'And death.'

'We are bonded with the Lorians now,' Sayer said. 'There is no going back.'

Ying added, 'Unless you accept this, you will understand nothing of what we face here.'

Sayer said, 'We have over seven thousand applications for the seventeen empty slots. All of them have been informed of our . . .'

'Losses,' Amanda said. 'Deaths at the hands of the sentient race.'

Sayer waved her words aside. 'All applicants have submitted written declarations stating they fully understand the required commitment.'

Ying said, 'The only things we require from you are supplies and transport for those applicants we decide are our best hope of moving forward.'

Hamoud's voice held to the same calm monotone as when he

guided them through the logged report. 'Major, ask them why the deaths happened.'

When she did so, Sayer and Ying nodded together. 'That is the crucial issue we face,' he replied. 'That is our link to the planet's Prime Directives.'

'That is what makes their deaths so important,' Ying said.

'Absolutely vital,' Sayer agreed. 'Each of them provides a crucial element of our study.'

Ying finished, 'And why your presence is such a threat to our progress.'

EIGHTEEN

Amanda was still digesting this when the Lorian appeared. 'Observe the other scientists,' Hamoud said softly. Amanda watched as the semi-circle of humans reached forward, craned, sought to touch the alien as it passed through. The Lorian walked in an almost drunken fashion, a gentle careening from one side to the other. Amanda thought the walk most resembled an infant's motions, hands open to either side, the legs not quite capable of balancing the body.

Sayer offered the alien a half-bow. 'Diplomat.'

Up close, the Lorian's expression also resembled an infant's. The wide pink eyes seemed to show a mild astonishment. As though it could not quite understand what it saw. The alien's bland surprise only heightened Amanda's unease.

Amanda's voice remained soft, but something in its timbre forced both humans back a pace. 'The action of murdering humans is *forbidden*. The deaths of scientists will *cease*. It will *never* happen again.'

The Lorian remained poised there before her, examining the suit. Then it lowered itself. The motion was another bewilderment. The alien did not bend. Instead, it flowed downwards until the eyes were at sand level.

Nasim said, 'What just happened?'

Hamoud said, 'It appears boneless.'

The alien resumed its stumpy form and turned to the two humans. 'This one's words carry an . . . emotion?' The final word was elongated and clearly required effort.

'Emotion,' Sayer confirmed. 'Yes.'

'This has a name?'

'Rage.' Sayer appeared embarrassed. Mortified, in fact. 'Anger.'

'This implies an action?'

'Conflict,' Sayer replied.

'Threat,' Ying said. She appeared even more embarrassed than Sayer. 'Argument.'

'These terms are unknown to me,' the Lorian replied.

The two human scientists shared a look, then Sayer shrugged and said, 'Separation.'

'This one is not of our tribe?'

'Definitely not,' Sayer replied.

'Not now, not ever,' Ying agreed.

'I seek understanding.' The Lorian's manner of speech was not unpleasant. It breathed each word, a soft punctuation that carried a low musical quality. Amanda was reminded of instruments she and her brothers had carved as children from sugar-cane stalks. 'This one seeks to remain apart?'

'It is permanently separate.' Ying gestured with one nervous hand. 'Separation defines its manner of existence. The suit. The machine. Separate.'

'So. Not of our tribe.' The Lorian turned back to Amanda. 'Why are you here?'

'Why . . . Did you hear my command?'

Again the Lorian showed gentle confusion. 'Command?'

Sayer's voice carried profound misery. 'Prime Directive.'

'I do not understand.'

Ying seemed equally despondent. 'She says that to cause one of our tribe to cease functioning is a breach of her Prime Directive.'

'But . . . You are of our tribe now.'

'They are still human,' Amanda said. 'The Prime Directive stands.'

'Your words are noted, Separate One.' The Lorian turned and drifted away.

Only when the Lorian left the beach did Sayer hiss, 'You threaten *everything*. You understand *nothing*.'

'Years of work,' Ying said. 'Decades. Gone.'

Amanda looked from one to the other, so astonished that she needed a moment to gather her thoughts. 'I want you to pay careful attention. Either you address the issue of those seventeen deaths to my satisfaction or I am shutting this outpost down.'

'Shut . . .' The pair showed genuine outrage. Sayer demanded, 'Did you not hear *anything* I said?'

'Absolutely,' Amanda said. 'My answer is the same. Either you present me with satisfactory answers, or this outpost will be closed and every one of you shipped out. You have six days.'

Sayer's response was cut off by one of the others calling softly, 'The Diplomat is coming back.'

The Lorian showed the same ungainly motions as it returned to stand before the two scientists. 'This one is to observe the dawn process.'

With that, Amanda was surrounded by a semi-circle of utterly astounded faces.

Sayer weakly addressed the Lorian, 'I don't understand.'

'This ending of breath, you call . . .'

'Death,' Amanda replied. 'Murder. Our first Prime Directive.'

'Your words are a mystery, Separate One. Join us for the Gathering. Then perhaps we will all understand better.' The Lorian turned away. 'Until the dawn.'

Amanda demanded, 'What just happened?'

Sayer seemed incapable of speech. Ying replied, 'You took the words directly from my mouth.'

'Explain.'

'We waited thirty years before we were permitted to observe a Gathering. Tomorrow marks the first time we are invited to join one.' Ying's features were tight in the island's glowing illumination. 'You show up, spout your nonsense about a human Prime Directive—'

'Another murder and you'll experience my Prime Directive to *shut you down*.'

'You have *no* idea what you just said.' Ying looked ready to strike her. 'Be here at dawn.'

Amanda was still standing there as the entire collective drifted away. She saw a number of resentful glances shot at her, a good deal of collective anger.

Hamoud said, 'Major?'

'I'm returning shipside.' Suddenly, she was very tired. Exhausted by strain and confusion both. And it was all made worse by the fact that she had apparently turned the entire outpost against her. By seeking to protect them from alien killers.

She was the enemy now.

NINETEEN

They slept through a shortened night. Amanda took first watch, certain she needed time to recover from the day, wanting her sleep to be unbroken once it began. Two hours before dawn reached the island, Nasim woke her and the three of them shared a quietly subdued meal. They were probably breaking a dozen regulations, using an ammo locker for a pot holder and setting mugs on the controls between hers and Hamoud's chair. The setting was oddly comforting, however. Amanda's back was to the viewport and the glowing pink world and the streamers linking two suns. Amanda had so many questions, and so few answers, but she found a genuine contentment in setting it all aside and enjoying Nasim's one-pot meal. For the moment, she was content.

Amanda insisted on clearing up. As she passed around fresh mugs of tea, Hamoud said, 'I've been remembering something from my childhood.'

'Now that's very interesting,' Nasim said.

'Not you too.'

'Our return to the Rift,' Nasim said. 'The games.'

Hamoud smiled. Amanda settled back into her chair, thinking how handsome these two men were when they dropped their guards. Hamoud said, 'As a boy, I hardly slept the week before the games.'

'Shame you always lost,' Nasim said.

'I won more than you.'

'You cheated.'

Hamoud re-aimed his smile at Amanda and went on, 'When I

was very young, my father served as adviser to the planetary emir. I grew up with the palace guards for friends. Nasim's father was a merchant who rose to lead the regional guild. We were best friends.'

'It's true,' Nasim said. 'Though I can't remember why.'

'My father hated serving as Lord Chancellor,' Hamoud said. 'But the emir asked and my father had no choice but to agree.'

Amanda asked, 'What did your father do, you know, before?'

'Before and after, he was a lawyer.'

'He was the *best* lawyer,' Nasim said. 'My own father was threatened with bankruptcy because other merchants had ganged up against him. My family came from nothing and rose because of my father's talent as a businessman. He threatened their clique, so they set out to destroy him. Hamoud's father saved us from ruin.'

Amanda said, 'You were thinking about the games too?'

Hamoud responded with that upraised chin, the polite negation. 'It was an event that changed everything about the games.'

'Before, families treated it as a rite of passage,' Nasim said. 'After, it represented our freedom.'

'That spring, the human empire sent another delegation. They came every decade or so. Oman is the de facto leader of the Arab systems. My father had been appointed Lord Chancellor soon after we were alerted to the delegation's arrival. I had never seen him so worried. He knew the pressure would be intense.'

'The empire threatened the Arab Protectorate's independence,' Nasim said. 'Any means to slow down the invasion was a good thing.'

'Invasion. Please. We were being formally invited to join the assembly of human planets. Without further delay.'

Nasim snorted. 'This time Hamoud speaks of, those delegates arrived with eleven ships of the line. Two thousand soldiers.'

'Three thousand,' Hamoud corrected. 'And a hundred heavily armed troop carriers.'

'Some invitation,' Amanda said.

'The emir knew he would go down in history as the ruler who lost the protectorate its independence,' Nasim said. 'Enlisting Hamoud's father was a stroke of genius. All blame could be passed on to the Lord Chancellor.'

'My father aged ten years in nine months,' Hamoud recalled.

'He sent my father off to speak with the other systems,' Nasim said. 'Tell their leaders they had no choice. The Protectorate must sign. Else we would be invaded.'

'Nasim's father saved all our lives,' Hamoud said. 'He spoke to the business leaders first. He convinced them of the reality that our rulers wanted to ignore. That we must accept the inevitable, and negotiate the best terms possible. Which meant acting together.'

Amanda waited. It was good to feel this sense of ease, even with the clock counting down to their own mysterious invitation. She glanced out of the front windows, watching the line of the sunrise trace its way across the globe. Soon.

Hamoud went on, 'My father refused to enter into formal talks until Nasim's father returned from his mission, and only if all the rulers agreed. As a result, two things happened. Nasim's father was carried from system to system by a GSA battleship, with six battlecruisers as his official escort.'

When Hamoud went silent, Amanda pressed, 'And the second thing?'

'My father invited the GSA delegates to join him on a trek across the Great Divide. That is my clan's name for the Rift.'

'This trek forms the heart of our annual games,' Nasim said.

'Nasim and I went as my father's personal aides. I was fourteen, Nasim thirteen.'

'Twelve,' Nasim corrected. 'My thirteenth birthday was the day after we returned.'

'Our planet has a valley that runs almost from pole to pole, nine kilometers deep and sixteen wide. Seven thousand waterfalls. Five different changes to climate and vegetation. It was fought over for centuries. Now it is a global park, open to everyone – all tribes, all clans, all classes. No one may live there, though the emir keeps a tent, as large as a palace. Nor may it be mined or farmed. A tribute to our future, and our peace.'

'We hiked in from a station at the boundary of our harshest desert,' Nasim recalled, smiling now. 'We rode beasts from the books of my childhood.'

'We remained there for two and a half months,' Hamoud said. 'And when we returned, the delegates were our allies.'

'Our friends,' Nasim corrected. 'The deputy leader offered to adopt me. Show me life in the inner realms.'

'My father sought to show these strangers what it meant to call ourselves Arab,' Hamoud said. 'To have a way of life that was powerful enough, beautiful enough, to deserve our separate status.'

'That was why he sent Nasim's father on the mission,' Amanda realized. 'To give him time to convince the delegates not to consume the protectorate.'

'They succeeded,' Nasim said. 'The two of them working together did the impossible. We are now officially allied to the empire, but we still retain our independence.'

'They made a song in our fathers' honor,' Hamoud said.

'The Song of the Rift,' Nasim smiled. 'Shame neither of us can carry a tune.'

Hamoud said, 'Still it is sung on the day of our treaty's signing.'

Amanda nodded slowly. What she thought was how desperately glad she felt to have Rickets send these two men. What she said was, 'You think that is why the Lorians invited me back this morning. To make me accept their methods. To force me to understand their Prime Directives.'

'It is possible.'

'What do you think is going to happen?'

'Something that the scientists have waited sixty years to witness,' Nasim said.

'We don't have the three and a half months your fathers had to figure things out, or change the Lorians to our way of thinking.'

'Six days,' Hamoud agreed. 'Not long.'

As she rose from her seat, she told Hamoud, 'I want you to come along.'

She feared the two men would object. And to be fair, the decision was risky from start to finish. But Nasim merely nodded and said, 'Having you both witness whatever this is might help solve the mystery. And fast.'

Hamoud stood. 'You can handle both sled and probe?'

'Why do you think I was given two hands?' Nasim slipped into the pilot seat. 'Dawn is coming. Hurry and suit up.'

TWENTY

Amanda became increasingly nervous as they departed. Nasim's voice came through the helmet's speakers, so clear he might have been stationed on Amanda's other side. 'Probe and sled are both armed and in position.'

Growing up in Florida, sunrise had been Amanda's favorite time of day. Her first year after the Academy, stationed one hundred and nineteen light years from Earth's system, her mother still seldom communicating with her, Amanda had often dreamed of her childhood dawns. Once or twice each week, she and her eldest brother had slipped from the house and danced their way down the trail connecting their home to the Inland Waterway. They had fished or canoed or paddle-boarded and watched the world come alive around them. There was a special breed of dolphins that thrived in the brackish waters, smaller than their ocean-going cousins and very friendly. They often slipped in alongside Amanda's craft, carving pastel prisms from the calm waters. Amanda dreamed of how they would glide at an angle, so that one brilliant eye was aimed straight at her, and chatter softly. On board the GSA sector headquarters, dominated by a superior she despised, Amanda normally woke from these dreams with her pillow wet from tears, certain the dolphins were telling her to come home. Back where she belonged. Back where dawns beckoned and life held few surprises. Back where she could reduce all dangers because she knew their names.

There was no comfort to be found in the Lorian dawn, however. Nor beauty. Instead, the dual suns rose and drew back a crimson robe.

Amanda and Hamoud passed through the same cloud cover as the previous day, the same shade as the mist that had coated Amanda's faceplate. When they popped through and the pinkish-blue sea became visible, up ahead the island was still rimmed by the bright underwater illumination. As they approached the beach, the sun crested the horizon and the sea went dark.

Their arrival at the human-inhabited island was uneventful. Nasim spoke for the first time since she and Hamoud had begun their descent. 'All the heat signatures are gathered in the center of the island.'

Amanda halted twenty meters before the beach met the tree line. At very low speeds, the scooter's movement could be directed by subtle shifts to her body. Amanda found it similar to cycling or surfing or skateboarding, where the tiniest motions were sufficient. She tilted to her right and leaned in, and instantly the craft began a silent circuit of the island. Hamoud settled in five meters to her right, with the island to her left. When they arrived at the human compound, she slowed and checked the seven structures. All were empty. She halted by the beach and said, 'Ready?'

Hamoud replied, 'On your word, Major.'

Nasim said, 'Probe positioned five hundred meters above and north of the central peak. No threatening movement. All the human heat signatures are stationary.'

'Here we go.'

She lowered herself to a meter above the pink sand and followed a distinct trail through the undergrowth.

As though in response, the island up ahead began to glow.

Amanda stopped. 'Nasim?'

'I see it, Major. But only on the visible range. There is no change to the infrared.'

'The humans are holding steady?'

'They are all clustered at your two o'clock, about fifty meters from the . . .'

'Call it a device.'

'The Lorians form a circle around it. No heat signature, as before.'

'What are the Lorians doing?'

'Nothing that I can see, Major. No detectable movement.'

'Where's their weapon?'

'The conical top has not shifted position.'

Hamoud shifted position so as to travel directly behind her, for the pinkish trees were dense and tight to either side of the trail ahead. She said, 'Proceeding.'

'Roger.'

Two hundred meters, three, and now the light was so strong
Amanda had to squint. Then they broke through the trees, and
there in front of them the same pink sand formed a broad ⌐⌐⌐ring
around the central hill. Up close, it was utterly clear that this was
not a hill at all. Instead, it appeared to be some form of beacon
The structure was perhaps two hundred meters in circumference
at its base, rising to a pointed cone. It was made from the same
sand as the beach and the clearing, compacted in perfect symmetry,
without crease or opening. The entire structure emitted a powerful
glow. And something more. Amanda felt herself drawn forward,
as if the light held a magnetic quality, one that *invited.*

She whispered, 'Hamoud, do you feel it?'

'Most certainly.'

Nasim asked, 'Feel what?'

When Amanda did not respond, Hamoud said, 'There is a force,
or communication. Something that pulls at me.'

Amanda pointed to her left. 'Look there.'

One of the Lorians broke away and started towards her. Amanda
thought it was the one the scientists called the Diplomat, but she
could not be certain. At a gesture, a human woman reluctantly
turned and followed.

The Lorians formed an almost solid ring around the conical
structure. She could only estimate their numbers by the size of
the structure at their center. There were probably several thousand
of them, but it was extremely hard to be certain. They seemed to
have partly melted together, forming a single body with thousands
of heads.

The Diplomat halted in front of them and said, 'You are
welcome, Separate One. But you must come no closer.'

Amanda realized the woman scientist's face was streaked by
tears. 'What's the matter?'

When the woman did not respond, the Lorian said, 'Speak for
us all.'

'We've waited sixty-seven years,' the woman said.

'Waited for *what*?'

'Your position is the closest we've ever come before today.'
She turned to the Lorian. 'Thank you so much. I can't tell you
how much this means . . .'

'Go and rejoin.' The Lorian started to turn away, then said to

Amanda, 'Observe what is never to be yours, Separate One. Here is the cost of your existence.'

Amanda watched the two of them return to the Gathering. The Lorian melded slightly and refashioned itself into the conglomerate. The scientist slipped back to where the other humans opened and then refolded themselves around her. Doing the best they could to mimic the Lorian's act of joining.

Hamoud muttered, 'I hear the words. But I understand nothing.'

Amanda had difficulty observing the human scientists. No matter how hard she tried, they remained slightly out of focus. If she did not know better, she would have said they were *melting*.

Then she realized the light had strengthened.

Amanda was suddenly very frightened. She prized herself on being extremely observant, no matter what went on around her. Her first year at the Academy, all cadets were run through a battle-field obstacle course under live-fire conditions. Afterwards, the instructor had passed out exam sheets and ordered them to diagram the position of all enemy combatants, human and otherwise. Amanda had been the lone cadet to pass on her first run. Yet here she was, so involved in studying a group of scientists that she had failed to notice the change.

This was not some mere shift in gradient. While Amanda had not been paying attention, the light had become *ferocious*. The conical hill was now a beacon that defied the rising sun. She turned to ask Hamoud if he had noticed anything in the moments she had not been paying full attention. But her question died unspoken.

Hamoud stared straight at the beacon. The illumination showed a man utterly transfixed. His eyes appeared unfocused, his jaw was slack. As she watched, a faint line of moisture ran down from the corner of his nearside eye, across his cheek, and dappled the inside of his helmet.

Amanda turned back and squinted at the humans, and . . .

She was lost.

TWENTY-ONE

A manda coughed. She breathed. She opened her eyes.
The female scientist who had approached earlier stood
watching her. Ying's eyes were clear, her gaze calm. The
scientist said, 'Now perhaps you will understand. If there is any
hope of teaching you at all.' Then she turned away.

Amanda realized the clearing was empty. 'Wait!'

The scientist merely smiled over her shoulder. 'Farewell,
Separate One.'

Hamoud coughed weakly. His limbs shifted. He tried to speak
but did not actually form any words.

Amanda could not understand it. She had only been out for a
few seconds. The conical hill had resumed its bland pinkish
coloring, melding smoothly with the empty clearing.

Nasim spoke through the headset, 'Major?'

'I'm here.'

'Hamoud, can you hear me?'

Hamoud gave another feeble cough in reply.

Nasim sounded very tense. Angry, in fact. Furious. 'Hamoud,
talk to me.'

'Give me a minute.'

Then Amanda saw the probe positioned directly in front of them.
It constantly shifted position, carving a tight semi-circle from the
air. Then it moved up thirty meters and repeated the process. To
her left, the sled with its double-barrel armament faced in the
opposite direction, making the same semi-circular scan. The sight
drew Amanda's world back into sharp focus. It was the standard
pattern of weapons on autopilot. Weapons *hot.* Weapons in *combat.*

'Nasim, where's the threat?'

'I have no idea. Hamoud, are you certain you're OK?'

'Yes, yes.' He lifted a feeble hand and tried to wipe his face.
When his glove touched his helmet, he realized what he had
done, dropped his hand, and stared around him. 'Where is
everybody?'

Nasim replied, 'The Lorians and the scientists left hours ago.'
'What do you mean, *hours*?'

Then Amanda realized. 'Hamoud. Look at the suns.'

'I don't . . .' Realization dawned in shocking swiftness, drawing
clarity back to the pilot's dark gaze. 'That's impossible.'

'Nasim, how long have we been out?'

'I've been trying to raise you for *seven hours*.' Nasim's tension
now had a name. Amanda realized the man was afraid. 'I let you
stay as you were because the woman who just left assured me this
was normal and you needed to wake up naturally. Your vitals
remained solid – no change from full wakefulness with either
of you, I thought . . . When you didn't respond to my calls, I drew
the probe in and pushed at Hamoud's shoulder. The woman scientist
who just left told me the first experience required a longer period
of recovery. That you would come around at sunset.'

At *sunset*. The first sun was almost below the horizon, the
streamers binding the two suns glowing like pink rivers. Overhead, the sun's light was closer to the white scale. But refracted
through the horizon's atmosphere, the planet tinted the light to
where it seemed to join with everything else on this world.

Then Amanda realized she desperately needed to use the fresher.

She powered up. 'We're returning now.'

They flew back to the lander, cycled in, and rushed through the
fresher. By the time both had showered and dressed, Nasim had
a meal ready. They ate in silence, the atmosphere tense from
Nasim's unspoken questions.

Amanda felt like her brain remained only partially connected
to her body. She had to make a conscious effort to lift her fork,
open her mouth, chew, swallow, again. Nasim remained seated in
the pilot's chair, swiveled around so that his back was to the pink
world. Amanda positioned her own chair to match his, so that they
both faced Hamoud. Anything was better than watching the curtain
of night draw over another lost day. Amanda's gaze was repeatedly
drawn to the shipboard clock. Remorselessly counting down to
failure.

Her back and legs and neck ached from having held a stationary
position for so long. *Seven hours*. Her head pounded softly. As
she drank Nasim's tea, her gaze fastened upon the clock above

the side station. The absence of answers and the pressure of diminishing hours only added to her pain.

Hamoud still looked utterly shattered. He seemed only partly aware of where he was or what he did. Nasim watched his friend with a tight, worried expression.

Finally, Nasim served them both another mug of tea, then pressed the button to bring up the video-cam.

'No,' Hamoud said.

Amanda wanted to agree, but she said, 'Nasim is correct. We must file a report.'

Hamoud sighed.

Nasim said, 'I suggest we record all three of us constantly, so that our responses can be taken on the first round.'

'There won't be a second,' Amanda agreed.

Hamoud coughed so hard he doubled over.

Nasim waited for him to straighten, then asked, 'All right, my friend?'

Hamoud rocked his hand back and forth. *So-so.* 'Let's get this over with.'

In truth, Amanda wanted nothing more than to unroll her pallet and disappear into sleep. But this needed to be done. Even now the memories seemed to be slipping from her, like tendrils of a dream forgotten upon awakening. 'I'll go first.'

'Rolling.'

Amanda took her time, starting from the point when she descended through the pink clouds. The records were mostly for themselves; they would be trimmed and reworked and discussed at length once they returned to base. For now, she carefully described the sequencing, as it helped draw the incredible day into focus. By the time she finished speaking, night cloaked the globe below. Nasim shifted the camera angle. 'Hamoud?'

'I agree with everything the major has said.'

'You have nothing to add?'

'One point. No, two.' He paused to cough. 'Sorry.'

'You don't look well.'

'I'll be all right after a night's rest. Point one. When the light strengthened, I heightened the magnification so I could study the Lorians.'

'I should have thought of that.' Amanda instantly realized what she had said, and blushed furiously. The complete novice who forgets the attributes of her own suit. 'Sorry.'

'No problem.' Nasim typed. 'Erased.'

She sighed. 'I am such a total beginner.'

Nasim touched the keyboard. 'Rolling.'

'Two things,' Hamoud repeated. 'I am certain the Lorians did not melt, as you wondered. They remained independent. But the strengthened light coursed between them in a very defined pattern. It was quite beautiful, actually.'

Amanda asked, 'Did you see the same light pattern connected to the scientists?'

'The angle was not good, and most were behind the hill from where I was positioned. But I thought so. Yes. Perhaps not as strong.' He coughed again. 'Sorry.'

'This light from the hill,' Nasim said. 'My instruments noted no change.'

That drew them both around. Amanda asked, 'What are you saying?'

'The hill's level of illumination remained stable throughout,' Nasim replied.

'That's impossible,' Hamoud said.

'Even so, it remained constant through the entire Gathering. When the people left, it faded.' Nasim shrugged. 'I can play back the feed from the probe, if you like.'

'Tomorrow,' Hamoud said. 'I want to see it. Very much. But not now.'

Nasim nodded. 'And the second point?'

'The major said the period when we were unconscious seemed very short. I can be more precise. It lasted three breaths.'

'Seven hours, my friend,' Nasim said. 'I was very worried.'

'Three breaths,' Hamoud insisted. 'I use breathing to count time in combat. It is second nature. I shut my eyes against the illumination, counted three breaths, and the light faded, and the clearing was empty.'

Nasim rocked softly in his seat, back and forth, then reached for the controls. 'This is all very—'

'And something more. When I opened my eyes and saw everyone had left, I felt a great loss.' Hamoud must have seen the surprise in Amanda's face, for he asked, 'You did not sense this?'

'Disorientation,' Amanda replied. 'It was hard to refocus. Soreness from staying in one position that long. But nothing else.'

'Loss,' Hamoud insisted. 'I felt a huge vacuum at the center of my being, so strong my bones ached.'

Amanda studied him. The handsome features appeared more drawn now, the shadows created by the interior lighting almost cavernous.

'What the Lorian called you. The Separate One. It makes sense now.' Hamoud coughed, harder this time, and waved at the camera. 'Turn that off. I for one must rest.'

TWENTY-TWO

A manda woke as the first sun rose over the eastern horizon. She raised her head far enough to check the galley's chrono. She had been asleep for six hours. Her body ached more now than when she had laid down. Even so, she regretted having rested that long. The gradual sweep of sunlight over the planet served as a relentless and unforgiving timer. They were entering into their third day on Loria, and she was nowhere near answering the questions they had brought with them

Amanda lay on her pallet and imagined herself re-entering the *Invictus*. Captain Barrat would no doubt assign her the lowliest, most odiferous station his ship possessed, probably one that had most recently served duty as a corral for farm animals. And that would be nothing compared to her arrival at GSA sector headquarters. Rickets would take her report and dismiss her with a nod. Then she would be back serving under a staff officer ready to end her career.

She rose to a seated position and gave the unwanted fears a mental shove. She was not alone in this. The problem was shared with two men whom she both liked and trusted. The pile of equipment formed a bulky wall separating Amanda's pallet from Hamoud and Nasim. She heard Hamoud cough softly, and realized he had done so off and on all night. The sound had drawn her repeatedly from deep sleep without actually waking her. She stared at the

sunlit viewport and allowed herself to consider her two compan-
ions. They were both intensely handsome and very appealing. And
yet it was only now, as she idled away a quiet few minutes, that
she thought about them in a remotely romantic way.

Back when she was in her final year at the Academy, Amanda
had befriended a young subaltern temporarily assigned to teach a
class of recruits. The subaltern was recuperating from an injury
suffered during an investigation that had gone awry. Amanda
recalled the two of them seated in the corner of an empty classroom, discussing what it meant to lead a planetary mission made
up mostly of men. The woman had described how she had been
one of only three females, alone with forty-one male soldiers. And
yet she had never felt threatened. Just the opposite, in fact. The
subaltern had struggled to describe how the bond between soldiers
had meant everything. It was only after, when they had extracted
her and the other four wounded, and her team had visited her in
the hospital, that she had thought of them as, well, men.

At the time, what Amanda had heard most clearly was a subaltern leading a mission into unknown terrain. Her yearning to be
in that woman's position had been an almost physical pain. Now,
though, as she lay in her pallet and stared at the metal ceiling, she
understood. And was comforted by how she did not face the
mysteries down on Loria alone.

Nasim whispered, 'Major?'

'I'm awake.'

'Hamoud's fever is spiking.'

Their portable health scanner was originally designed for battle-
field use. This was both good and bad, as far as Amanda was
concerned. Good because the device was so simple a panic-
stricken untrained trooper facing incoming fire could operate it
correctly. Bad for all the same reasons.

The health scanner was a medium-size case, sculpted into a
tear-drop shape with four indents intended as handholds at top and
bottom and either side. After activation, a series of nine questions
appeared on a translucent screen that rose from the top. When
Amanda had trained with the device as a recruit, the questions
had fueled a lot of late-night laughter. Now, crouched beside
Hamoud as he sweated and twitched and groaned, the humor was

lost. *How many patients have life-threatening wounds? Select the patient closest to death; can a heartbeat be detected?* And so on.

When the machine pinged ready, Amanda followed the protocol she'd learned as a cadet. She scanned him from head to toe, keeping the machine about a hand's breadth from Hamoud. This close, the pilot did not look at all good.

The body scan complete, she held the machine as it extended a device from a hidden alcove and took blood from Hamoud's arm. Then a little white spoon emerged from another portal, and the screen flashed with instructions for Amanda to obtain a sample of Hamoud's saliva. That done, she stood over the body and waited as two quick flashes signaled X-rays and MRIs.

The machine hummed softly, then chirped.

Nasim demanded, 'What does it say?'

'No known infection. A planetary nanovirus is expected to be the cause of his illness but cannot actually be detected. Hamoud's genetic structure remains intact.' Amanda knelt and set the device beside Hamoud's left forearm. 'He is receiving injections of immune-system strengthener, antivirals, vitamins, fever reducer, and a calming sleep agent.'

The injections completed, the machine encircled Hamoud's wrist with a narrow plastic band. The machine began emitting a soft light in time to the patient's heart rate. The monitor showed oxygen intake and breathing, and a gradually reducing temperature. Hamoud sighed once more, spoke fragments of words that Amanda thought were Arabic, and slipped into a deeper sleep.

She asked, 'What did he say?'

'Separate One.' Nasim glanced at the planet dominating their front viewport and shook his head. 'These Lorians have much to answer for.'

Amanda rose to her feet. 'I need to travel back to the surface.'

'Breakfast first. Then we both go down together.'

'You are staying.' Amanda held up a hand, halting his protest. 'Hamoud needs monitoring, and you can guard my progress just as well from up here. Better, in fact.'

'Major—'

'The probe tracks me. The sled holds position directly by the Lorian weapon.'

Nasim looked down at his friend. 'I don't like this.'

Amanda decided there was no need to state the obvious. That they were no closer to answers. Even less to a solution.

TWENTY-THREE

As she suited up, Nasim protested once again that they should perhaps send the probe for a recce. But when Amanda did not respond, Nasim did not insist. The mission deadline weighed on them both. Hamoud's illness changed nothing.

She flew down alone. The suns were well over the horizon, the connecting light-ribbons strung across the eastern sky. Her descent into the planetary atmosphere was uneventful. The clouds were just clouds. The island sat in a placid coral-colored sea. The sky was precisely the same, thinly veiled, the wind calm. Amanda paused thirty meters off the shoreline and scouted.

Nasim said, 'Sled is in position.'

She wondered when it rained on this planet, and whether the rain fell in pink drops. 'Where are the scientists?'

'Everyone appears to be in the central structure, the one we assume holds the lab.'

Which was also the building they had dragged the woman from. 'And the Lorians?'

'Almost impossible to track them, since there's no heat signature. A dozen or so are outside the lab. A few by the central hill. Otherwise . . .'

Amanda decided, 'I'm going in.'

Amanda noticed the change within seconds of her arrival. The scientists' camp held a distinct difference. She positioned herself just outside the lab's central window, the platform hovering a few centimeters above the beach. Two of the scientists looked up from their work and waved in greeting. The others ignored her entirely.

The seven buildings appeared to be constructed entirely from beach sand. They extended out from the shore into open water, resting upon stubby columns that rose a meter or so above the

sea. The walls and window shutters and roof tiles were all solidified sand. As were the steps and pathway connecting the buildings
to the island.

The scientists appeared utterly unconcerned by her arrival.
Amanda was more than content to sit on her lander and observe.
It was the first time she had been given an opportunity to study
them at their routine. The central structure was over a hundred
paces long, with nine broad windows on either side, overlooking
the island and the sea. Through the open windows Amanda could
see a dozen lab tables that ran perpendicular to the shoreline,
each holding a number of instruments being operated by scientists
and research assistants. Power was supplied by solar panels lining
the roof.

No one spoke.

The silence was intense. Amanda heightened the feed to her
external mikes until she could hear their footsteps scrape across
the lab's floor, their fingers tapping the computer consoles. An
instrument portal was opened, a glass beaker of some kind was
set inside, the door shut, and the machine began softly whirring.
Otherwise, nothing. No insects. No birds. No waves. No wind.
The Lorians gathered along the shoreline were so motionless that
it was possible to ignore them entirely, as she would mounds of
sand with eyes and lipless mouths. Their bodies were featureless.
She shifted over slightly so as to examine them more closely. She
could see faint lines where the arm-like appendages extended from
their bodies. Same for the fingers. And their stubby legs. Almost
like suggestions of where the limbs would emerge and reform
when required.

Sayer stepped into the lab's entryway and hurried down the
ramp. He was followed by the exobiologist, Ying. 'Major Bostick.
Sorry to make you wait. I was in the middle of a very complex
investigation. Why didn't you let us know in advance that you
were coming?'

'I wanted a chance to observe you at work.'

'Would you like to come inside?'

The room's silent confines seemed almost claustrophobic,
despite the open windows. 'Maybe later. Does it rain here?'

Sayer followed the direction of her gaze. 'Ah. The absence of
glass in our windows. Rain yes, storm never.'

Ying said, 'No moon. No tides. No wind. No waves.'

Amanda asked, 'Who serves as your medical specialist?'

'I would,' Ying replied. 'If there was a need. Which there hasn't been.'

'One of my crew has become very ill.'

They both nodded. Sayer said, 'The man who accompanied you yesterday, yes? It's quite normal.'

'About half the new arrivals suffer from a fever after observing their first Gathering,' Ying said. 'It passes in a day or so. No lasting side effects.'

'Except a massive headache,' Sayer offered. 'I was out of commission for almost three days.'

'You and no one else,' Ying said.

'Barry was too.'

'Barry.' Ying huffed. 'I suppose every scientific mission must have at least one hypochondriac.'

Amanda looked from one to the other. Their former hostility, the tension, the resentment over her lack of understanding . . .

Gone.

Amanda asked, 'You haven't had any illnesses in sixty-seven years?'

'I've only been here for eleven,' Ling replied.

'Twelve,' Sayer corrected. 'Almost thirteen.'

Ying shrugged. 'Loria holds no transmutable bacteria. No viruses of any kind. The ocean is apparently void of all life forms. We grow all our food in the two hydroponics sheds.'

'What about normal things, you know . . .'

'Oh, sure. The occasional broken appendage or sprains.'

'Headaches,' Sayer insisted, his tone easy. 'Heart attacks, some cancer.'

'Everyone dies of something eventually,' Ying said. 'No one since my arrival has been under seventy at their passage.'

Amanda started to mention the deaths at the hands of the Lorians, but decided she would gain more by holding back.

Sayer said, 'We have a standard-issue health scanner.'

'Probably out of date now,' Ying said.

Sayer asked his associate, 'When was the last time you turned it on?'

Ying frowned. 'Three years ago? Four?'

Amanda had heard enough. 'Where is the one you call the Diplomat?'

'Behind you.'

She glanced back. The six Lorians remained stationary. And utterly identical as far as she could tell. 'Which one?'

'The one on the right. Do you need to speak with her?'

'Later. The Lorian is female?'

'We have no idea. Professor Darian called the first Diplomat a her. It stuck.'

'You haven't researched their biological make-up?'

Neither scientist responded. Amanda half expected the sort of angry retort she had known previously. But their bland expressions did not shift. In fact, she felt as though their response was, well . . .

Alien.

She tried again. 'I've read all your published research. Nothing has been said about the Gatherings.'

'We do not discuss those matters,' Sayer replied.

'This is another of their Prime Directives?'

'Yes, exactly.'

'Understanding these rules of existence has occupied most of our time here so far,' Ying added. 'Being permitted to fully enter the Gathering was our reward for getting things right.'

'Finally,' Sayer said. 'At long last.'

'We have a long way to go, but we've made a good start.'

'But . . . Your papers are published off-planet.'

Sayer shook his head. 'Telepaths, remember?'

'They would know,' Ying calmly insisted.

'They read your thoughts?'

'Before yesterday, definitely not. Now . . .'

'Probably not yet,' Ying said. 'But it is coming.'

Sayer turned to her. 'You think?'

'I have no evidence to back this up,' Ying replied. 'But after yesterday I am fairly certain it is only a matter of time.'

Amanda looked from one to the other. The ease of this conversation was so unexpected it left her at a loss as to how she should proceed. She asked the only thing that came to mind. 'So the deaths your colony has suffered—'

Nasim broke in with, 'Major, you must return shipside.'

Her first response was a drench of terror that her question had caused the cone to lift off the central hill. She cut off the external feed and demanded, 'Is their weapon on the move?'

'That is not the issue. Major, you need to get back here *now*.'

TWENTY-FOUR

When she was a kilometer above the surface and five klicks away from the island, Amanda pushed the go-stick to redline. Fifteen seconds later, she passed through the sonic barrier. 'Is it Hamoud?'

'Negative.' Nasim's reply carried an uncommon tension, worse even than when they had been attacked by the hilltop. 'You're now on my scanner, Major. I need you to relinquish control.'

'Wait, what?'

'I've shifted position. Speak the command "link controls to main vessel."'

Amanda did so and watched the go-stick take on a life of its own. 'What's wrong?'

'Hold one, Major. You're docking in ten seconds.'

She started to protest that it was impossible; she was nowhere near the cloud cover yet. Then she spotted the lander. Hovering just *beneath* the clouds.

When she cycled through the lock, Nasim was not there to help her unsuit. Nor was he watching over Hamoud. Instead, his gaze was fixed on the horizon beyond the front viewport. The internal gravity was on, a useless expenditure of energy this close to the planet. But it allowed Nasim to point the lander straight up.

'Tell me what's going on.'

Nasim pointed at the clouds. 'We have company.'

Amanda walked over with the suit's upper half dangling behind her. She did not need to ask if it was their ride home. GSA transports operated by a set of strict rules when it came to recoveries. If the timeline shifted, they would send an n-space alert.

'Military,' Nasim said. 'A Surrus-class battlecruiser.'

'But Surrus-class vessels haven't been in operation for years
. . . Oh.'

Nasim nodded. 'The pirates are back.'

They settled the lander down alongside the easternmost structure,
one of the hydroponics farms. The pirates no doubt were already
aware of the scientific mission and had probably discounted it as
of no immediate concern. Once they took over the planet, Amanda
knew, this would change. These scientists would be wiped out or
enslaved.

Amanda used the fresher, then suited up once more and cycled
back through the airlock. Sayer emerged from the lab building,
waved a greeting, and met her on the beach. 'Why don't you get
out of that suit? The water's fine.'

She realized the man had just made a joke. 'My orders require
me to maintain a quarantine-style distance.'

He nodded agreeably. 'Orders are orders.'

'I need to warn you that an evacuation may be required.'

'Sorry. That's not possible.'

'A heavily armed battleship is in orbit around this planet. We
have to assume they are pirates.'

'Oh, we know all about them.' Sayer waved it aside. 'They'll
get the same treatment as the last time.'

'You know about that?'

'Obviously.'

'Does that mean you're in telepathic communication with the
Lorians?'

'You heard what Ying said. Not in the way you suggest. Not
in thoughts. At least, not yet. But ever since this last Gathering,
when they have something they want us to know, they send an
image. Or impression. Or suggestion.' Sayer shrugged easily.
'It's hard to describe.'

'Try.'

'You know how an infant struggles to be understood? It's like
that in reverse. We are struggling to learn a new language.'

'A new *thought* language.'

'Precisely.' He beamed. 'For the first time in human history, we
are bonding with a telepathic alien race on *their* terms.'

Despite the imminent threat, Amanda's need for a clearer

understanding burned brightly. 'You've been expecting this telepathic transition for some time?'

'Hoping, more like.'

'I've read every article published by your group. You've said nothing at all about this possibility.'

'Oh, no,' Sayer said cheerfully. 'They wouldn't approve.'

'You're saying they censor what you study and everything you send off-planet.'

'It is a small price to pay, wouldn't you agree?' When Amanda did not respond, Sayer went on, 'We are bound by their Prime Directives. These go much deeper than mere laws. They've defined our existence. Even being allowed to know the Prime Directives exist took over thirty years. Now that we are tentatively accepted, we must pay the price for not following these unspoken rules. Whenever a Prime Directive is broken, the offending individual must relinquish their life. The difficulty we've had, the reason for these losses, all comes back to the simple fact that we have not been able to understand what the Lorians require in order to fully accept us.'

Nasim broke in, 'Major, perhaps you should return to the point.'

Amanda cut off the external comm-link, so Sayer could no longer hear what she said, and asked Nasim, 'Any shift from the pirate vessel?'

'Still patrolling pole to pole.'

'Let me know if anything changes.' She resumed contact with the chief scientist. 'You do realize everything we discuss will go into my planetary report.'

Sayer seemed to waver slightly, as though he shifted momentarily out of focus. Then the smile returned. 'You are a Separate One. You are not defined by our restrictions.'

She took a mental step away from the scientist and the island and the mysteries they represented. The presence of a heavily armed illegal vessel, Sayer's calm acceptance of this new threat, the pressure of vanishing hours, all came together in her mind. Her thoughts became compressed, caught in a vise that squeezed and squeezed, forcing her to see . . .

On one hand, she now had enough to supply headquarters with a full report. She could return and officially count the mission as a success. Any question Commander Rickets might put to her, in regard to this group and their strange attitudes, she could answer in a manner that would secure an up-tick on her record. She should feel satisfied. Whether this report would halt the threat of military invasion was not directly her concern. But she suspected her report would form ammunition for Rickets and her allies.

The comm-link clicked on and Nasim asked, 'Major?'

'Hold one.'

Although she remained stationary, Amanda felt as though she shifted her scooter out over the placid sea. Putting miles between her and the buildings and the island and the chief scientist and his strange smile. Hamoud's voice resonated through her mind. The *real* crisis. The *true* issue.

She did not know what that issue was. But she knew she was moving in the right direction. One step at a time. And her gut told her that the pirates actually played a role in uncovering the hidden truth.

Sayer broke in with, 'Can I ask you a question?'

Another first. 'Of course.'

'If we were to be evacuated, that is, assuming we don't all simply vaporize upon departure, how would that happen?'

'In a crisis situation, as mission commander I could order you to be transported to our retrieval ship. By force, if necessary.'

Sayer showed no response to her implied threat. Instead, he gestured to the lander and asked, 'How many people does your vehicle hold?'

'Thirty-one plus my crew.' She searched his placid expression. 'If necessary I could request assistance from the retrieval ship. And its bevy of marines.'

'Would it cause problems, taking on so many extra passengers?' Sayer's tone remained amiable, unconcerned. 'Though I suppose we could bring produce from our hydroponics.'

Amanda studied him intently. Sayer seemed utterly disconnected from what was happening. Involved in a casual conversation with a colleague. As if the previous day's events had never occurred. 'These questions of yours. Do they come from you or the Lorians?'

Sayer quavered once more. It was the only way Amanda knew to describe what she observed. It was more than a shudder. The man actually seemed to go out of focus. The shift was so quick it was possible to pretend it did not happen. Sayer stilled and replied, 'I suppose . . . It is not one or the other, Major.'

Nasim broke into her next question. 'Major, Hamoud has woken up.'

TWENTY-FIVE

Hamoud asked, 'So what's been happening?'

Amanda hesitated. Hamoud seemed totally disinterested. His voice suggested the question had been spoken on automatic pilot. Hamoud remained seated on his pallet, sipping from a mug of Nasim's soup. It was the first nourishment he had taken in almost a day. Nasim looked worriedly at Amanda and did not respond.

Amanda asked, 'How are you feeling?'

'Terrible. My head is pounding. My stomach keeps threatening . . .'

She squatted down beside Nasim. 'I think you should take a pain reliever.'

'My neck and shoulders are so stiff it's hard . . . I'm sorry, what did you say?'

Amanda watched her pilot struggle to focus. 'You need relief from your discomfort and another full rest period.'

'I . . . Yes . . . Perhaps . . .'

Amanda shifted so Nasim could fit the med-scan on Hamoud's left arm. She watched him order two injections, one for the pain and the second another sleep inducer. As Nasim worked, Hamoud's gaze drifted to the front viewport. 'Why is the light so diffused? Or is it me?'

The question was all the confirmation Amanda needed that they were right to be knocking him out again. Nasim snorted softly, as if in agreement with her unspoken thoughts, and hit the button. The scanner whirred, then chirped in confirmation. Amanda said, 'Lie back down and close your eyes.'

Hamoud did as he was instructed. 'Oh. That's better.' He sighed a long, 'Sorry. So sorry.'

Amanda waited until his breathing was steady, then asked, 'Any change?'

Nasim did not need to ask what she meant. He set the scanner to one side, rose, and stepped to the pilot's controls. 'The battle-cruiser is still doing its pole-to-pole.'

Which meant they were mapping the surface. It was only a matter of time before her lander was detected. 'Help me out of my suit.'

She ate two mugs of Nasim's soup seated in the co-pilot's chair. Nasim shifted back and forth between Hamoud's pallet and the monitors tracking the vessel overhead. She was glad for the silence. Several elements had started coming together while she had show-ered and changed. The soup was as thick as stew and spiced with some distinctly Arab herbs; she thought it was probably tarragon and ground cardamom seeds. As she finished the second mug, Nasim again inspected the monitors, and said, 'No change to the battleship's course.'

'Their planetary survey can't take much longer.' Amanda rose and carried her mug to the cooking station. 'Tea?'

'Please.'

'I think we need to assume our position has already been noted.'

'There's nothing we can do about it,' Nasim agreed.

She over-sweetened Nasim's tea, the way she knew he preferred, gave him the mug, then stood over Hamoud's silent form. Thinking.

'Is he resting easy?'

She sipped from her mug. *The hidden crisis*, she heard their pilot say again. *The secret mystery*.

'Major?'

Amanda slipped into her chair and said, 'I have an idea.'

'I'm relieved to hear it,' Nasim said.

'You might not be when you hear what I have in mind.'

Nasim squinted at the pink clouds. 'Major, we have hostiles repeatedly crossing overhead. There's every chance the pirates will blame us for their missing ship. I am at a complete loss.'

Amanda stared at the digital clock. The pressure continued to mount. 'I want to take the initiative.'

Nasim turned from the viewport. 'A planetary lander. Going up against a heavily armed battlecruiser.'

'Right.'

Nasim replied, 'No doubt they will be as surprised as I.'

'It all comes down to why Rickets ordered us here.' Amanda could almost see the plans take concrete form as she spoke. 'If our ultimate aim is to keep GSA forces from invading the protect- orate, we must take any opportunity, no matter how dangerous, to engage with the pirates.'

Nasim studied her a long moment, then said, 'Rickets was right to trust you with this mission.'

Amanda downloaded all their reports to an emergency pod, including one she hastily prepared while Nasim checked on Hamoud. The pod was too small to be detected by most systems, and transmitted an alert signal on a frequency only accessible to empire vessels. She watched the little pod drift away from the airlock, then hit the switch breaking the link and sending it into low-alt orbit. It blinked twice in silent farewell, then vanished.

She turned her chair to where Nasim knelt beside Hamoud. 'How is he?'

'Totally out. Monitor shows him resting easy.'

'Maybe we should suit up. Unless you think it might send the wrong message, a peace mission showing up in battle armor.'

But Nasim was already up and moving. 'Help me get Hamoud into his gear.'

TWENTY-SIX

'Surrus battlecruiser, this is Major Amanda Bostick, temporary head of the GSA scientific mission on Loria. Come in, please.'

Amanda hoped her tremors of fear were not detectable to the ship passing overhead. Nasim focused on the monitors and remained silent.

Amanda repeated her alert a second time. Third. Fourth. Then, 'Surrus commander, please note, I may have information regarding your missing vessel. Come in, please—'

'Explain yourself.'

The voice was most likely alien. There were certain traits shared by all non-human species when speaking System English. Either a roughness to the words, as if they were being sawn from stone. Or a sibilant texture, as if drawn from a wet and clinging muck. Amanda was almost certain she was being addressed by a species communicating through a highly sophisticated voder. 'May I ask with whom I speak?'

'Questions later. First explain.'

'I arrived three days ago from Galactic Space Arm to investigate a similar issue to your own. One-fifth of our scientific staff on this planet has been wiped out. We are only now beginning to understand why. I think the evidence we uncovered may help explain your situation.'

Nasim said softly, 'The vessel is now stationary directly above us.'

Amanda said, 'Captain, may I suggest that you do not enter the planet's atmosphere.'

'You threaten me?'

'We are an unarmed lander. I am trying to save you from further losses.' When the Random officer remained silent, Amanda said, 'Request permission to come on board.'

Forty years back, the empire's vessels underwent a drastic shift. Related technology had been gradually transitioning for a century, ever since a new species had been drawn into the Stellar Alliance. They had brought with them a novel way of manipulating energy. The human's usage of this technology came together the year Amanda's parents were married, and made headlines throughout the Human Empire. By the time she was old enough to dig a shallow tunnel under the spaceport's perimeter fence, the new generation of ships dominated Port Canaveral's military and commercial landing fields. Even so, Amanda had grown up building models of Surrus-class cruisers. Their vast array of armaments and sensing equipment reached out like a space-going porcupine. There was no question what they were designed to do: grip the fabric of space, shift position fast, and destroy whatever form the enemy took.

The new breed of vessel was something else entirely.

The same technology that formed her translucent vehicle had caused the redesign of every modern spaceship. All those external probes and cannons were no longer required. On the new craft, the instruments and weaponry were fashioned from focusing the ship's energy upon a minute suggestion of an appendage. Using a larger physical structure did not help the process in any way. In fact, the ship's shields were strongest when the physical surface was not just smooth but polished. Which resulted in the new class of vessels being built without hard edges of any kind. The sensors and weapons and n-space drive were fitted into shallow indentations.

For reasons that only interested quantum physicists, a creamy silver coloring worked best.

Amanda had often hunted and fished the swampy Seminole lands with her brothers and father. Her greatest triumph had come from finding artifacts, especially the flint arrowheads that had been imported from other tribes. That was what the new vessels reminded Amanda of – giant polished arrowheads.

They were awesomely beautiful crafts. Great star-going works of art. The latest emblem of human advancement through peaceful trade with other species. A declaration that mankind had, at long last, come of stellar age.

But the Surrus-class vessels still took Amanda's breath away.

Their lander broke through the cloud cover and flew towards Loria's north pole. Three minutes later, Nasim said, 'Target is dead ahead.'

'I see it.'

The Random battleship was a fearsome metal beast that cut a jagged silhouette from the stars. As they closed, Amanda thought it could only be a pirate vessel.

TWENTY-SEVEN

They were ordered to enter amidships, on the largest of the vessel's landing decks. Amanda watched the blast-doors close behind them, sealing them in. She studied the array of cannons lining the two side walls, and saw how the two nearest troop transports were shifted around so as to aim their shipboard weapons at them. She muttered, 'Maybe this wasn't such a good idea.'

In response, Nasim hissed softly.

She tracked the direction of his gaze. 'Oh, no.'

The interior portals drew back, and their escort entered the docking bay. At their head was a pair of . . .

'Glyphs,' Nasim said. 'So the rumors are true.'

She swallowed against the electric dread. 'Maybe you're mistaken. Maybe they're—'

'No. Those are glyphs. Their merchants visit Oman's largest moon from time to time. Trading.' Nasim must have felt her stare, for he shrugged. 'They pay in gold.'

'What do we do?'

Nasim shook his head. 'No idea.'

The Human Empire was linked by treaty with seventy-three alien races. Warlike species were relatively rare. Historical records now available to humans revealed that most highly aggressive races destroyed themselves long before they achieved interstellar flight. Developing a star-drive required a planetary-size effort. Which meant the system was required to rise beyond its primitive roots before it could join with other races.

But there remained exceptions to this galactic rule.

A few species hunted other races as a part of their transition to full adulthood. Still others considered war and planetary conquest to be normal components of trade and expansion. Any such race, or those who enslaved intelligent species and treated them as goods to be traded, was banned from joining the Stellar Alliance.

One reason why entry into the Alliance took so long was that current members had to vote on every new race. And accepting them also meant accepting their enemies. Which created some very real conflicts among existing members. So each new race had to prove they were genuine allies, and also carried with them sufficient value to justify naming all their foes as enemies.

And then there were the glyphs.

This particular forbidden race treated humans as food.

The glyphs. It was hard for Amanda to separate her childhood terrors from what she had learned as a cadet. Especially since this species fueled any number of late-night bull sessions at the Academy.

The military's own records made for brutal reading. Very few species were interested in the narrow band of planetary requirements that sustained human life. What before had been called the Goldilocks zone was now classed simply as HER – Human Environmental Range – grades one through three. Grade one meant liquid water, balmy weather, adequate mineral resources, absence of any conflicting sentient species, and so forth. The Lorian system was classed as grade three because of its lack of arable land, the silicate-based environment, and the presence of a telepathic race. HER-3 planets were used for transport and supply hubs, little else.

Unfortunately, the glyphs shared the same planetary requirements as humans.

But that was not what made them so terrifying.

Soon after first contact, the glyphs discovered a peculiar trait unique to humans that made them not just edible but a unique delicacy. When a human was forced into a state of extreme terror or pain, the adrenal glands drenched the muscles and blood with a distinctive blend of proteins that created an overpowering aphrodisiac for glyphs.

Needless to say, glyphs only ate flesh that was still alive.

Glyphs were oxygen breathers and preferred flat terrain covered by shallow waters, with stable temperatures in the semi-tropical range.

In other words, they were swamp dwellers who would have been right at home in the Everglades.

The three glyphs stood on two stumpy legs, with a third appendage that stretched flat behind them and supported their weight when stationary, like a portable stool. Their expressions were of constant astonishment, their eyes round and somewhat protruding. They breathed via gills running down their necks. Their mouths were as circular as their eyes, like giant suckerfish, and lined with dagger-sharp teeth.

Amanda whispered, 'I'm so sorry.'

The three glyphs were accompanied by a bevy of some smaller gray-skinned species that Amanda did not recognize. The glyphs waited while their minions set the portable weapons on tripods and took aim at the transport.

Amanda said, 'Talk about overkill. Why do they need another weapon?'

Nasim shook his head. 'I have heard of these. They are called pain amplifiers.'

'Oh. Great.'

One of the glyphs carried a voder attacked to a chest belt. The mouth writhed, the teeth glistened, then the transport's communicator said, 'Open your portal.'

Amanda pressed the respond key and said, 'I formally protest your show of force. We come in peace. Our sole aim is to assist you in avoiding further losses.'

'That is the wrong answer.' The glyph turned to the minions. 'Fire.'

TWENTY-EIGHT

The weapon passed easily through the lander's shields. Amanda's skin crawled with a million electric bees, burrowing and stinging. She heard one of the men scream, or perhaps both of them, and she shrilled in response.

The amplifier did not just magnify physical pain. All the emotions she had so tightly compressed and stored away, the years of guilt and loneliness and longing, these too were magnified. The intensity threatened to tear her apart. She screamed, and screamed again, for it was the only way to release a tiny shred of all that distress.

Then, nothing.

The relief was exquisite. Amanda had time for one great heaving sob of a breath, then the glyph said, 'Open your portal.'

'No! I protest—'

The bees attacked again.

When they stopped, her head was filled with Hamoud's hoarse moans. The pilot gasped, 'What is happening?'

'Quiet, brother,' Nasim replied. 'Be still.'

'But . . .'

The glyph repeated, 'Open your portal.'

Amanda pressed the button that released both sides of the airlock, and said again, 'I'm so sorry.'

The gray minions swarmed inside. They lifted her and the men and carried them out. The glyphs wheeled about and led them into the ship. Amanda saw little besides the corridor's metal ceiling. When she raised her head to look forward, hands gripped the point where her helmet connected to the suit's neck and hauled her back.

Eventually, they arrived at an annex to the control room. The minions fitted them into racks that stretched along the rear wall, holding them in three starfish patterns. A metal protrusion jutted into the small of her back, forcing Amanda into an extremely uncomfortable position. She and the men breathed in tight gasps.

The annex formed a sort of holding room for the gray minions. They were dwarfish figures scarcely taller than her waist but equipped with appendages that accordioned out to three times their height. A shallow sleeve rose from the floorplates, grooves through which the blast-doors would slide shut. The minions did not pass that line and enter the control room beyond. Directly in front of her, through the open blast-doors, Amanda saw the pink planet suspended in a velvet black sky.

The glyph equipped with a voder stepped in close and observed as the minions struggled to release the catches on Nasim's suit. Finally, they failed and stepped away. Amanda thought she saw them shudder, and wondered how many of them had been strapped in where she now hung.

The glyph said, 'Open your suit.'

'No. We come in peaceful . . .' Amanda watched the minions carry in one of the pain amplifiers and set the tripod directly in front of where she dangled. The prospect of swarming electric bees drew her brain into hyper-speed. 'Wait! We are suited because we carry an extremely contagious infection!'

The glyph spoke a single word, and the minions froze in place. The sound of its speech was sucking, wet, voracious. Through its voder, the glyph said, 'Explain.'

Amanda turned to her right and saw that the man hanging next to her was Nasim. 'The man furthest away from me. He contracted a terrible sickness. We think it is a nanovirus. We are both now infected. We have not found a cure—'

'Enough.' The glyph moved out of her field of vision. When it returned, it stepped close enough for Amanda to see the flecks of yellow dotting its hide. 'First we will harvest the other humans. Then we will study this infection. If it exists.'

'It does, really—'

'Silence.' He studied her a moment longer, then decided, 'I will devour you first. And during. And last of all.'

TWENTY-NINE

When the glyph spokesman returned to the control room. Hamoud moaned slightly and asked, 'What happened to us?'

The glyph stepped back into the connecting passage and ordered, 'One more word, and we turn the weapon on. And we leave it on through the harvest.'

Hamoud went silent.

Their suits were not intended to be bent backwards, which meant the starfish arch was restricted somewhat. Plus the internal balancing mechanism helped support Amanda's weight. Even so, the metal hump bent her spine and kept her joints stretched taut. Her helmet was strapped to the wall like her arms and legs. But at least the electronic bee stings had mostly worn off.

She risked another glance to her right. Nasim met her gaze and grimaced. Seeing that good man stretched out on the wall rack hurt worse than any physical pain she had ever known. She turned away. Another dozen or so empty racks extended out to her left. Waiting for the harvest.

Directly ahead of her, the command center's view-screens formed an unbroken vista that curved along the front wall. Loria drew so close it filled the entire wall. Only in the top right corner was a sliver of space still visible above Loria's northern pole. Amanda watched as the ship entered the cloud cover, and thought of the unarmed scientists clustered on the island below. She had never felt so helpless.

Amanda's tears began falling in a steady stream.

Then the ship groaned.

*   *   *

Multiple alarms began clanging throughout the vessel. Amanda's internal speaker system was designed to mimic the outside environment. The placement of external sounds was essential in identifying threats, and now this meant that she heard alarms from all directions. A glyph appeared in the command room's portal and roared. The gray minions not manning the pain amplifier scattered. The control room became a hive of frantic activity.

The ship gave a violent shudder. The alarms shrieked at a painful volume. The control room's viewports became rimmed by brilliant flashes as the ship's cannons fired. Streaks of energy flashed in every direction, but Amanda could not identify their intended target. It seemed to her as though the glyphs fired at nothing except . . .

Clouds.

The shaking grew violent, as powerful as an earthquake. Those glyphs still standing clung to control stations and roared in angry protest. The destroyer's weapon streamers became as constant and brilliant as the alarms.

Abruptly the shudders stopped.

Amanda took a steadying breath. Another. She had to assume the cruiser's firepower had eradicated the Lorians' defense.

There was a massive shriek of rending metal. Sparks and flames and explosions erupted on all sides.

Then the strongest quake of all *slammed* her from behind and above.

THIRTY

Amanda must have blacked out, because the next thing she knew, she was slipping through tendrils of pink webbing. The cloud veil was much thicker than during her first descent, strong as tensile fingers. She felt as though she was being passed gently from hand to hand. Her suit and her body and her limbs and her helmet were probed, inspected, then released. Her descent was slow, steady, calm.

The sensation was one of being scrutinized. Taking her measure through the touch of a million tiny hands. All fashioned from the pink clouds.

Her thoughts seemed fragile and partly disconnected. In her addled state, it seemed as though the clouds also probed her *mind*. Which was just crazy, she knew. And yet . . .

The sky around her was filled with debris. Minions and parts of the battlecruiser fell in slow motion, caught and released in the same pattern as herself. And yet not the same at all.

Above her and slightly to the right, Amanda watched as the clouds gripped a trio of glyphs and . . .

Tore them apart.

'Major!'

'*Nasim!*'

'I can see our transport! It appears to be intact.'

'Will it respond to voice command?'

'Pilot to EV, approach my position. Yes! Yes! Pilot to EV, prepare airlock for pickup!'

'Nasim, do you see . . . *Hamoud!*'

About five hundred meters to her left, a limp space-suited figure slipped through the cloud tendrils, spinning slowly, limbs outstretched, graceful as silent ballet.

'Nasim!'

When he did not respond, Amanda assumed he was cycling through the airlock. Then she realized the baton forming her individual scooter was still attached by her left collarbone. She pulled it free, powered up, and cried in relief when the oval platform took shape and the instrument panel illuminated her helmet. She halted her descent, drew up the shields, and took aim for Hamoud.

The pilot continued to fall, with limbs and head rearranging themselves each time they passed through more webbing. Amanda's own mental state was much clearer now. She began consciously registering a multitude of factors she had totally missed before then.

'I have you in sight, Major. I'm three klicks out and closing.'

'How's the EV?'

'No apparent damage. Amazing.'

Only it was not amazing. It was . . .

Impossible.

The debris field stretched out in every direction. Components as large as their transport, but torn to fluttering metal ribbons, went through the same pattern of catch-and-tear-and-release. Fragments as small as her hand, tiny as a fingernail, spilled down in a constant metal rain. She slowed her approach as a partially shredded battle cannon fell between her and Hamoud. She was close enough to actually see the cloud form into dozens of tendrils – hundreds – and probe the cannon before tearing away another shard. Shredding carbon-tempered titanium as easily as it had torn limbs off the glyphs.

Just as she reached Hamoud, she watched a dozen or so gray minions fall to her left, then become caught in the webbing, where one was plucked out and torn apart. The rest were released to continue falling. They shrieked in one unified voice as they fell through the pink webbing and vanished from sight.

Amanda said, 'I have Hamoud.'

She drew him onto the scooter's narrow platform by holding him in a fierce embrace. They passed through the debris field untouched. Hamoud's head lolled against the suit's neck-frame. She said, 'He's still unconscious.'

'Fifty meters and closing. Airlock is open and ready for retrieval.'

Amanda drew her platform into the airlock. 'I am cycling Hamoud through alone.'

'Say again.'

'I want to check something out.' She settled Hamoud onto the narrow floor, then moved her scooter back into the sky. 'Take up station by the scientists' lab. I'll join you shortly.'

In truth, she wanted nothing more than a long hot shower and a solid rest. But first she had to see if what she thought was happening was real.

Amanda waited until the transport started its descent. When she was fully alone, she tilted the platform slightly, so her vision was almost straight up. It was a very uncomfortable position, as it compressed the bruises caused by the wall rack. She remained as she was, watching. She did her best to ignore the pain and sought to make sense of what she saw.

All around her, the metal rain continued. And yet she remained utterly safe. The scooter's shield was superfluous. Nothing came within several meters of where she hovered. Directly overhead, the remaining mass of the destroyer was being held in place and gradually shredded.

By clouds.

Over and over she watched pink cloud-tendrils pry off yet another component of the gradually diminishing battlecruiser. There was no question in her mind that this was happening. The destroyer's shields were rendered completely useless. The cloud tentacles took their time. Inspecting.

All the while, the metal rain never touched her.

Nasim's voice sounded inside her helmet. 'We have taken up position at sea level.'

'How is Hamoud?'

'His head is severely bruised. Possible dislocated shoulder. I can't unsuit him alone.'

Amanda caught the hint of disapproval in his voice. She tilted the scooter towards Loria. 'I'm coming in.'

THIRTY-ONE

The lander's airlock was a tight compartment, only slightly larger than the fresher. Amanda knew they were probably being overly cautious, completing a full disinfection every time they cycled in. But as she listened to the anabolic spray wash over her, she found she liked this in-between space. It separated her from all the confusion and mystery that loomed outside their transport. It granted her time to reflect on everything she had just learned, and confess aloud, 'I don't understand.'

'Major?'

'Nothing.' The interior portal sighed open. She stepped in, stripped off her suit, then knelt beside Hamoud. As they unsuited him, Hamoud drifted in and out of consciousness. The scanner confirmed a dislocated shoulder, as well as a mild concussion and severe bruising. But at least his fever was gone.

Amanda and Nasim bound Hamoud's head, then followed the scanner's instructions and worked on his injured shoulder. They injected doses of painkiller and sedative and anti-inflammatory, then left him softly snoring.

Nasim asked her help in removing his undergarment. His upper body appeared to be one massive bruise. But the skin was not broken, and only his right elbow caused him severe distress. He refused an injection against the pain but allowed Amanda to rub on an unguent combining an anti-inflammatory and local anesthetic.

Nasim said, 'Now you.'

'I'm fine.'

'Oh, is that so?' He pointed to where the suit's padded under-garment met her hairline. 'I suppose the stain on your collar here is from the suit leaking.'

Only then did she notice the pain. She touched her neck and saw her fingers come back sticky and glistening red.

'And there's a scrape on the back of your head.'

'Ow. That hurts.'

'Of course it hurts. You've been wounded.'

She stepped into the fresher and clenched her teeth against the pain of lifting her arms. The shower was exquisite. Washing her hair only made her head hurt worse, but she did not mind. She toweled off, groaned softly as she donned a fresh overall, then stepped out and allowed Nasim to apply antiseptics and local anesthetic. Nasim then held the scanner so that it could apply clips to the wound on her neck.

Nasim ran the scanner over her, and said, 'It reports a possible sprain of the atlas. That's the top vertebra connected to your skull.'

'No injections,' she insisted. 'We've already lost too much time.'

He responded by setting down the scanner and applying the same unguent from her hairline to her collar. The salve felt icy and Nasim's touch was remarkably gentle. He asked, 'A pill against the pain?'

'Maybe later,' she replied. She waited as he stowed the scanner and checked on Hamoud, then asked, 'Do you feel able to suit up again?'

'With your help, of course.'

'One of us needs to speak with the scientists about what just happened. I don't want to talk with them yet. I need to figure something out.'

Nasim nodded. 'Glad to know at least one of our minds is still functioning.'

She helped him don his suit, moving with him, taking it as slow as he required. 'I'll make dinner. If they ask, say I'm busy and you don't have the authority to make any decisions.'

He stepped up to the airlock and pressed the button to open the portal. 'Understood.'

'Say we wanted to check on them. Find out if any debris hit their island.'

Nasim entered the airlock, closed the portal, and said, 'The Lorians just tore apart a battlecruiser. Surely they could protect the island.'

'That's the logical answer. Just the same . . .'

'What?'

'I have an idea . . .' She shook her head. 'It's not something I can put into words. Yet.'

Nasim opened the outer lock and powered up the scooter. 'After what we just witnessed, that almost makes sense.'

Amanda considered herself a barely passable cook. She lacked the patience and dexterity required to combine ingredients so that they created the delicate artwork of fine cuisine. Her mother and father were both excellent cooks, and her brother was head chef in one of her home region's top restaurants. Amanda could follow instructions and she had the discipline of timing down cold. Which meant she would probably never starve.

She used a tiny fraction of her mind to prepare a meal, while the remainder of her attention hovered over the unseen. Every time she checked on Hamoud, her mind returned to his words. *The hidden crisis.* It actually helped to keep her hands busy with a task that could be done by rote, freeing herself to fit together more fragments of this planetary puzzle. She selected a trio of vat-grown protein packs flavored as steaks. She set the main cooker to broil, and placed the meals on a rack and applied salt and pepper and a packet of spices. She filled a pot with water, set it to boil, and placed freeze-dried vegetables in a strainer so they could be steamed awake. Bread was readied to be softened by juice from the broiler. Satisfied with her preparations, she shifted to the transport's other side and again ran the med-scan over Hamoud. It suggested another pain suppressant and a second injection to accelerate the collarbone's healing. When the needle entered his forearm, Hamoud opened his eyes.

He asked softly, 'Where are we?'

'Safe.'

He winced. 'My shoulder . . .'

'I know. That's what the injections are for. That and your bruises.'

His eyes tracked her as she set the scanner on the footlocker. 'Truly, we are safe?'

'For the moment.'

That appeared to satisfy him. 'It all happened, didn't it? The glyphs, the assault, and the invasion . . .'

'Yes. It did.' She settled her hand on his good arm, swallowed hard, and repeated what she had said before, 'I'm so sorry, Hamoud.'

'For what?'

'I radioed the pirates and asked permission to dock with their ships. I thought . . .' Amanda blinked and felt the heat course down her cheeks. 'I don't know what I thought.'

He studied her carefully for what felt like hours. Finally, he said, 'My people say bravery is best measured in an impossible situation. One that cannot either be controlled or predicted, and from which there may be no return.'

Amanda's response was cut off by Nasim's asking, 'Major, are you there?'

She stepped to the controls. 'Go ahead, Nasim.'

'Their scientists' responses to the attack are all the same. They either don't know or don't care. I'd like to speak with the Lorian, the one they call the Diplomat.'

'I should have thought of that,' Amanda said. 'Go ahead. And keep it on speaker so I can monitor.'

She watched as Sayer pointed Nasim back to a dozen or so Lorians standing where the vegetation met the beach. When Nasim shifted the scooter, Sayer and Ling followed. Amanda heard him clear his throat, then ask, 'Are you and your people responsible for demolishing the ship?'

The Lorian stared at Nasim, as if the question confused her. 'What other explanation could there be, Separate One?'

Nasim said, 'Thank you for not killing us.'

'Why would we want to do that?' Amanda leaned closer to the viewport so as to observe the Lorian's response. The Diplomat made what to Amanda looked like a human gesture. It extended its left arm, the three digits open wide, and swept out in a move that took in the entire island. 'You are welcome.'

'How did you do it? Break through the battleship's shields and take them out?'

The Lorian dropped its arm and stepped to one side, so as to look at the scientists standing behind Nasim. From her position inside the ship, Amanda could not be certain, but it appeared to her that Sayer and Ling were both smiling.

The Diplomat turned back to Nasim and said, 'The threat is no more. The . . .'

'Invaders,' Sayer said.

'Enemy,' Ling said.

'They are gone,' the Diplomat went on. 'You are safe. Your . . .'

'Spaceship,' Sayer said.

'Lander,' Ling said.

'That which is required to maintain your separate status, it too is intact.' The Diplomat tilted its head, just like a human would when wanting to study a confusing element from a different angle. 'Is this not enough?'

THIRTY-TWO

Nasim returned, stepped through the airlock, and said, 'I understand none of what just happened.'

Amanda prepared their meal while Nasim unsuited, used the fresher, and changed into singlet and shorts. They elected to eat on the floor by Hamoud's pallet. The pilot needed both of them to help him to sit upright. Nasim folded his legs and leaned against the bulkhead. Even in his damaged state, Hamoud showed genuine interest in their discussion. He positioned his plate to his right, waited while Amanda cut his food, then tore off fragments of the microwaved bread and folded it around each bite.

As he ate, Nasim gave a detailed account of meeting the scientists, and their utter disinterest in what had just happened and the glyphs' threat. Their only response was to say that they were glad he and the others were safe. They shrugged off his questions about what forces had been applied to demolish the pirate vessel.

'It is not spoken of,' Hamoud said.

'I actually didn't hear them say those words,' Nasim replied. 'They just didn't seem to care. Another mystery.'

Hamoud said, 'After all we have been through, a quiet mystery is fine by me.'

Nasim took another couple of bites, then said to Amanda, 'That last time you met with the scientists, you asked about the papers they had written.'

'Twenty-three have been published.' She nodded. 'I've read them.'

Both men were watching her now. 'You found anything that might help us understand what is happening here?'

'Nothing.' She set her plate aside. 'They publish a scientific report every few years. Signed by all the scientists and researchers. Each one a complete and utter bore. Soil samples, water structure, absence of sea life, an island civilization without competing species or airborne bacteria. Organic structure of all the vegetation.'

'What did they write about the Lorians?'

'Very technical, but also peripheral. Studies on their telepathic link. Domestication of the environment. You heard me ask the scientists. Nothing about the Lorian biological structure, or the ferns draped from the trees after a death, what they represented, or the Gathering . . .' She went quiet.

Hamoud demanded, 'What are you thinking?'

'There was one thing. I requested permission from the head of my division to show their research to one of the exobiologists. See if there was something in the data that I needed to understand. This was after the earliest three deaths. My superior forbade me to involve anyone else. He said it was a total waste of other people's time.'

'Your superior,' Nasim said, 'is a loon.'

'No argument there.'

Hamoud said, 'You did it anyway. Didn't you?'

She nodded. 'I covered my tracks as best I could. I started frequenting a café down on H-Deck, just opposite the exo-lab's main entrance. I made friends.'

'No one can fault you for being friendly,' Nasim said, smiling.

'One of them took an interest in my little planet,' Amanda said.

'Correction,' Hamoud said. 'He took an interest in you.'

'Whatever. He said most of what had been observed on Loria was typical of systems with telepathic races. None that we have so far identified have interstellar flight.'

'What, not one?'

She shook her head. 'There is apparently a shared need to remain closely linked with their species. None seek to go off-planet. The scientists did mention two items of interest. Trade is often welcomed by telepathic races, but they never willingly invite off-worlders to live among them. If an off-worlder settlement is permitted, they are built within exclusion zones.'

'Which explains why these scientists were so excited to live among the Lorians,' Nasim said. 'Despite the death sentence.'

Hamoud asked, 'And the second difference?'

'Loria is unique among dual-sun systems,' she replied. 'Virtually all others contain several massive gas giants and enormous debris fields. Early in a double-sun system's life, planetary orbits are extremely erratic. Smaller planets are drawn into contact with the giants and are demolished. Only the strong survive.'

'But not here,' Nasim said.

'One planet, no debris,' Amanda said. 'Which is how Loria maintains a stable orbit in the dead center of the life zone. No debris, no moons, no other planets. Unique among all the known systems.'

By the time they finished eating, exhaustion had settled on Amanda like a physical weight. She cleaned up, then was there to help Nasim return Hamoud from the fresher to his pallet. Hamoud sighed hard as they lowered him. But his eyes were clear and his skin had lost its clammy sheen. He declined another sleep agent and only accepted the pain injection after Nasim insisted and Amanda backed him up.

When she lay down, Amanda had difficulty finding a comfortable position. Her wounds throbbed now, particularly the place on her neck where the skin had been clipped shut. Eventually she fell into a fitful sleep. Her dreams warped into glyphs taking hold and opening their sucker mouths and revealing the circular rims of tiny dagger teeth, then leaning in close and feeding on her neck and head. Then the pirate ship's alarms sounded once more, but the glyphs kept on feeding . . .

Amanda jerked awake. She realized the transport's alert was pinging softly.

She took her time rising, testing each set of muscles before applying her weight. The two men kept snoring, testimony to everything they had endured. She seated herself in the pilot's chair, dry-scrubbed her face, and checked the monitor. She had been asleep for four and a half hours. It felt like twenty minutes. Less. She tapped the key to silence the alert, then discovered they had received an n-space message. She typed in her command code, read the terse message, and hissed softly.

The rules governing planetary missions were carefully defined. Any GSA transport captain was entirely in his or her rights to shift their retrieval time. Anything up to and including seventy-two hours in either direction was part of the skipper's official remit. Amanda did a swift calculation and hissed a second time.

The n-space alert brought their retrieval forward by seventy-one hours.

Barrat's orders were equally precise. She was required to be fully ready and in position, with a thirty-minute window for extraction.

They now had less than five hours to complete their mission.

Amanda decided to give herself ten minutes, make herself a cup of coffee, and try to work out a way to salvage her mission. The serrated schedule and the captain's determination to wreck her chances left her filled with a terrible mixture of rage and fear. Added to this was the suspicion that Captain Barrat was working under orders from the generals opposed to Rickets and their own peace initiative. If the *Invictus* skipper had been unable to wreck their mission going in, shaving three days off their timeline was an equally effective weapon.

Unless she came up with a solution.

Immediately.

Her hands shook as she measured the water and coffee. She tried to tell herself that she had enough to record a successful mission. But she could feel Commander Rickets' implacable gaze bearing down on her already. She heard the commander ask questions for which Amanda had no answer. The cold shadow of defeat loomed over her.

Then the monitor chimed a second time.

Amanda rushed back, spilling hot coffee over her hands. She hoped against hope that the cruiser had sent through a second message, a correction . . . One more day, she frantically hoped. Two would be great – superb, in fact. But one full day more just might . . .

But when she coded in, the second alert froze her bones.

When she managed to unlock her chest, it was to shout, 'Hamoud! Nasim! *Alarm!*'

THIRTY-THREE

A manda stood between the two men. All of them watched the electronic array superimposed over the front viewport.

'Nine ships,' Nasim said. 'One less than a full flotilla.'

Hamoud said, 'Whoever thought a pirate's crew could put together a fleet this size?'

Nasim pointed to the upper left quadrant. 'Four are relics from bygone eras.'

'I doubt,' Hamoud replied, 'they would find our lander much of an adversary.'

Amanda found having the two men standing to either side, feeling their tension and their worry heat, actually helped clarify things. 'There's more.'

They both looked at her. 'More?'

She drew up the n-space alert and displayed it on the portal. She found it somehow fitting, adding the captain's message to the enemy's presence.

But her former semi-paralyzed state was gone. She studied the two threats, the transport's timing and the pirates, and there beside them appeared the steps they needed to take. All of them laid out as sharp and vivid as if they were illuminated on the portal.

'Listen up. Here's what we're going to do.' Amanda spoke in the same terse bites she had used in addressing Commander Rickets. Walking them through her objective in tight stages. She kept her gaze on the front portal throughout. Reading the invisible battle plan.

Nasim responded with an expression of genuine horror. 'I can't believe you would even think such a thing.'

But Hamoud, weak as he was, could at least see part of where she was headed. 'This plan, it has merit.'

Nasim gaped at his friend. 'Your brain is still addled from the drugs.'

'I have never thought more clearly.' He lifted his good hand and pointed at the enemy ships. 'Nine battlecruisers arrayed from pole to pole. With another Surrus-class warship poised directly overhead.'

'I can see that as clearly as you,' Nasim countered. 'It still does not excuse an act of sheer insanity!'

'They won't try to invade.' Hamoud's eyes shifted about, directing the battle plan. 'They've already lost two ships. They won't risk a third close approach.'

'They won't need to,' Amanda agreed. Knowing she was right to take the risk she proposed. Even though it probably meant she would not survive the day. 'They'll stand well off and bomb the entire surface.'

'Destroy the cloud cover with flame bursts,' Hamoud said, nodding now. 'Hold off their heavy armament until they're certain it will all get through.'

'Eliminate the entire Lorian race,' Amanda said. 'Claim the planet as their own.'

Slowly, reluctantly, Nasim turned back to the illuminated array. 'Terrible, terrible idea.'

'Actually, I think the major is correct,' Hamoud said.

'Which brings us to the other issue,' Amanda said.

Hamoud nodded. 'The GSA transport.'

'It's due here in . . .'

'Four hours and twenty-two minutes,' Hamoud said.

'The pirates would consider this a prize worth the losses they've suffered,' Amanda said. 'We can't let that happen.'

Nasim protested, 'Surely there must be a different way. One that does not require the major to sacrifice her life.'

'We do not have the time to find it,' Hamoud replied. 'If indeed a better plan exists. And one thing more.'

Nasim looked ready to do battle with his friend. But all he said was, 'What?'

'The major was not asking our opinion,' Hamoud said. 'She was issuing our orders.'

Amanda prepared an n-space alert to Ricckts. When she showed it to her team, Nasim merely grimaced and turned away. Hamoud smiled at his friend's response, then handed it back and said, 'It's perfect, Major.'

The message read: *Killings resolved. New agreement with Lorians achieved. I hereby confirm presence of Random colony. Am seeking direct contact with their leader. Report to follow. Bostick.*

'No changes? You're sure?'

He shook his head. 'The commander would be proud.'

Over a final mug of tea Amanda recorded a message for the men to submit on her behalf. She did her best to ignore the console's digital clock. She explained herself fully, calmly. Hamoud remained seated beside her throughout, his silent presence a mighty source of strength. Namid hovered in the back, but did not speak. Though clearly both men knew what she was doing. Fashioning an end-of-mission statement. In the likely event she did not make it back.

Her suiting-up carried a somewhat formal note. Nasim kept silent, but his disapproval reverberated through the lander. Hamoud's left arm remained strapped, which hindered his actions. But he did all he could to both help and shield her from Nasim's bitter displeasure. Hamoud asked, 'Water canister full?'

'Check.'

'Best if you carry extra rations.'

'Good idea.' She accepted his handful of energy bars and stowed them in the neck pouch, where she could easily pull them out. 'Thank you.'

'How's the head?'

'It hurts,' she admitted.

Nasim muttered, 'At least you won't need to worry about that for much longer.'

Hamoud said, 'You could take half a dose; that shouldn't cloud your judgment.'

'Better not.'

He did not insist. 'You have a full med-pack?'

'Roger.'

Hamoud watched her seal the helmet, walked her to the airlock, then said, 'Nasim.'

'This is insanity.'

'Nasim.' Hamoud saluted, waited for Nasim to follow his lead, then said, 'Good hunting, Major.'

THIRTY-FOUR

When Amanda directed her scooter away from the airlock, the beach fronting their lander was empty. Amanda shifted over and saw the scientists all busy in the lab building. She spoke softly. 'Any heat signatures?'

Hamoud said, 'There are no discernable signatures outside the central building.'

Then she heard Sayer call from inside the lab, 'Just a second, Major. I'm coming!'

It was only now, as he rushed across the lab and appeared in the central window and waved to her, that Amanda could give a description to the scientist's actions. Everything he did seemed theatrical.

The closeness of danger brought a sharp clarity, a sense of looking beneath the surface, deeper than ever before. Amanda knew she only had a few moments of relative safety left. She desperately wanted to use them well.

She said, 'Confirm you are recording this.'

Hamoud said, 'Roger that.'

She found herself thinking of Commander Rickets and her grimly impatient drive. Amanda felt closer to the woman than ever before. The colony's chief scientist, she decided, lied with every breath, every step, every cheery word. If she was to make any headway in the few moments remaining, she had to do what the commandant was best at, and look *beyond*.

Amanda turned away from the lab and stepped past the boundary of palm-like trees. Away from the narrow trail leading to the central hill, the vegetation grew in a tight but orderly manner. The beach gave way to waist-high plants with tiny flowers bright as pink gemstones. Then trees growing in clusters of between four and ten. Amanda was reminded of how the Lorians had stood by the lab entrance, and, before, around the glowing central hill. There was the same connection at the base of the trunks. Amanda shifted her platform closer. The faint lines of demarcation continued up to about where the Lorians' heads would have emerged.

'Major! There you are!' Sayer scampered over the sandy beach in the disjointed manner of a man who had never given much time to exercise. 'Sorry to make you wait.'

If anything, Sayer seemed even more cheerful than at their last meeting. Amanda asked, 'Is this one tree or five?'

'Is . . .' He seemed taken aback by her question. 'Why do you ask?'

She really didn't care about the island's vegetation. But she was keenly interested in how her question had wiped away Sayer's blithe manner. 'I am simply curious, Doctor. Isn't that what drives a good scientist – curiosity?'

'I suppose, yes, of course. That and careful definition of the cases and a clearly repeatable pattern of study and—'

'Back to my question. Is this a single plant?' She watched him struggle to restore his smile. Amanda found herself thinking of a clown she had seen as a child, when the man's eyes had given him away. They had held a nightmarish glint, a latent rage that had terrified her.

The scientist's gaze held no anger. Instead, they looked . . .

Pink.

'That is a more complex issue than you think, Major.'

Amanda shifted closer. The man's eyes definitely had a pink tint. And there at the point where his neck emerged from the tattered shirt, the skin held a pinkish pigmentation that had not been there before. 'But you've studied the plant's DNA, right? The Lorians can't keep you from studying plant life.'

'Major, there are examples all over the known system of plants that share—'

'I know all about that.' She moved in closer still. Wanting to keep him unsettled. 'I was born on Earth. I know about birch forests that are all one single giant entity. My question is, does the same thing happen here – yes or no?'

Sayer stopped trying to hide behind his smile. He replied stiffly, 'I can share with you the preliminary data for an article we are currently preparing—'

'Good. Please do so. I'll wait here.'

'What, now?'

'This very instant. And while I'm waiting, ask the Diplomat to join me.'

'I . . . Ah, yes . . . That is . . .'

'Hurry, Sayer. Now means now.'

As the scientist started off, Nasim asked, 'Should you not stay on point, Major?'

She turned back to the island's interior. 'I never left it.'

By the time she spotted the Lorian moving down the beach towards her, Amanda had worked out a tight line on how to proceed. As Sayer walked down the lab building's ramp and pointed in her direction, Amanda asked, 'Hamoud, can you direct our med-scan to examine the scientist?'

'You mean, from inside the transport? Sorry, no.'

'The directions instruct us to hold it no more than ten centimeters from the body,' Nasim reminded her.

'What if I draw him over by the airlock?'

The two men went silent, then Nasim asked, 'You're not asking us to suit up and join you.'

'Correct. They have a med-scan. Which means the scientist will know what we're doing.'

'You don't want him to realize you're scanning?'

'Right. That can't happen. So try this. I'll shift around so Sayer's back is to the lander, then you try to scan through the front viewport.'

'Roger.'

Amanda watched the Lorian's approach. She had noted an absence of greetings before, something she had read about in her study of telepathic races. None of them had words for either hello or farewell. Which meant she could safely continue to try to unsettle the scientist. She hoped. She shifted the scooter closer to the lander, waited for them to join her, then asked Sayer, 'Have the documents been forwarded?'

'My assistant Ling has broken off from crucial work in order to collate the data and—'

'Excellent. Please make sure I am informed the *instant* this goes through.' She shifted toward the lander a fraction at a time, drawing them with her, and said, 'Nine pirate battleships are arrayed above your planet.'

The news pushed Sayer back a step. 'I thought there was just one.'

'How could he possibly know that?' Hamoud said.

The Lorian glanced over. Amanda detected a faintly human aspect to the motion. As if the Diplomat intended the look as a rebuke. Sayer took another step away, as if in confirmation. Amanda went on, 'You are partly correct. One is stationed overhead, just beyond the atmospheric boundary. Eight more arc in higher stationary orbit.'

The Diplomat spoke for the first time. 'Explain that. Further out?'

'I'm sorry. I don't understand the question.'

'Where precisely are these other eight . . .'

'Vessels,' Sayer supplied, frowning. 'Warships.'

'One moment.' Amanda cut off her exterior feed and said, 'Nasim, give me the coordinates one vessel at a time. Wait. Anything further from the GSA transport?'

'Not a peep. We're monitoring on all frequencies.'

Amanda turned the exterior mike and speaker back on and pointed to a branch lying on the sand by the plant boundary. 'Hand me that, please.' She used the action to turn them further around, so their backs were now to the lander. 'OK. Nasim, the coordinates. Hamoud, the scan . . .'

'On it, Major.'

She squatted on the platform and began drawing in the sand. She drew the dual suns and the planet Loria, then positioned the ships as Nasim fed her the coordinates. She then rose back to full height and used the stick as a pointer. 'This is your planet's mid-morning position. The closest ship is here, midway between your island and the north pole. My guess is, they're planning a double-strike.'

The Lorian tilted its head back and forth, clearly having difficulty with Amanda's drawing. 'Explain.'

'One barrage will be directed at this particular island, a larger strike at the pole. Their intent would be to destabilize your orbit and wreck the cloud cover.'

The Lorian looked up. 'They will not survive.'

She decided not to point out that the entire Lorian race would most likely be wiped out, making the pirates' survival a moot issue. She drew a line back from the ship's current position to where it would probably lead the armada. 'They'll send out the first strike, then probably fall back to here. They'll have your world in a pincer, and be able to bombard the entire globe. All the islands and both poles.'

The Lorian studied her. 'You are knowing this how?'

'I have studied these tactics.'

'You are a . . .'

'Student,' Sayer said, frowning. 'Of war.'

'No. My mission is peace.' Amanda stabbed the sand again. 'Theirs is not.'

The Lorian returned its attention to the drawing. The silence stretched out until Hamoud said, 'Sorry, Major. We're getting no readable data. The scanner isn't equipped for ranging beyond half a meter.'

Nasim said, 'I saw it. The scientist's pink skin. And hair. Very strange.'

The Lorian looked up. 'We must arrange a Gathering.'

Sayer looked genuinely stupefied. 'But we just had one. Plus you say it can only happen at dawn.'

'But we do not have a dawn. Do we, Separate One?'

'My name is Amanda.'

The Lorian gave another curiously human response. A half-step away, a turn to its head, as though taken aback by her change of direction. 'You have suggested that time is an issue.'

'So is my name. Amanda. I ask that you say it.'

'Your . . . name.'

Amanda decided that was close enough. 'You need a lesson in some of the Prime Directives that rule my system.' She glanced over at the scientist, who had started a hand-waving two-step. 'Sayer, either you freeze or you leave. Now.'

Sayer froze.

Amanda went on, 'My species is driven to learn and to understand. Which means asking questions *regardless* of what your Prime Directive says. We will try to adjust our questions, but these issues do not grant you the right to eliminate one of my kind. As I stated before, our key Prime Directive is that human life is precious. And your own. All sentient species hold a special relationship within the galactic empire. That is what differentiates us from the pirates orbiting your planet. They kill. We protect.'

Nasim asked, 'Is this truly a time for such discussions?'

'Leave her be,' Hamoud replied. 'The major is on a roll.'

'Learning, inspecting, studying,' Amanda went on. 'That is why the scientists were sent here. So that we could learn through them . . .'

Amanda stopped because the Lorian responded precisely as it had at their first confrontation. It flattened down to a gelatinous two-eyed puddle.

Sayer groaned, 'What have you done?'

'What you should have done sixty-seven years ago.' Amanda knew it was time to press home. She stabbed the sky. 'There is a pirate battle fleet up there. They will *take us out*. Now I have a plan to save us and protect this planet. But it means you and your Diplomat pal must do *exactly* what I say.'

The Lorian resumed its full height. 'Say what it is that you require.'

THIRTY-FIVE

'This Gathering,' Amanda said. 'It is part of your protection?'

'It is for you,' the Lorian replied. 'You can speak with these . . . others?'

'I intend to. But I need to accomplish something first.' She chose to ignore how Sayer's distress was again rising to near-explosive levels. 'Look. I can't afford to be knocked out for another seven-hour stretch. We need to communicate with those pirates as soon as possible. And what I'm here to discuss with you is *vital* to making that happen.'

Sayer subsided. 'The Diplomat has asked what you need.'

'First of all, if we're going to have this Gathering, it needs to be shortened. A lot.'

'Your requirements are noted,' the Lorian said. 'We will reduce this Gathering to . . .'

For once, Sayer was not there with the proper word. Amanda asked, 'A brief time like the space of one breath?'

'Perhaps two. Will you come?'

'OK. Yes. But one thing needs to happen first.' Swift as she could, Amanda outlined what was required. And why.

Their response surprised Amanda as much as anything had that day. The scientist started to speak, halted himself, then rubbed his mouth with a trembling hand. The Lorian turned and looked inland. It was the sort of action Amanda might have expected from a human confronting a problem and needing to disengage and think things through. Only a human would look seawards. Out to the unbroken horizon.

Amanda's attention returned to the scientist. She had the impression that Sayer was trying to stifle a laugh. 'Did I say something funny?'

He dropped his arm. 'What? No. Of course not.'

But the smirk and the false cheeriness was back now. She wasn't a child any longer, though, and the clown no longer scared her. She snapped, 'You promised me an answer to my question, Professor. We don't start this Gathering until you have delivered the data.'

Sayer showed her a frustrated rage. 'You have *no* idea what you're asking.'

The exchange drew the Lorian back around. 'Go and tell all the new ones of the Gathering.'

Hamoud said, 'What did the Diplomat just call the scientists? The *new ones*? Did I hear that correctly?'

The Lorian dismissed Sayer with a wave that was distinctly human, then said to Amanda, 'This new . . . craft, the one meant to . . .'

'The transport ordered to retrieve us.'

'Yes. Where are you to meet?'

Amanda heard the subtle shift: the pause and then the heavy application before certain words. She suspected it meant not just learning a new term, but also accepting what this word signified. The Diplomat was learning of separation in a new degree. Another fragment of her invisible puzzle fitted itself into place. She shifted her platform further from her drawing of the two suns and poked another hole in the sand. 'Interstellar travel, journeys between planetary systems, delivers ships to a point in space that is not warped by solar or planetary gravity. These arrival points are very specifically defined. We meet here, about ten times the distance from your planet to the suns.'

The Lorian studied the drawing for a long moment.

Nasim said, 'Major, the scientist Ying is here with your data.'

Amanda glanced over, saw Sayer's aide standing by the airlock. 'Have her put it in the keyhole portal. Be sure to disinfect.'

'Roger that.' Nasim hesitated, then added, 'Major, the woman's skin looks pink to me.'

Hamoud said, 'I confirm that.'

The Lorian drew her back with, 'The method you used to hide your very small . . . craft when it departed earlier. This will not work on those who arrive?'

Hamoud demanded sharply, 'How can they possibly know about the communication pod?'

Amanda asked, 'You detected the small craft's departure?'

'This is our world. We detect all things.'

'How far out can you search?'

The Lorian nodded, another distinctly human act, one Amanda had not seen before. 'Far enough to detect one ship only.'

'I told you the truth about the others.'

'I accept your words as genuine . . .'

'Amanda.'

'This is a word intended for you . . . alone?'

'Yes. Each human has a distinct label, or name.'

The Lorian responded with a visible shudder.

Amanda went on, 'Back to our pod. It was a small communications satellite, made mostly from a material similar to this sand. Its size and make-up hide it fairly well. Then cameras on one side illuminate the other with a duplicate-image, so it can pass unseen by visual means. We used it to send out information about this mission, in case we did not survive the pirate craft. Thank you again for keeping us alive.'

The Lorian responded with another human-like wave. 'Go on.'

'Our lander is metal and so large that the visible mask would not work. I was hoping . . . To be honest, I don't know what to even ask.'

'You want to hide the . . . craft.' The Lorian pointed to her hole in the sand. 'So it can go there.'

'Right. And alert our interstellar transport so the pirates don't capture it.'

The Diplomat nodded. 'This we can do.'

'Really?'

'Observe . . . Amanda.'

She glanced over and gasped. It took her a long moment to find her voice. 'Hamoud, Nasim, are you OK?'

'Of course. What's wrong?'

'You've just vanished.'

The Diplomat said, 'This is a temporary state. Do you understand? The effect will only last until your . . . craft leaves our planet's boundary.'

She studied the empty space where her lander had previously rested. 'The pirates will have technology that allows them to see . . . beyond the visible light spectrum.'

'The masking is total.'

Amanda decided she had no choice but take the Diplomat at its word. 'Hamoud, did you get that?'

'Loud and clear.'

Nasim said, 'Major, are you certain—'

'Hurry. The transport will arrive in . . . How long?'

'Two hours and fifty-one minutes,' Hamoud said.

'Go now. That's an order.'

'Good luck, Major.'

'Thanks. And you.' She waited a moment, then asked, 'Are you still here?'

'We are fourteen klicks away from the island's surface and accelerating. We will leave the planet's atmosphere directly opposite your current position. As per your orders.'

'Roger. Out.' She forced herself to turn away, and watched as the scientists spilled out of the lab building. All of them seemed to hold a slight pinkish tint to their skin, some also to their hair.

She had never felt so alone.

THIRTY-SIX

Amanda entered her second Gathering with a sense of battle-field awareness. She had heard of this numerous times during training. The difference between a good officer and a dead officer was the ability to parse the seconds and observe with a clarity that only existed in extreme situations. Like now.

She stood in more or less the same position as before, only without Hamoud's comforting presence. She missed her two friends, and yet she didn't mind the solitude. She watched the Lorians gather with unaccustomed haste, then make room for the humans. The scientists milled about like nervous cattle before finally settling. As she watched the conical hill's light strengthen and the Lorians seemingly merge into a single unit, Amanda sensed that she was planting one fragment after another into the puzzle of mysteries. She could not see the whole picture yet. She could not name it. But she knew in her gut that . . .

She was gone.

One breath followed another . . .

And she returned.

Only this time it really *was* just a pair of breaths between departure and opening her eyes. She knew because her first act was to check her suit's monitor.

She had been gone precisely fifty-one seconds.

The Lorian stood before her. Amanda had to assume it was the Diplomat. 'Did you witness?'

Amanda had no idea what the words meant, nor did it matter. 'No. Nothing. I shut my eyes, and now you are standing here.'

The Lorian responded with yet another human-like action. The point where its upper appendages met its pink body slumped, and its head lowered, then it released a long breath. A sign of a very real dejection. 'Then there is nothing more to be done.'

Amanda had no idea how to respond to such an act of defeat except to say, 'I'm sorry.'

'As am I, Sep— *Amanda*.' Once again, there was far more than the mere learning of a new word. The impact of using her name was so deep that the Lorian shuddered. 'Know this. We do not wish to extinguish any life form. Most especially one who thinks and feels.'

'What about the dead human scientists?'

The Lorian straightened. 'You should already know the answer to that.'

Amanda nodded. 'You've been culling them. Disposing of the ones who don't measure up to whatever is required for this joining.'

'They *chose* to be here. They have *asked* to join. For years and years, they have asked. We simply seek to do as they wish.' The Lorian made yet another human motion. 'Go and do your best to save these other lives. While you still have time.'

'Calling the Surrus cruiser stationed above the planet Loria. This is Major Amanda Bostick, requesting permission to dock. I have information that is vital to your ship's survival.'

She had been broadcasting the alert on all channels since leaving the planet's surface. Every now and then she switched to the rarely used GSA frequency, repeating her message, simply to let Hamoud and Nasim know she was moving into the next phase.

So far, the pirate battleship had not responded.

She remained somewhat overwhelmed by the Gathering's impact. Which was the primary reason why she kept her speed low. Her mental state was nowhere near as unsettled as after the first go. But her mind again felt slightly disconnected from her body. The experience weighed on her like a bad hangover. She did her best to shove it aside. She needed to be alert. She needed to be fully *on*.

As she approached the dense cloud layer, she felt a strong wind buffet her scooter. Above her, the pink veil roiled and rippled, like froth over a storm-tossed sea. It was the first real weather of any kind she had seen on this planet. Amanda wanted to assume it was nothing more than a natural offshoot of planetary rotation. But she could not help wondering if this was part of their preparation for assault.

Then a thought struck her, one carrying such force she drew the sled to a halt.

Who precisely were *they*?

She had been working on the assumption that a telepathic race was in control of virtually every aspect of their environment. She saw them as individuals and a group both.

But what if there was no *they* at all?

All around her the mist boiled and rippled, a pink reflection of her mental cauldron. She was not certain precisely how, but she became convinced that this question was essential to linking all the puzzle fragments together. Once more she heard Hamoud's voice. The unseen threat. The *real* crisis.

She pushed through the upper layer of clouds. The top layer puffed upwards with her, as if the planet was sighing a silent farewell at her passage.

Then she saw the ship.

Away from the dual suns and their ribbons of power, the stars shone with a unique brilliance. Amanda had heard from other officers how death's approach magnified the vital nature of each sensation. She heard her breath sigh inside the helmet. She felt the tensile strength of the suit that allowed her to stand here, on the invisible platform of a craft formed from pure energy. And call to a pirate vessel that carved a deadly silhouette from the stars overhead.

'Calling the Surrus cruiser—'

'Why are you here, Major?'

The voice carried a distinct accent. Amanda was again certain the pirate skipper was not human. 'Who am I addressing?'

'Captain Kiril. Skipper of the battleship *Darrow*. Now answer my question. Why are you here? Respond or be fired upon, Major.'

'I have information that may be vital to your survival.'

'Why should you care whether I live or die? I am your enemy, no?'

Amanda halted where the cruiser's many appendages cut deadly shadows from the sky. 'Do you have glyphs on board?'

'I do not.'

'Then no, Captain. You are not my enemy.'

He went silent for a moment, then, 'Permission granted. Board via the central flight deck.'

*   *   *

The Surrus battleship was a truly mammoth beast to be approaching alone, exposed, and unarmed. Despite the suit's automatic extraction of her body moisture, Amanda felt perspiration drip down from her temples and burn the edges of her eyes. Nor was she able to wipe it away. She shook her head hard, determined to take in everything.

'Our central hold is illuminated.'

'Roger that.'

A trio of fighters drifted from the bow portal and formed a close-kill escort as she approached. Then her radio clicked and she heard, 'Hamoud here. Check. Repeat. Check. Hamoud out.'

The main portal was a vast illuminated rectangle. She flew inside and followed the rippling lights to the central landing platform. The cannons guarding the entry port swiveled and tracked her progress. A clutch of guards stood behind blast shields with their weapons at the ready. Behind her, the entry portal slid shut.

No one moved.

Kiril's voice came through her radio. 'Explain the message you just received.'

It was one thing to decide she would be entirely open and honest with the pirates when planning strategy. Back when she was seated with her two new friends, eating a final portion of Nasim's wonderful Arab-style stew. Back when she was safe and comforted by knowing she could trust these men with her life. She could make plans and know there was a slim chance that she might not just be right, but actually survive.

Now, she was surrounded by the very real terror of having gotten it all completely wrong. Again.

'I'm waiting.'

There was no time to rethink her strategy. Nor any room for maneuver. She had committed to her course when she sent Hamoud and Nasim on their way.

She was going to be completely and utterly honest.

With pirates.

Who had every reason to blame her for the loss of their ships.

Amanda replied, 'The communiqué was from my pilot. We were scheduled for retrieval. My pilot and his number two flew out to the rendezvous point. He radioed to confirm the pickup was successful, and the transport has retreated out of the system and gone dark.'

Amanda held her breath. She feared the skipper would respond by sending off a bevy of his craft on a hunter-seeker mission. Which had very little chance of success, since Barrat would now have every sensor on high alert and keep his ship ready to go interstellar the instant an incoming pirate vessel was detected. Not to mention the fact that the transport's crew had been given all the pirate vessels' coordinates, and the attackers had no way to know where to hunt.

Kiril came back on line. 'Take off your suit.'

The command was expected, but still it was hard to comply. She stripped down to her wrinkled and sweat-stained uniform. And waited. Her sense of utter isolation grew stronger still.

THIRTY-SEVEN

The guards encircled Amanda in a rather loose array and marched her through one long corridor after another. About half were human, and these wore odd components of military garb. Most of the others were Merphesians, a race Amanda had come to know while at the Academy. They were silent, watchful creatures, generally about two-thirds Amanda's height. Their home planet circled a brilliant blue-white star, and Merphesians lived most of their lives underground. They had two sets of eyes, one for life in dimly lit terrain, the other for their brief forays in full daylight. Their limbs were supple, their musculature and tendons attached to a springy-soft skeletal structure. Over this was a thin pelt of palest gold, the same color as their underground eyes. They moved in an almost liquid flow, and when among their own kind they tended to cluster like furry puddles. They were known as a sincere and trustworthy race and possessed an empathy that Amanda had found most endearing. Their presence left her mightily assured.

This time the guards led her across the antechamber and through the blast-doors and into the control room. The same massive view-screen dominated the chamber, curving slightly as it swept around the front wall. Amanda shuddered tightly as she recalled the last time she had viewed Loria from a pirate vessel's bridge.

A Merphesian slipped from the captain's chair and started over. It was slightly taller than the others, perhaps a bit heavier. But the real sense of authority came from how the guards straightened at its approach. 'I am Captain Kiril. You are Major Bostick, correct?'

'Yes, Captain.' The manner of address comforted Amanda mightily. The Merphesian spoke to her without the benefit of a voder. It had adopted a human name beginning with K. The sound did not exist in their language, and most Merphesians were fascinated with how the K and hard C reshaped their mouths. 'Thank you for seeing me.'

'I am ordered to determine what weapons the planet used on our ships. You can help with this?'

'I think so, Captain.'

'You will tell me what you know?'

'I will tell you everything,' Amanda confirmed.

The Merphesian studied her a long moment, then said, 'You will take liquid?'

'Thank you, Captain, that would . . .'

Amanda froze. She felt incapable of breathing, much less uttering another word.

'Major?'

The ship had resumed the pole-to-pole orbit taken by the destroyed cruiser. As it rounded the Lorian equator, the dual suns came into view. In that instant, everything changed.

A tiny fraction of Amanda's brain realized this was what the Lorians had wanted her to take away from the Gathering. An understanding of what they were fully capable of. A weapon so monumental it could not be *explained*. She had to *witness*.

Which was precisely what happened now.

She knew at some deep level that what she saw was not actually happening. But it did not matter. For she did not mentally envision this weapon. She *experienced* it.

The streamers that bound the two suns shifted.

The ribbons of light reached out in the same manner as the clouds. The flow tightened into brilliant tentacles, hundreds of them. Thousands. They flickered with the intensity of pure rage, hunting.

One by one, the battlecruisers were gripped, melted, blasted, destroyed.

Neither the shields nor their weapons meant anything. After three of the vessels were demolished, the others went into retreat. Amanda saw their stellar drives light up, but the power was so feeble, so *slow*. The tentacles moved with impossible swiftness, intent upon total destruction. Their weaving force held the capacity of demolishing entire planets. Not even a massive gas giant could withstand its power, nor a hundred million asteroids. The Lorian system contained only one planet because the Lorians . . .

Amanda was jarred back to the immediate moment by the realization that something she thought, a mental item she had just formed, was *wrong*.

But she was only partially reconnected. It felt to her as though she viewed her body from some fractured distance. She realized she was trembling and weeping both. Her vision was partially melted. Relief at seeing the *real* view-screen, and realizing the image was not yet upon them, was counter-balanced by the conviction that it was coming. Destruction was almost upon them.

'*Order a retreat!*'

She screamed the words so loud it forced the guards and captain to back away. The act of screaming again drove her into the vision. She felt her head begin to pound, sensed the sweat pouring from her, knew a fever like Hamoud's had now taken hold. But none of this mattered. She could not tell if she was actually shaping the words anymore. Her entire consciousness was gripped by the vision of the twin suns growing tentacles and attacking. She hoped she was still capable of speech. She could not hear anything. But it felt as though her throat was in as much pain now as her head, which she took as a good sign, for it meant she was shrieking her warning, trying to explain how the Lorians had warned her at the Gathering, and she was only now seeing that they only had a few moments at most before they were destroyed, torn apart, melted and blasted and killed . . .

She dove headlong into a blackness so complete she feared the warning had come too late to save any of them.

THIRTY-EIGHT

Amanda awoke twice that she was certain of. Perhaps there were other moments when she swam so close to the surface that she could see light and register voices. Then down again she dove. The two clearest times carried oddly jarring notes, such that they jolted her to momentary alertness. The first was when a needle pricked her inner elbow, and an icy substance began flowing into her vein. Amanda heard a human voice say something about no infection to match her fever. But before she could explain about the Gatherings and their after-effect, she was gone. The second time, she felt her body compress into some form of pallet, and heard someone say, 'Engineering didn't properly synch the fields before acceleration.' Amanda wanted to smile, because she had the same thought, and because it meant they were underway. Departing the system.

All the dreams that followed the second awakening were exquisite. Blissful. Because they were safe.

Which was why, when she next opened her eyes and saw Hamoud smiling down at her, Amanda said, 'You're a dream too.'

'I have been called many things in my time,' Hamoud replied. 'Never that.'

'Nightmare, most certainly,' Nasim offered from behind him. 'Big mistake. I recall my lovely cousin saying those words. Many times.'

'Your cousin thinks I am wonderful.'

'We are obviously speaking of different cousins.'

Hamoud's dark gaze remained upon Amanda. 'Welcome back, Major.'

'You're really here? Both of you?'

'The stories we have to tell you,' Hamoud said.

'Starting with where "here" is,' Nasim said. 'Tell her that first.'

'We are on Random,' Hamoud said.

'Actually, "in" Random is more precise.'

'Indeed.' Hamoud extended his arm in a sweep of formal invitation. 'Welcome to the pirate's lair.'

They took incomplete turns, regaling her with their adventure. Hamoud used that very word. How exciting it had all been. Like some great interplanetary lark they had been on ever since leaving her on Loria and going in search of their only way home.

The GSA transport *Invictus* had actually arrived early. Which was evidence, according to Hamoud, that the captain had every intention of downchecking her for being late to retrieval. No matter what success she might have gained on Loria, such a black mark would also go into her record. Barrat's displeasure at being hailed by the lander gave both Nasim and Hamoud reason to smile. But that was nothing, they declared, compared with Barrat's fury when he learned that Hamoud had no interest in boarding.

'The man screamed like a little girl,' Nasim said, grinning hugely.

Amanda realized what she was hearing. 'You disobeyed a direct command from a GSA transport captain?'

'He might have ordered me at some point,' Hamoud conceded. 'He was yelling so much I had difficulty understanding anything.'

'Oh, he ordered all right,' Nasim said. 'Many times.'

Hamoud sniffed. 'Details.'

Nasim said, 'It gets worse. At least from Barrat's perspective.'

'I explained that we were arriving merely to save his ship, and his crew,' Hamoud went on. 'And that we carried a vital n-space message for the commander.'

'Which we revised, but only slightly,' Nasim said. 'Something about our being required to join you for the meeting with Random's leader. I forget the exact words.'

'Barrat accepted the n-space message and full report only because to do otherwise would be a court-martial offense,' Hamoud said.

'The skipper is in cahoots with the commander's opponents,' Nasim said. 'No question.'

'Cahoots,' Hamoud said. 'The word fits Barrat like a glove.'

Amanda looked from one to the other, trying to build up a bit of her own wrath. 'I specifically ordered you—'

'To meet the transport, report in, and pass on the message and report,' Hamoud said.

'And warn them of the pirates,' Nasim added.

'Which we most certainly did,' Hamoud said. 'It was the only reason Barrat stopped yelling.'

'You didn't say anything about leaving you behind,' Nasim pointed out. 'I know because we were listening very carefully.'

'Both of us,' Hamoud confirmed.

'You know that was exactly what I meant,' Amanda replied.

Hamoud shrugged. 'Who are we to interpret our commander's unspoken intent?'

She saw the spark in their eyes, the humor and the defiance. And fought off a sudden urge to weep. 'I should have you put in chains.'

Both men smiled, understanding her clearly. 'It's good to see you too,' Hamoud said.

'So we are stranded.'

'Oh, no,' Nasim said. 'It's much worse than that.'

'We're prisoners,' Hamoud said. 'We're told that as soon as their leader has what he wants, he'll offer us two choices. Join his crew or be sold into slavery.'

'Which is more than any other GSA officer has ever been granted,' Nasim said. 'He only offered that because you saved his fleet from certain destruction.'

'We're here,' Amanda pointed out. 'They don't know for sure . . .' She stopped talking because both men lost their smiles. 'What?'

'The fleet captain left three unmanned battle probes on patrol,' Hamoud said.

'They were destroyed,' Nasim said.

'A cruiser remained just outside the system to monitor the probes,' Hamoud said.

'What they saw has become the talk of all this planet's inhabitants,' Nasim said. 'How the suns grew arms, or tentacles, and tore apart three probes.'

'Just as you warned,' Hamoud said. 'The admiral has been waiting for you to wake up, so you can tell him how you knew.'

THIRTY-NINE

Amanda waited through another two standard days before leaving her safe haven. Their guards granted the men some freedom of movement, probably because she remained locked inside her rock-walled cabin. Every time they visited, Amanda listened carefully and gave nothing away. But with each additional hour, she grew increasingly certain of what was about to happen. Which was why she played at sickness. The fact that the admiral's medical staff could not identify a reason for her fever granted her room to maneuver. Which was good. Because Amanda had to get this right. Much more than their survival depended on her next move.

She had to assume Barrat had sent the message, and Rickets had received it. So much depended upon this. The n-space alert not only excused them for taking the required time for this second foray. She hoped it also granted Rickets the ammunition to defuse her opponents. At least temporarily.

Amanda had never considered herself good at deception. She secretly feared she lacked some essential gene that was required to lie well. She suspected this might prove to be her downfall, were she ever offered a shot at the Diplomats' Academy. Of course, given the fact that they were prisoners of a pirate king, on a planet that did not officially exist, some might say that should not register on her list of concerns.

What she learned from Hamoud and Nasim's visits also added pieces to the other puzzle. As in what was behind the mysteries that awaited them back on Loria.

The *real* crisis.

Random was a planet with neither sun nor fixed orbit. The pirate admiral – Durant Leclerc was his name – had discovered it while on regular patrol outside the Lorian system, waiting for ships using the transit point to the Arab systems, hunting prey. And he had thrived as a result. One ship had become two, then four, and at that point he had sent part of his fleet out exploring. Seeking whatever else resided in the neighborhood, another quarry he might take down.

Nothing could have prepared him for what they found. Not in his wildest dreams.

The only way they found Random at all was because of a huge gravitational anomaly. And there it was, swinging through empty space, cold and dark and waiting for them to take control.

Gravity remained a problem on Random, because it was shifty and unstable over the planet's surface.

'Say that again,' Amanda told them.

Random's standard gravity was not standard at all. It was merely an average, a fraction above Earth-norm, though the planet was scarcely as large as Earth's moon. The pirate's lair was located in a crater cut seventeen kilometers deep, the result of some massive meteor blast, which was perhaps what had cost Random its sun.

Hamoud and Nasim had been granted no view of the planet's surface. They had asked, once, and their escort had responded that such matters needed to wait for Leclerc's decision.

'Repeat that,' Amanda said.

Having Leclerc grant them this level of restricted freedom was completely without precedent. Anyone captured in raids was given the standard choice. Join Leclerc's crew or be sold. The richest regained their freedom through massive ransom payments. Everyone else became subjects of the wandering planet.

Yes, all right, Amanda had apparently saved the pirate fleet. Everywhere Hamoud and Nasim went, people stopped and stared at these GSA officers who had shielded the pirates and their battle fleet from destruction.

The pirate crew was not too bad – at least, those the two officers had met. Neither Hamoud nor Nasim had spotted more glyphs. In their one meeting with Leclerc, they had asked about the carnivorous aliens. Leclerc had apologized in what Hamoud had described as a very Arab manner, saying that unlikely allies were a hazard in his profession. And changed the subject.

Which was the point when Amanda announced she was ready to leave her underground haven.

Leclerc responded by sending down servants with armloads of . . . Gowns.

And jewels.

And crowns.

And shoes.

And an invitation to dine with Durant Leclerc, pirate king.

Amanda accepted the invitation, then asked Nasim to fetch her a working uniform from the lander.

FORTY

The banquet hall was as royal a setting as could be had on a pirate world of barren rock. The chamber was a hundred and twenty paces long, with a galleried ceiling so far overhead the upper pinnacles were lost to shadows. Torches of living flame rested in braces that appeared to be carved from solid gold. The flickering light made the battle standards appear to shift, as if caught in a sudden breeze.

Hamoud and Nasim entered the chamber one pace behind her. As they surveyed the vast hall, Nasim murmured, 'Isn't that our ruler's crest?'

Amanda followed the men's gazes, up to the third standard hanging from the opposite wall. Four Omani standards hung between those of the Urami system, the French, the . . .

'Look up,' Hamoud murmured.

Amanda did so and felt her breath freeze.

Their side of the hall held over a dozen flags bearing the GSA seal.

'A standard for every ship of the line they've taken,' Nasim guessed. 'Or destroyed.'

Amanda did her best to ignore both the standards and the guards by the four exits. She walked to where floor-to-ceiling windows lined the opposite wall. She touched the surface and felt what she thought was glass, which meant this was indeed her first view of the outer world.

Random's surface defined hostile. Their position was midway up a vast cliff. There must have been lights rimming the windows, for the view was astonishingly clear. Amanda overlooked a barren and molten world. To her right, a ribbon of rock traced its way down the ridge like a frozen waterfall. The base of the crater stretched out before her, a stone plain ribbed by volcanic mounds and rivulets whose bottoms were lost to shadow.

Hamoud pressed a finger to the glass, pointing out into the distance. 'What is happening out there?'

Nasim stepped up close to the pilot's other side. 'Must be their docking station.'

Amanda remained silent. But she suspected the bright yellow lights represented something else entirely.

To her mind, the lights said she had a distinct hope of getting this right.

One of the guards shouted, '*Ten-shun!*'

Admiral Leclerc had the solid stance, the broad shoulders, the massive jaw, and scarred hands of a man born to fight his way to the top, then lead a company by strength of will alone. His silver-black hair was cropped short, his face clean-shaven, his gaze sharp as an onyx blade. Amanda guessed his age at late fifties, standard Earth years, almost double her own. Even so, she found herself enjoying his flirtatious manner. The offer of gowns and jewels made perfect sense now. As did the formal manner in which their dinner was served. Four dark-suited servants poured their drinks, laid out their courses on plates of solid gold, then stood in white-gloved attendance behind their chairs.

They were seated at the head of a table capable of holding sixty or more. A fire burned cheerfully in a vast fireplace carved from the cavern's wall. Torches lit the entire chamber. Amanda had to assume they were fed by some local power source, for there was certainly neither wood nor charcoal on this bare-rock world.

The first plates were whipped away and replaced by a second course. The portions were small, the flavors exquisite. Amanda ate with a good appetite. The admiral watched her with evident approval. 'You did not agree with my choice of gowns, perhaps?'

'I was hoping we might discuss business, sir,' she replied. 'The uniform seemed more appropriate.'

'Then regretfully to business we shall go.' He set down his fork, waited as the servant plucked away his plate, then demanded, 'You transmitted a message before entering my cruiser. I have to assume it was in code.'

'It was. Yes.'

'When my captain asked what was the actual message, you had your fit. Or whatever it was.'

'"Fit" is as good as anything I can think of, Admiral.'

'So this was not some act to keep you from responding.'

'No. Definitely not. But just the same, I did have time to answer your captain with the truth. I received word that the GSA transport had been warned of your vessels orbiting the system and was safely on its return journey.'

'So you divided your meager force in order to save your only way to return home . . . Where is home, by the way?'

'We are based on the GSA sector headquarters, Admiral. I am originally from Earth.'

He watched the servants remove their plates. As their next course was set down, Leclerc said, 'I have visited Earth. Twice, in fact. I wished to see if my native region's cuisine lived up to its reputation. I was most pleasantly surprised. I became somewhat addicted to the wines of Bordeaux.' He lifted his goblet. 'A ridiculous indulgence, and most expensive.'

'Life is best enjoyed when we look beyond today's cares,' Amanda said. 'And savor pleasures both large and small.'

'That was a quote, yes? Who said that?'

'My father. A very good man.'

'And wise.' He lifted his glass. 'To all good fathers everywhere.'

She drank. 'How was yours?'

'Not so good, I'm afraid. His addictions were less pleasurable and even more expensive. He sold me to pay off debts.'

She set down her glass. 'I'm so very sorry.'

'Ah. Well.' His gesture took in the cavern and the meal. 'I am here.'

'And this life suits you.'

'Indeed.' At a gesture, the servants exited the chamber. 'Now that we have dined, perhaps we should return to the matter at hand.'

'Three matters,' Amanda replied. 'What I know about your missing ships. And the Lorians' defense system.'

'And you will tell me?'

'Everything I know, sir.'

'I believe you, Major. Of all the approaches I have known from those facing the prospect of my company, yours is unique. You are my enemy, yes?'

'Officially.' She pointed to the GSA standards lining the wall. 'My superiors would certainly confirm that.'

'And you? What do you say?' When she hesitated, he pressed, 'Are you seeking to become a soldier of fortune? Join my ranks and know the riches of the illicit life?'

'No offense, sir. But I am happy where I am.'

Amanda expected him to threaten. Say the obvious. That she and her two friends might have little choice.

Instead, he toyed with his glass, drained it, set it down. His actions were careful and deliberate. 'And yet you speak of the official position. Which means you must also hold an alternative.'

Amanda felt the electric thrill of very real hope. 'That, sir, brings us to the third matter.'

FORTY-ONE

Leclerc led them into a side chamber of more comfortable portions. A massive desk dominated the far end, and three walls were covered by hand-stitched tapestries. Leclerc dismissed his servants, set out glasses and a crystal decanter, and poured them each a measure of something he called cognac. Amanda sipped cautiously and decided it tasted like liquid fire. And delicious.

At his request, Amanda walked Leclerc through their experiences on Loria. She left out their sending down the probe and the missing island. Instead, she began with their arrival at the colony. Leclerc interrupted only once, to question her more intently about her first contact with the Diplomat. She then described the top of the conical hill and its ability to stop a shielded heart. This was followed by the evaporation of the scientist when she tried to step onto Amanda's lander. Leclerc did not speak again, not even when she described watching his ship being peeled apart by fingers made of pink clouds.

When she finished, Leclerc turned and studied the flames. She was content to sip from her goblet and wait. She knew she should be tired. But just then the anticipation of what might come next kept her not just awake but fizzing with repressed excitement.

Finally, Leclerc turned back and said, 'The third matter.'

Amanda was as ready as she would ever be. 'Given what I know of you and your situation, Admiral, I suspect that you recently have had a major change of circumstances.' She felt Hamoud stir beside her. She glanced over, and rather than confront a silent protest, she saw very clearly that the pilot was astonished at her ability to piece together the hidden. He had suspected something, she realized. Which probably meant he had been granted direct access to news from their missing spy. All this only added to the moment's thrill.

Leclerc said merely, 'Go on.'

'Something has shifted in your current status,' she repeated. 'Otherwise there is no logical reason to continue probing Lorian defenses. The loss of two ships would have been enough. You survive by bringing in wealth for all your subjects and minimizing danger. And yet twice you have returned in force to a planet that offers you no riches. So why bother?'

Hamoud said, 'I thought . . .'

Amanda nodded agreement to the unfinished words. 'We all thought you wanted a planetary base. One closer to your field of action. But to do this also meant granting the GSA a target. Right now, you remain safe because no one is certain where you are. A planet without a sun, lost to the reaches of space beyond any planetary system, you are as well hidden as you could possibly be. It is why you have survived as long as you have. And yet now you are risking everything. And for what?'

Leclerc's only response was to turn and stare into the fire. The flickering shadows revealed his age. Leclerc looked not just worried but exhausted. Perhaps it was the hour. Leading a pirate kingdom could not be an easy task. But Amanda thought she had succeeded in uncovering his secret agenda. Which only made her blood fizz more strongly still.

'Something has changed,' Amanda went on. 'The shift is so drastic that what has worked for decades no longer suits you. Your options are limited now. Either you change or . . .'

Leclerc addressed the fire. 'Or what, Major?'

She took a breath. 'You find a way to adjust or you lose control of your population.'

Leclerc's gaze remained held by the flames. 'You have described a specific set of circumstances. Have you extrapolated this further? Have you pierced the veil?'

She nodded slowly. The answer was in how he refused to meet her gaze. 'I think so. Yes, sir.'

'Tell me.'

'I suspect Random was formerly a gas giant orbiting the double stars. The Lorians pushed both this planet and the entire array of asteroids and comets out of their system. Thus eliminating any threat to their planetary orbit.' She gave him a moment to object, to criticize, then went on, 'A gas giant's core has been debated for centuries. No probe has ever survived a descent. We have no idea what really lies there. But the thinking is, it is a liquid ball of heavy metals. The force that shoved this giant off its orbit also blasted away the gasses, and left . . . What?'

Hamoud murmured, 'Of course.'

'Instead of pirating, you are now bringing in a new army. A mechanized one. Specialist mining robots. Almost all your population has been refocused upon this new venture,' Amanda said. 'And what they have found . . .'

She stopped because Leclerc rose to his feet and said simply, 'Come with me.'

FORTY-TWO

The cavern they traveled was as broad as a city's main avenue. Illumination came from curved lights planted into the ceiling every twenty meters. The pavement was polished stone, with two lanes for fast-flowing traffic and two more for those on foot. Amanda had no idea what time it was, nor did she think it much mattered to these people. Some of those they passed shouted greetings; others planted fists to chests in a semblance of ancient salutes. A few, she noted, scowled and spat. If Leclerc noticed the disrespect, he gave no sign. One of their servants drove the high-sided vehicle, but the top was open to the cavern, and there was no shield that Amanda could detect. She decided any planetary leader who could travel with just two guards in an open-topped vehicle was in good shape indeed.

Their destination was a portal taller than the dining hall was high. Everything in this cavern kingdom appeared oversized to Amanda. The guards alighted, checked wrist instruments, scouted in all directions, then nodded to Leclerc. He stepped from the transport, pulled a gold chain from beneath his uniform, and inserted a key into the portal. An electronic eye emerged, scanned him, then the others. Leclerc said, 'I enter with two guards and three guests.'

The electronic eye inspected them in turn, then the blast-doors rolled back. Leclerc said, 'Follow me.'

They entered a cavern so vast the dimensions could not fully be gauged. Amanda estimated the far wall had to be several kilometers away, the ceiling further still. A medium-sized city would have fit comfortably inside. Leclerc led them to a smaller flat-bed vehicle, pointed Amanda to the front passenger seat, waved the other four into benches behind them, and handled the controls himself. They cruised past dry-stone warehouses with cages for doors. At each Leclerc pointed and declared their contents. On and on the names went.

Heavy metals.

The definition had changed somewhat as humankind entered the galactic realm. What before had been known as the atomic table now had two distinct sections. The second portion, heavy metals, were known by a second name.

Stardust.

The rarest elements in the known universe all shared the same birthplace. Blasted out of dying stars, blown through space by the cataclysmic explosions that defined stellar death. The fiercest battles, even between otherwise close allies, happened over unclaimed planets who were found to be repositories of stardust.

Leclerc stopped before just another stone building. He unlocked just another barred door. He waved them into just another warehouse.

Only this one was filled with gold bars. He hefted one and passed it to Amanda. 'The next twenty warehouses all hold this.'

She accepted the brick, which was surprisingly heavy, then passed it to Hamoud.

Leclerc said, 'I have managed to maintain unity by granting my crew a level of luxury most would never have dreamed was possible.'

Amanda said, 'You've also pledged to find a way to make this not just theirs, but legal.'

'The glyphs you destroyed were the last of their race in my employ,' Leclerc said. 'You rid me of a very difficult issue.'

'It was not us,' Amanda said. 'But you're welcome.'

'I invited you here because I need you to tell me how to conquer Loria,' Leclerc said. 'I wanted you to understand how urgent is my need. How crucial.'

'I'm sorry. Truly. But I can't help you.'

'I need Loria in order to petition the empire and gain admittance as a bona fide system. Either this happens immediately or my people will revolt.' He waved a hand at the wealth that surrounded them. 'Regretfully, this means that I must have an answer that suits me. Help me, and everything this warehouse contains is yours.' Leclerc dropped his hand. 'You will not refuse. You cannot.'

Amanda nodded slowly. This was the moment she had spent two standard days planning for. The only reason she had remained content to stay flat on her back. Trapped inside a windowless sickbay. So she could meet Leclerc's gaze and say, 'The power the Lorians hold, their ability to turn even their suns into weapons, is unlike anything the galactic empire has ever faced. You cannot conquer that world. It is simply not possible. But I do have an answer to your question.'

Leclerc had grown increasingly somber as she spoke. There, in the pirate king's craven features, dwelled a force that could condemn an entire fleet to slavery or worse. He was a man of two distinct natures. And here now was revealed the other visage.

Still she waited.

'You don't think I would have found another course of action?'

'There is an alternative,' Amanda insisted quietly. 'I am certain of it.'

'You're bluffing.'

'No, Admiral. I am not.'

'Then you're shielding the colonists. They've managed to settle Loria for almost seventy years! You know their secret! I demand that you tell me what it is!'

'Sir, the colonists are not the issue. Your motivations are. The Lorians are a telepathic race. They may not read your mind, but they most certainly knew your crew's motives. And this is why—'

Leclerc closed the distance between them. Furious at her willingness to defy him. 'Tell me you understand how close you are to death.'

She did her best to keep her voice steady. 'Closer than when I was trapped by the glyphs.'

They were both surprised by Hamoud saying, 'Admiral, if I may.'

Leclerc remained as he was, so close Amanda could smell the cognac's sweet aftertaste on his breath. Close enough for her to see the flecks of black fury in his unblinking gaze.

Hamoud took the admiral's silence as permission. 'I have only known Major Bostick for the length of this mission. But it is long enough for me to be certain that she holds a rare skill at finding the unseen. What she says about the colonists is true. I attest to the fact that they have survived this long only because they seek to join the Lorian race.'

Leclerc's response was a volcanic rumble. 'Impossible.'

'And yet it is happening. Those who cannot do so are killed, and the colonists accept their deaths as part of the price they must pay. But, Admiral, that is not the issue. If Major Bostick says she has an alternative for you, I urge you to listen.'

Nasim said quietly, 'She has a gift for uncovering the hidden, true enough.'

Leclerc took a step back. 'Very well. Speak.'

Amanda took a breath and launched in.

The first indication she had made the right move did not come from Leclerc. Instead, it was delivered by her pilot.

Hamoud startled them all by clapping his hands and laughing out loud.

Amanda dragged her gaze away from Leclerc, knowing it was as dangerous a move as ignoring a crouching carnivore. 'You think it will work?'

'Do I *think*?' Hamoud laughed again. 'Major, you have solved a dozen interplanetary crises with one word!'

'Actually, it was quite a lot of words,' Nasim corrected.

'And what words they are!' Hamoud applauded once more. 'Genius!'

Amanda swallowed her smile and turned back to Leclerc. The admiral glared at her a moment longer, then said, 'Major, you and your allies are granted permission to breathe one day longer.'

Following the enclave's sleep cycle, Leclerc kept them waiting for hours. Amanda found herself surprised by her own calm. The pressure she had endured since boarding the *Invictus* and heading to Loria was . . .

Amanda felt as though time had been suspended. All the elements beyond her control, even the need to meet Commander Rickets' time constraints . . .

Gone.

Either Barrat delivered her report, or not. Either Rickets accepted the current situation, or . . .

Whatever happened, it was beyond her control. And something more. To survive, she had no choice but suspend worry about all external issues. And focus totally upon the here and now.

Amanda spent the hours working on details with Hamoud and Nasim. She assumed everything they said was being monitored, and did not care. She had made it this far by being completely open. They developed a step-by-step strategy, assuming the admiral would accept Amanda's idea, knowing they were not dealing with a patient man. Success or failure would depend upon not only bringing him a concrete resolution, but doing so as fast as humanly possible.

When the guards came for them, they were taken straight to Leclerc's study. The admiral was seated at his desk, eating while studying a sheaf of documents. A uniformed attendant hovered at the admiral's elbow, pointing to lines of numbers and murmuring quietly. Leclerc forced them to stand there before him. Neither he nor the attendant glanced their way.

Finally, Leclerc waved a dismissal. The servant cleared away the meal's remnants and the file. When he departed, Leclerc said, 'Yesterday you mentioned missing ships. Plural. But we only lost the one plus our probes.'

'Thanks to the major,' Hamoud pointed out.

Leclerc glared at the pilot, but when he responded, it was only to say, 'Explain.'

'We are aware of your first ship going down, sir.'

'What ship would that be?'

'There was a spy on board the first vessel you sent to Loria. He notified the Omanis of your mission. He has not reported in since.'

'Perhaps we identified the spy and gave him the same punishment I am considering for you three.'

Amanda did not respond.

Leclerc let the threat hang in the cavern's air for a time, then went on, 'If indeed there was a spy – which I am not accepting, mind. But if there was, why did the empire not attack me? You yourself said we were sheltered only because the GSA has no idea where we are located. A spy would change all that.'

'Because the spy was a soldier of fortune. One who was granted a trip to the Omani moon. But not entrusted with Random's location.'

Leclerc crossed his arms. 'So when you first arrived in Loria, you hunted for evidence of my ship.'

'And found nothing at all.' Amanda described their probe's overflight of the drop zone. The missing island. The Lorians who observed their probe's passage from three thousand meters away.

When she went quiet, Leclerc remained very still. Watchful. Intent. Like a lion on full alert. Deadly.

Finally, he said, 'Tell me what you require.'

Amanda allowed herself a tiny breath. 'Two voice n-space messages. And a fast ship.'

FORTY-THREE

N-space messages required enormous expenditures of power. Standard interstellar data streams were milliseconds long and still cost more than Amanda's annual salary. But in some rare cases, where voice confirmation was required, these hyper-space bursts were extended. Amanda had compacted

her message to Rickets to seven sentences. Twice she wrote out
an eighth, begging the commander to excuse her for ignoring their
time restriction. Twice she threw it out. If Rickets needed
persuading, no n-space entreaty would make any difference
whatsoever.

Leclerc insisted upon reviewing the communication and struck
one sentence entirely. Those six sentences would cost more than
a Florida condominium with a view out over the Atlantic.

Hamoud's message was forty-one sentences long.

Leclerc pondered it for a long time. 'Explain to me who is the
recipient.'

They had been through this already, but Amanda did not object.
She knew Leclerc was in truth examining the risk of this entire
approach. Permitting these unknown officers of his primary enemy
to represent him. And thus allowing them off-planet. Amanda
said, 'Flight Captain Hamoud's father has served as adviser to
the Omani system's emir.'

'Actually,' Nasim corrected, 'he did so twice.'

'He is the ruling council's most trusted ally within the private
sector,' Amanda went on. 'If anyone can make this happen, and
quickly, it is him.'

Leclerc handed back the second message without change. 'Your
ship is standing by. You depart in one hour. Your number three
stays here.' He stifled Amanda's outburst with an upraised hand.
'Do not even think of objecting.'

FORTY-FOUR

At Hamoud's request, Amanda packed all the gowns.
'And the jewelry.' He was seated next to Nasim on a
narrow wooden bench by the wall opposite her bed. A
guard slouched just outside her open door. The admiral's gifts
made a glittering pile over her coverlet.

'Hamoud, no, really. I don't . . .'

Nasim said, 'Major, you don't know what you will face. Or
who. Hamoud is right. Take them all.'

Amanda found it difficult to even glance Nasim's way. He leaned against the wall with his hands laced behind his head. His legs were extended so that she had to step over them to move from the pile of stolen items to the valise Leclerc had given her.

Loaned, Amanda corrected herself. She was taking no gifts from that man.

Then she realized Nasim was humming.

The sound irritated her mightily. 'What could *possibly* make you so *cheerful*?'

'I was thinking,' Nasim said, 'of nights before battle.'

'Cringing in your bunk,' Hamoud said. 'Weeping with fear.'

'Preparing our gear, checking our armament one final time.' Nasim pointed to the pile on her bed. 'Just as you are doing now.'

She dumped the jewelry into the valise. 'I *hate* this.'

'For once, Hamoud is correct,' Nasim said. 'Take the jewels.'

'I'm not talking about the jewels and you *know* it.'

Both men smiled at her. Nasim said, 'Leclerc was right to order me to stay behind on Random.'

'You would have done the same in his position,' Hamoud said. 'As would I.'

'My presence may even grant you a bit more time to make this work,' Nasim said.

Amanda fought the valise's latches. 'I should never have agreed.'

'You had no choice,' Nasim said. 'None of us did.'

Her response was cut off by the guard entering the room and announcing, 'It's time.'

The main hold was the largest cavern Amanda had ever seen. A dozen football stadiums from her home planet would have been lost inside. Their destination, a medium-sized cruiser, was docked next to a Surrus battleship. Beyond them stretched an armada of battle-ready vessels, too many to count on fast approach. Amanda spotted some so ancient she had only read about them in history books. But there were also a number of sleek fighters from the current era, some of which were being readied for another assault.

As their vehicle halted by the cruiser's loading platform, Leclerc broke off conversation with a pair of non-humans and strode over. 'You will be sequestered for the duration of this journey. Only a handful of my most senior officers know Random's location. That is how it must remain.'

'Until the Major's plan is successfully put in place,' Hamoud corrected. 'And Random's position enters the galactic record.'

'Let us hope your optimism is well founded,' Leclerc replied. 'For all our sakes.'

Amanda stepped closer. 'I agree to take on this mission, but on one condition.'

'Major, you are in no position—'

'If I fail, you will allow me to return and be the one facing punishment. You will let Nasim go free. You will see him safely to his home world.'

Nasim protested, 'Major, I can't allow—'

'Silence!' When she was certain of being obeyed, Amanda continued, 'In return, I pledge to do my utmost to bring you a treaty you will find acceptable.'

Leclerc studied her for a long moment, then turned and called, 'Captain, allow our guests the use of your cabin for this voyage.'

'Aye, sir.'

Leclerc turned back. 'Very little manages to surprise me, Major. And yet you continue to do so at every turn.'

'Admiral, do we have a deal?'

He offered Amanda his hand. 'You have the word of a pirate king.'

FORTY-FIVE

Amanda had no way of knowing the exact length of their journey. The cabin's chronograph and vid-screen had both been disabled. Soon after departure, guards arrived with meal trays. While they ate, Hamoud related how his and Nasim's journey to Random had taken place with them locked inside the lander, which had been fully powered down before takeoff. But he thought the voyage had lasted about a day and a half. Amanda wondered if it had cost him as much to speak Nasim's name as it did her to hear it.

They slept, ate again, and pushed through the hours with work.

Her knowledge of the Arab systems was founded upon books and documentaries. Hamoud spent the entire journey from Random to the Lorian system continuing the education he had started in her windowless sickroom, explaining the political mess on Oman. There was no other word to describe the current situation. The government was in chaos. Which made their chances of success slim indeed.

Hamoud introduced her to the people and system and etiquette. Her status as a serving GSA officer might be a detriment, he warned. But with the ruling council in such turmoil, very little could be said for certain. The emir whom his father had served was dying, and the crown prince was rendered toothless by the ruling council. The prince had been named heir to the throne more than thirty years ago. Three decades was a long time for anyone to wait for power. Hamoud had met him only once. He described the pretender with grave concern. Amanda became infected by his worries, and yet she welcomed it. At least that kept her from fretting over the man she had been forced to leave behind.

The two guards who had brought their meals now led them down a series of empty corridors. Amanda assumed they were headed for the main transport hold. But when Hamoud asked their destination, the guards did not respond.

The battlecruiser was enormous. Amanda estimated they walked at least a kilometer and a half. The corridors were wide enough for two landers to pass each other. She wanted to ask why they did not ride, but decided there was nothing to be gained from giving the guards another reason to ignore them. They were both humans, these pirates, and very big. They dwarfed Hamoud, and he stood almost a head taller than she.

They rounded a corner, and massive blast portals loomed before them. As they entered the flight deck a trio of fighters passed through the sally port, heading out on patrol. The double shields used to maintain atmospheric conditions inside the hold flickered like electric webbing, one after the other. Amanda remembered how, during her first descent, the clouds above Loria had clutched at her before granting passage. So much had happened since then.

The launch station's control room formed a metal protrusion about two-thirds up the wall to Amanda's left. A pair of blaster cannons positioned on its roof tracked their progress. Other than the cannons and the departing fighters, there was no movement in the vast hold. The flight deck was about three-quarters full, mostly one-man fighters and battle drones. But a trio of military-grade transports formed a wall directly in front of them. The ships were mostly a generation out of date, but all appeared to be in battle-ready condition. The absence of life or sound spooked her. She saw how Hamoud frowned as he searched the hold, and knew he felt the same.

Beyond the transports loomed several mountains of equipment and armaments, all strapped down with pale netting. They threaded their way through in single file, Amanda in rear position. Up ahead of her, Hamoud stopped and murmured, 'Oh, my sweet word.'

The pilot's expression was almost comical. Hamoud looked pole-axed, as if he had just fallen in love. Then Amanda stepped past the equipment and saw what he saw. 'What is *that*?'

'That,' Hamoud said, 'is an Octavian-class space yacht.'

She knew the name, of course, and had seen numerous photographs. Several cadets at the Academy had decorated their walls with Octavian posters. But seeing one up close like this was something else entirely.

One of their guards waved to the control tower. The yacht's portal opened, and a ramp slid down to land at her feet. And she realized, 'This is *ours*?'

Their evident excitement finally released the guards from their compressed silence. The larger of the two said, 'I am ordered to say you are free to go. The vessel's rear hold contains the gold bullion you requested.' His voice was a rush of cold rage. 'For myself and everyone else on this vessel, I say the admiral was wrong to trust you.'

The other guard snarled, 'He'd be better served selling you to the detrinium slavers.'

'The admiral is the only reason you're still breathing,' the first guard went on. The force required to break silence left him sounding slightly strangled. 'My father and brother and the rest of my clan were murdered in a raid by empire forces. My sisters . . .'

'You're scum and always will be,' the other guard declared.

'The admiral wishes you a speedy and successful voyage,' the first guard said. 'I for one wish you a slow and agonizing death.'

Amanda and Hamoud stood planted at the ramp's base as the guards stomped away. The blaster cannons remained aimed directly at them. Hamoud said quietly, 'Perhaps we should make way.'

FORTY-SIX

Travel through n-space was still a new enough experience for Amanda to enjoy watching the yacht's monitors perform a slow dance of stars. Human physicists had long accepted that n-space portals were the final gift of a dying black hole. Those massive beasts of space and time had a life cycle just like everything else in the positive universe. Whether dark matter followed a similar route was hotly debated. But such mathematical conundrums counted far less to Amanda than the poetry of light now on display.

N-space portals were generally larger than the orbit of Mercury, the closest planet to Amanda's home sun. This was why most vessels passed safely through the Lorian transit point, even with a pirate fleet on patrol. But not all. The Octavian yacht was a case in point.

Their vessel had been holed in several places. A blaster cannon had carved a substantial cavity from the cockpit by the port monitors. Aft of the private cabins, three spots on the hull by the crew's galley and another next to the ship's defense cannons had also been carefully repaired. Hamoud pointed these out while Amanda accompanied him on a careful inspection of their borrowed vessel. His explanation helped her focus beyond the luxury on display. He explained how these precise strike zones meant the ship had been rendered helpless while not killing the wealthy patrons. The power train had also been left intact, thus not turning the vessel into a miniature star. It was the work of an experienced crew, operating with surgical precision. Their strike window would only have lasted a few seconds at most. After the ship emerged from n-space, the yacht's crew would have immediately gone weapons hot, as anyone rich enough to afford such a craft would also know this was a high-risk region. Hamoud fingered one of the points where the cockpit's hull had been split open, and added there was always the chance that one of the crew had been bribed.

The space yacht was, in a word, magnificent. Nothing could fully erase Amanda's awe. Not the guards' blood-chilling farewell, nor Nasim's hostage situation, nor Hamoud's description of the pirates' assault. Amanda had never known such luxury could exist, much less be hers, at least for this one journey.

The empire's largest shipbuilders all had specialty divisions that dealt exclusively with the super-rich of many species. Humans had a hard-won reputation for crafting vessels that were as much priceless works of art as the means of moving between planets. Everything Amanda saw or touched redefined her concept of what money could buy. The cockpit's control deck, the star monitors, even the frame of her co-pilot's chair were all chased in sterling silver. The doors, including those to the yacht's nine closets – closets! – were polished burl. The deck was fashioned from tongue-and-groove wooden slats rimmed by tiles of semi-precious stones. The master bedroom's fresher was larger than the cabin she shared with four other subalterns.

With a tub.

Amanda left Hamoud humming in the galley and took her first bath in months.

She emerged wearing a one-piece outfit taken from the bathroom pantry – pantry! – a long-sleeved house-suit of some thick beige material, soft as a cloud. Hamoud greeted her with the finest meal she had ever eaten from freezer packets. As they were cleaning up, repeatedly Hamoud started to say something, then clamped down. The internal struggle left him scowling.

'You might as well go ahead and tell me what is wrong.'

'Perhaps we should both rest first.'

'Hamoud, look at me.' When he reluctantly lifted his gaze, she went on, 'Whatever it is, do you really think waiting until after we've slept will make it any better, or easier to discuss? Out with it.'

'My family . . . No one on Oman knows of my . . .'

'Demotion.'

He nodded miserably.

She did her best to stifle her smile. If only all their problems were this easy to resolve. 'Hamoud, I have always considered you a flight captain. Nothing has changed.'

The first sign they had of Hamoud's message having reached his father came when they passed through Oman's n-space portal. A bevy of the emir's warrior fleet was there to greet them. Though 'greet' was perhaps too fine a word for the stern command. 'This is the Omani Space Guard. Identify yourself or die.'

'GSA Flight Captain Hamoud, son of Jaffar. Reporting as ordered.'

'You are expected, Captain. How many in your company?'

'Just one. Major Amanda Bostick, outbound from GSA sector HQ.'

'You are ordered to descend and report to the Palace Council.'

Hamoud hesitated and glanced over. As worried as she had ever seen him. And for good reason.

The longer Hamoud had described the current situation on Oman, the clearer her next step became. The ruling council regularly met in the emir's sickroom and fought viciously for control. Every trusted ally of the comatose ruler was suspect. Death by poison and assassination had become the norm. Throughout the system, conflict roiled just beneath the surface.

A visiting official from the Galactic Space Arm, bringing an offer of a new interplanetary treaty that could strengthen the emir's allies on the council, might as well arrive with a notice of her own execution.

Finally they had both reached the same conclusion. Their best hope of success lay in Amanda maintaining complete isolation. Hamoud would serve as her official representative. Leaving her, the GSA officer, the outsider, completely removed from system politics.

'Do it,' Amanda whispered.

Hamoud keyed the external comm-link and replied, 'Regretfully, sir, I must decline. The major suffers from an unidentified ailment. Possibly contagious.'

'Hold one.'

Amanda waited until Hamoud cut the comm-link, then said, 'It's a good plan.'

'So much depends on our getting this right,' he fretted.

The electric clarity was still with her, the sense of following the absent commander's lead. Doing her utmost to protect those placed in her charge. Peering beyond the bend of time. Moving forward.

The Omani commander came back with, 'One of my fighters has been assigned escort duty.'

'Roger, I see the beacon.'

'Follow the vessel to Oman City. Arrangements are being put in place.'

'Roger that.'

'Welcome home, Captain. Omani Space Guard out.'

The escort vessel led them to the rooftop flight deck of the capital's premier hotel. Their descent was through heavy cloud covering. A storm masked almost all of the planet's surface. Amanda caught glimpses of gray rain-swept structures and swaths of green city parks. There was a fantasy element to what she saw: fairy-like pinnacles that twisted as they rose, impossibly poetic and fragile. She yearned for the chance she knew would most probably not come. To escape from the bounds of responsibility and challenge. To go adventuring on this new world.

A group of emergency medical personnel stood just beyond the landing platform. They wore full isolation suits and bore a pair of translucent stretcher-pods. Hamoud was required to alight first, wearing his suit, which was sprayed three times before he was allowed to lie on the stretcher and be transported away. Then Amanda descended the ramp. Her single glimpse of Oman City was drenched in green disinfectant, then blue, before hands directed her to lie down. The pod was sealed, and her glimpse of a rain-swept vista was over.

The hotel's isolation wing contained rooms for aliens requiring a different atmosphere than human-normal. But most of the suites were intended for the sort of wealthy patrons who could afford to land private yachts atop the planet's most expensive residence. The wing also contained a full hospital service, with many of Oman's foremost doctors and clinicians on call. Amanda was housed in a suite larger than the Florida home where she and her four brothers had been raised. The dining hall held an oval table that seated fourteen. The suite's last occupant had been the senior wife to the ruler of Oman's largest moon. This she learned from the butler with whom she communicated through monitors in every room.

Hamoud was given a clean bill of health and released from confinement later that evening. Amanda's doctors clearly knew there was nothing wrong with her either. But no word was uttered suggesting she move out of the isolation ward. At least, not in her presence. Hamoud briefed her via the wall monitor. 'Your suite is isolated behind double doors similar to a ship's airlock. There are four guards on duty between here and the exit. Your windows face an interior courtyard and are blast-proof.'

'The doctors know there's nothing wrong with me.'

'You are far from the first guest who has needed security to stay in good health.'

'What about you?'

'The ruling council has assigned me a detail of the emir's own guards.' His smile was twisted slightly by the faceplate. 'I suppose a battle probe might make me safer. But it would hamper my discussions.'

Amanda glanced at the parlor's window. Her suite was on the second floor, and her view was of a blooming tree and of birds whose song she could not hear. Time, she knew, would hang very heavy. 'I need you to do something for me.'

'Name it.'

'There must be records from the protectorate's earliest explorers who visited Loria.'

'I suppose . . .'

'Think about it. Why would all the rulers in this quadrant not set up at least a guard colony on the planet closest to the lone n-space portal?'

Hamoud stared at her.

'Something happened,' Amanda went on. 'Something so definite that the idea of colonization was dropped entirely. Even when Oman lost ships to the pirates, nothing changed.'

'The empire promised us a protective force soon after the first ship went missing,' Hamoud replied.

'And they may eventually get around to that,' Amanda replied. 'Once the Arab systems bend to the empire's wishes and request full membership.'

'That will never happen.'

'Exactly.' She rose and walked over to the window, staring at the planet she was barred from ever seeing. 'The logical action would be for the Arabs to put a battle fleet on constant patrol.'

'Expensive,' Hamoud replied. 'It would also require a level of harmony between systems that does not exist. These rulers are a difficult and quarrelsome lot.'

'Even so,' she insisted. 'We're missing something.'

'I will ask my father,' Hamoud decided. 'If anyone can obtain the information you seek, it will be him.'

FORTY-SEVEN

Amanda dreamed that she floated on a pink sea, and watched two suns fashion a deadly web of light. She was surrounded by a wind that whispered a constant melody. When she opened her eyes, it seemed as though the music came with her, speaking of a mystery she had yet to uncover. About a pink planet and an entire system controlled by little telepathic beings who disliked taking life and yet could demolish entire planets . . .

She realized that something was chiming.

She sat up and shifted her feet to the floor. The bed was as big as a boat and the sheets were some mix of natural fibers – she guessed silk and cotton. As were her sleeping garments. She rubbed her face and said, 'Yes?'

The chiming continued. Amanda rose to her feet and padded into the central parlor. She followed the sound over to the desk by the window. A monitor she had not noticed before blinked in time to the chime. She tried several other commands, then had an idea, and said in Arabic, 'Speak.'

Her butler's face appeared on the monitor. 'Forgive me for disturbing your rest, my lady. But you have a call, and I am told it is most urgent.'

'Put it through.' Then she was caught by a sudden thought. 'Wait. Can you stay on the line?'

'Of course, mistress, if you will it.'

She had to assume her every utterance was recorded. Something classed as urgent needed to be publicly monitored. 'Split the screen so the caller will also see you.'

He was an older Arab, with the formal manner of one with a lifetime's training of answering every whim. 'As you command, my lady.'

A lovely young woman with liquid eyes and the stains of exhaustion appeared beside her butler. 'My sincerest apologies, mistress. But Captain Hamoud and his father the Lord Chancellor insisted you would want to hear this without delay.'

She said to the butler, 'Can I have tea?'

'Of course, my lady. Breakfast?'

'Later.' To the young lady, 'May I ask your name?'

'Laila, mistress. I serve as personal aide to the Lord Chancellor.'

'I thought Captain Hamoud's father had retired.'

'It is our custom for planetary officials to keep their highest title for life, my lady.'

The woman's System English was heavily accented, but under-standable. And far better than Amanda's Arabic. She heard the outer portal sigh open and shut, and was rising before the door chimed. 'Wait just one moment, please.'

She returned and poured herself a cup of strong black tea. Amanda breathed her way through three sips, then said, 'Proceed.'

'The documents you sought were hard to find, as they belonged in the private records of the last emir. Which were sealed.' The woman revealed a lovely smile. 'The Lord Chancellor can be most persuasive when he is provoked.'

'If he is anything like his son, I believe it.'

'The Pilot Captain would be a young duplicate of his father, if he had not been infected with the desire to fly among the stars.'

'I am guessing Hamoud's decision to join the GSA Fleet Arm did not go over well.'

The woman smiled more broadly still and shook her head as she replied, 'It would certainly not be in my remit to speak of such things.'

Amanda finished her cup and poured another. 'So you have the documents for me.'

'Indeed. These records date back almost three hundred and fifty years, when the royal court still kept all records in formal Arabic. I have transcribed them into System English. All seven hundred and twelve pages are ready for your inspection.'

The reason behind the woman's strained features became evident. 'When did you last sleep?'

The smile returned. 'If one works for the Lord Chancellor, one learns to go without.'

But reading Laila's translation proved very difficult. The language was extremely vague in places. The Lord Chancellor's aide had sought to make a *literal* rendition. Page after page was layered with references to the former emir and his lofty aims, protecting the system, expanding his subjects' fortunes, and so forth. Amanda asked for a tablet with the text embedded, and a stylus so she could make notes alongside. Before that arrived, however, she made her first discovery. One that raised the hairs on the back of her neck in an excitement that could only be described as electric.

Twice more her discoveries lifted Amanda from her chair and set her to pacing the parlor floor. Rain speckled her window and washed the interior courtyard of almost all color. The suite's air was sterile. The only sounds came from the passage of her feet across the carpet. For once, she did not mind the isolation. She was so lost in thought that the door chime caused her to jump. 'Yes?'

'The tablet you requested has arrived, my lady.'

'Outstanding.'

'Would you care for your midday meal now?'

Amanda had not realized how hungry she was until that moment. 'Absolutely. I'm starving.'

'At once, my lady.'

When the interior door flashed green, she opened it and pulled out a tablet and stylus in the same sterile wrapping that contained her meals. She re-read the initial hundred and fifty pages of the translation and made furious notes while she ate. The food was a bland and boring rendition of Arab cuisine. Amanda longed for the meal the two men had prepared for her, back on the GSA transport that had started them on this quest. She hoped Hamoud was finding success in his efforts. She longed to be reunited with Nasim. Then she pushed it all aside and dove back in.

An hour or so later, the desk monitor chimed again. 'My lady.'

'What . . . Yes?'

'The Pilot Captain is here and requests an audience.'

Amanda followed the butler's instructions to what she had assumed was yet another closet, this one situated between the dining hall and the bedroom. When she opened it, she discovered a small room encased in a pale gray velvet. Even the desk extending from the rear wall was covered in the same padding. But none of that mattered. For the rear wall was glass, and on the other side stood Hamoud. He offered her a weary smile in greeting. 'How are you, Major?'

'Not climbing the walls. Yet.'

'They are seeing to your needs?'

'For everything except the one thing I want most. My freedom.'

He gestured to the chair by her desk, waited until she had seated herself, then pulled back his own chair. 'All conversations within this booth are confidential. Do you understand me, Major?'

She read his grim expression and replied, 'Loud and clear.'

He leaned forward until his forehead almost met the glass. His voice came through a speaker in the ceiling. The words were flattened by the padded walls. 'I've failed miserably.'

She resisted the urge to tell him that what she had discovered might well make the voyage a success, just the same. If only they could rescue Nasim. 'Tell me what happened.'

'My father has used every connection he has left. I've met personally with half the council and two members of the royal family. They have all responded with the same message. Our government is in utter turmoil. Until a new ruler is crowned, there is no chance of negotiating anything so complex as a planetary treaty. None.'

Up close, she could see the hollow caverns surrounding his eyes, dark as bruises. 'Have you slept?'

'Some. A little.' He rubbed the stubble on his cheek. 'I forget when.'

'We've only been here a day. Perhaps with more time—'

'My father insists my own situation grows more precarious with every passing hour. And yours as well.' He shifted his hand around to rub beneath the back of his collar. 'There is one thing. He was granted permission to contact the French embassy. They responded an hour ago. If we were to travel to their system, their deputy prime minister has agreed to grant us an audience.'

To any observer, it might have appeared that Hamoud had located a crick in his neck. The jerk to his chin was that subtle. But Amanda recognized the quick up-and-down motion for what it was. She said carefully, 'In that case, we must first report personally to the admiral.'

Hamoud dropped his hand to the padded counter. 'Are you sure, Major?'

She saw the clarity return to that dark gaze, and knew she had guessed right. All this was mere theatrics to those who were not supposed to be monitoring their conversation. 'Our remit was very specific. Travel to Oman. Negotiate a treaty. Return.' She rose to her feet. 'Please thank your father on my behalf. How soon can you ready the ship for our departure?'

FORTY-EIGHT

Two hours later, Amanda was required to don an isolation suit and endure an intensive drenching from the disinfectant sprays between her two sets of doors. She was met by four guards in uniforms that Amanda thought garish. They silently escorted her to the rooftop landing platform. From their haughty demeanors, Amanda assumed they belonged to the same palace contingent that had been made responsible for Hamoud's safety.

A damp wind blew across the vast roof, scarring her vision. The yacht's entry-ramp extended at her approach, and Hamoud emerged wearing his pilot's uniform with captain brevets on the sleeves. Hamoud came to attention and snapped off a salute. Amanda's lead guard responded, then her guards turned as one and marched away. When they were alone, Hamoud said, 'I for one will not be sorry to be rid of this place.'

'But I have seen nothing at all of your home,' Amanda replied.

He hefted her valise, led her up the ramp, sealed the ship, helped her out of the clinging suit, and replied, 'When all this is over, you will return as my family's honored guest.'

'And Nasim's.'

'Of course with Nasim. How else could we declare this over?'

Amanda stepped into her cabin and donned a coverall. She entered the cockpit as Hamoud piloted them towards the cloud line. Amanda watched a dark tempest rush over the city center. 'Does it rain much here?'

'This is winter. Our rainy season.'

'Most of the image transcripts I viewed showed Omani deserts and ocher mountains.'

Hamoud used the hand not on the controls to wave to his left. 'The Dry Realm is further south.'

'The Dry Realm,' she said dreamily.

'Mountains form the Rift's southern boundary. Beyond those hills, it rains once in a decade. Perhaps less.'

Amanda waited until Hamoud officially cleared the city's air control, then said, 'I have something you need to see.'

'It really must wait, Major. I am soon to become very busy.'

Amanda watched him follow the escort's blinking light. 'Can't you switch to autopilot?'

'That will not be possible.'

She very much wanted to hand him the tablet and have him confirm that Laila had correctly translated the passages that most interested her. Amanda wanted to watch him grow as excited as she felt. She hoped that would be the case. But for now she sat in the co-pilot's chair and watched the planet's atmosphere turn pale and then vanish into the blackness of space. The planet's gently curving globe became fully visible. Hamoud activated the comm-link and said, 'Pilot Captain Hamoud to escort. You are cleared to disengage.'

'Roger that, Captain. Safe journey.'

'My thanks, escort. Hamoud out.'

Amanda watched as Hamoud accelerated away from the planet. He checked the chrono set in its sterling-silver frame, frowned, and pushed the engines harder still. Amanda observed the g-gauge climb to ten, twelve, fifteen, twenty-two. Behind them, the planet shrank smaller and smaller. The first moon swept past, then the second, and they entered interplanetary space. Minutes ticked by. Hamoud continued to watch the chrono far more than the monitors until . . .

Hamoud slowed.

Then he halted.

He clicked the comm-link. On and off. Again. Waited. Clicked it twice more.

The monitor to Hamoud's left had previously shown blackness. Suddenly, it pinged gently. A lavender light illuminated the nothingness of deep space.

Amanda demanded, 'What is *that*?'

Hamoud smiled as he accelerated. 'Surprise.'

FORTY-NINE

Hamoud maneuvered the yacht toward a mining asteroid shaped like a lump of gray dough. He swept past a number of unmanned diggers that clawed furrows over the surface, hunting rare metals. He halted perhaps a hundred meters above the asteroid's narrowest tip, and said, 'Just exactly where they said it would be.'

Amanda was about to ask what he meant when Hamoud sank their vessel into a crevice she had not noticed until then. The yacht's exterior light revealed pale gray rock to either side, not quite close enough to touch. Down and down they went, until the yacht's landing gear made contact with the asteroid's surface. Hamoud cut off the exterior lights and most of those inside. The cavern's shadows locked them in.

'Let's get you suited up.' Hamoud rose from the pilot's chair. 'You need to go and return within the hour. Any longer and your contact's absence may be noted.'

She felt weightless, as though she was already suspended in space. 'Why can't you come with me?'

'You do not negotiate with the likes of this one,' he replied. 'She demanded, I agreed.'

'But you're sending me over to do just that. Negotiate.'
'Correct.'
'Alone!'
'You'll do fine, Major.' Hamoud handed her the helmet. 'Ready?'

Amanda pushed away from the airlock and activated her nearly invisible scooter. As she rose from the crevasse, a lumpish freighter drifted slowly into position directly overhead.

No doubt she would one day consider such solitary journeys through deep space a normal part of her existence. Right now, though, the stark beauty left Amanda breathless.

Below her swept scarred gray stone, pimpled with meteorite strikes and wreathed in dust-clouds thrown up by the metal beetles. Ahead of her, a rocket-propelled container rose from the surface and began docking with the freighter. The Omani sun was off to her left, about the same distance away as her native sun would be from Mars, a brilliant orange-white globe that dominated its quadrant.

There was no pirate battlecruiser up ahead, no cannons tracking her passage. She was momentarily free to play space tourist. Amanda craned and twisted and searched in every direction. Up and to her right hung a double-helix galaxy, about the size of her palm. And beyond the freighter spun the Milky Way, a river of shimmering jewels.

A light began blinking on the freighter's stern, just aft of where the mineral container was docking. Amanda watched an airlock slide open, ready to receive her. She entered and powered down her scooter. The exterior portal shut behind her. The interior airlock door opened to reveal the most perfectly refined woman Amanda had ever seen. She was in her late fifties; Amanda knew this because Hamoud had told her. But she could easily have been fifteen years younger. She wore a midnight-blue suit of some elegantly rich material. Her only jewelry was a coiled necklace of gold and diamonds. She was flanked by guards in the same livery as those who had protected Hamoud. Behind them stood Laila, aide to Hamoud's father. Laila offered Amanda an impish smile but did not speak.

The older woman demanded, 'You know who I am?'

'The Princess Ismat, second in line to the throne after your brother, the Prince Regent.' Her space suit made bowing a cumbersome act, but Amanda gave it her best try. 'An honor, Highness.'

Ismat meant protector, or guardian, and was a word from beyond time. The princess addressed her in System English, heavily accented but very precise. 'How is the wayward pilot?'

'Hamoud sends you his regards, Highness.' Amanda glanced at the young woman behind her. 'I am fortunate to have him with me.'

Ismat gestured imperiously and walked away. 'Come.'

The freighter's tail section was sealed off from the rest of the vessel. What had previously been just another cargo hold was now a regal apartment containing private chambers, guards' quarters, galley, pantry, and conference room. All this the princess explained as they proceeded along the elevated walkway. But no amount of finery could hide the fact that this particular ship had seen decades of hard service. As they descended stairs connected to a rusting port bulkhead, Ismat said, 'No one would concern themselves over just another freighter carting elements mined from a drifting asteroid. This suits me quite well. Particularly when I must officially claim to be elsewhere.'

Two guards helped Amanda out of her suit. As they started away, Amanda said, 'One moment.' She released the scooter's baton from its catch on the suit's chest. She did not want to be separated from her ride home. No matter that the princess trusted her guards. They were strangers to Amanda, and that particular scooter was valuable enough to be considered booty by some.

She followed the two women into a conference room bearing the royal Omani shield. The room's only doorway and the connecting wall were glass. The guards took up station outside the entrance, their backs to the room.

Ismat seated herself, waved them to chairs, and said, 'Time is short. I suggest we dispense with niceties. Hamoud told you of the situation we face?'

'Hamoud says your father the emir is quite ill.'

'A subtle way of putting things. But we do not have time for delicacies. My brother has spent half his lifetime hovering in the shadows. If he had his way, he would remain Prince Regent for the rest of his days. The prospect of wearing the crown gives him nightmares.' The princess watched Laila as she spoke, as though the two women shared a secret far deeper than what Ismat actually said. 'Our opponents on the ruling council do their best to keep my brother utterly under their control. When they finally allow my father to die, they are determined that the current power structure will remain unchallenged.'

Amanda asked because she sensed it was expected of her. 'What about you?'

'I give the council no reason to suspect I am anything more than my brother's loyal subject. Which is why we meet here, and must hurry.'

'Forgive me, Highness. But the admiral will want to know, so I must ask. Who am I speaking with?'

Ismat nodded approval. 'Hamoud said you would make a worthy ally.'

'And friend,' Amanda replied. 'I hope.'

'A group that includes Hamoud's father seeks to establish a strong and stable government. We feel it is time for Oman to become a republic, with a figurehead monarchy. The current leadership is failing the people. I am here representing those on the council seeking change.'

Laila spoke for the first time. 'I have been sent here to confirm what her Highness says.'

'So.' Ismat folded her hands in her lap. 'Now you will tell me what you seek.'

'A treaty,' Amanda replied. 'Random officially becomes a planet within the Omani system.'

'I understand from Hamoud's father there are precedents for a distant planet to be legally joined with a system allied to the empire?'

'Four, to be precise,' Amanda replied. 'I've checked.'

Laila said, 'The Lord Chancellor can supply details, Highness.' 'Go on.'

'Oman's government will petition the empire,' Amanda said. 'Requesting a formal pardon for all Random's citizens. Admiral Leclerc is to be recognized as Random's official ruler.'

'The pirate captain is made king?'

'He already is,' Amanda replied. 'You officially recognize the reality.'

Ismat rose and faced the glass wall. 'And in exchange?'

'You have heard from Hamoud of Random's newly discovered riches?'

'It is why we meet. Hamoud deposited a crate of gold bullion in an account bearing his father and myself as co-signatories. The gold has been inspected. Most stardust minerals carry very specific tells, minor impurities which present evidence of their origins. The gold you supplied carries a signature that has been seen a few times by merchants on our largest moon, but until now the origins were unknown.' Ismat glanced over. 'Did this pirate king also show you booty from ships he captured, and the lives destroyed?'

'Just the gold he has taken from the planet's mines.' Amanda emphasized that word. Gold. 'A cavern full of gold. Not to mention all the other heavy metals they are discovering. In abundance, Princess. If you refuse, there will certainly be some other system—'

'I want half of everything he has mined, and the same of all his future riches.'

'Princess, a customs duty of one-tenth would be more in keeping—'

'This is neither a *duty* nor a *levy*.' She glared down at Amanda. 'This is a royal fealty *demanded* from a pirate world that has wreaked havoc for decades.'

Amanda thought it best not to respond.

The princess glowered at her for a time. When Amanda maintained her silent composure, Ismat finally turned back and said to the glass, 'Half for five years.'

'A one-time payment of half the riches he now holds. Followed by a proper customs levy—'

'That is outrageous!'

'Of ten percent,' Amanda finished.

'*Half!*'

'Twenty percent. That is the most, the absolute most, I could take back to him with even a shred of hope that he would accept . . .'

Amanda was silenced by an electronic scream of alarm.

FIFTY

Amanda's first real space battle could well have been her last.

Their chance of survival was nil. Her options to change the outcome utterly non-existent.

Amanda had been trained in warfare, both during basic and then again at the Naval Academy. But the pressure she knew then had all been about demerits and promotions and not letting her team down.

She learned many things in the attack's first split seconds.

Blaster cannons in space were, of course, perfectly silent. But what she had not expected, what nothing could have prepared her for, was how *loud* their impact was inside a spaceship. The first round sounded like a giant buzz saw attacking the freighter. The shrill screeches wrenched the freighter in patterns of four.

She suspected they were under attack by an older cruiser, one whose blaster cannons fired double rounds in sequence, then paused for eighteen seconds to recharge. Eighteen seconds of alarm claxons and people screaming and the freighter shuddering as it sought to make way.

Ismat's guards burst into the conference room with guns drawn. They shouted something that was lost to the claxons. The lead guard gathered up the princess as the other warriors hunted in every direction, desperate to fire on an enemy they could not see.

Amanda crowded in close to the rear guard, assuming they had some safer destination in mind. As she left the chamber, she gripped Laila and pulled her along. The young woman wailed a constant note, as though terror had rendered her capable of screaming without needing to draw breath.

The princess remained remarkably calm. When the rearmost guard started to shove Amanda away, she gestured once, a silent command. They continued on together.

Then the eighteen seconds were up, and the next barrage struck.

FIFTY-ONE

They almost made it.

The escape pod was a bulbous orb wedded to the stern bulkhead. They broke from the corridor just beyond the pantry and made a mad dash through the storage space when . . .

First the lights flickered. Then the entire ship lost power.

The darkness lasted a second. Less. But for Amanda that brief absence of light was far worse than the screaming cannon barrage. Which was much louder this time. A completely different sort of sound. And she knew why.

The hull behind them hummed like a massive tuning fork that was being wrenched apart. Then the lights came back on. But now they only emitted a sullen glow. Laila continued her unremitting scream.

When the barrage ended, a new alarm began moaning, deep and sour as death. The lead guard yelled, 'Hull breach!'

Then the gravity went out.

The pod was three paces away. Less. Just beyond the lead guard's outstretched hand, the one not gripping the princess. It might as well have been on the other side of the galaxy.

The guards roared in unison as their boots left the bulkhead. Laila's shriek climbed a full octave.

Amanda managed to perform four remarkable tasks in one split second.

She reached behind with her left hand, gripped Laila's collar, and . . .

She used her final foothold on the bulkhead to propel herself and Laila towards the drifting princess, and . . .

Using her right hand, she pulled the scooter's baton from her pouch just as she collided with the princess, who by this point had been released from the guard's hold, and then . . .

A line of deadly brilliance seared its way down the starboard bulkhead. Instantly, the hold was filled with a new sound, that of air whooshing out into the starlit darkness revealed through the breach.

It was the last sound any of them would hear, unless . . .

Amanda gripped both women in as fierce an embrace as she could manage, and punched the button on the end of her baton.

Air escaped through a breach in the stern bulkhead. As they were sucked forward, Amanda had no way of knowing whether the scooter's shield would expand to cover three bodies. The whole concept behind the device was that it served as an *individual* transporter. She knew a moment's terror that it would simply refuse to encase them, which meant a swift death-by-vacuum.

The freighter's bulkhead wrenched further open, revealing the asteroid's pitted surface directly below. And she kept breathing.

Which was when she was assaulted by the next fear.

Air.

The scooter had a very small oxygen reclamation motor, only there as backup in case the user's suit was breached. But for three women, all of whom puffed in frantic near-death terror, Amanda had no idea how much time they had.

Even so, she could not risk speed.

When Laila kept screaming, Amanda gripped the aide's collar with her hand not holding the baton. She wrenched the fabric until Laila's air was partially cut off. The woman's shriek died to a faint gasp. Which was very good, because Laila's mouth was jammed into the hair above Amanda's left ear.

The scooter's shield compressed them into a single tight unit of flesh. Someone started to complain, she thought it was probably the princess. Amanda hissed, 'Quiet for all our lives.'

She had no idea if her comm-link was transmitting. The arm holding her baton was trapped between the shield and the princess.

Laila moaned.

'Not a word. Not a sound.'

The baton's propulsion unit had a subtle indentation by her forefinger, placed there so acceleration and steering could be controlled without looking down. Amanda twisted the dial ever so slightly.

They passed beyond the fractured ship and the searing light of another barrage. Amanda gradually aimed them toward the asteroid

and the crevasse. Their passage had to appear as if they were
simply part of the debris field.

When the first corpse collided with their shield, the aide moaned
once more. This was no time for delicate measures. Amanda
tightened her hold on Laila's collar. When she heard Laila choke,
she loosened it a fraction. The aide huffed a tiny sob but did not
speak again. Not even when their passage brought them into contact
with Ismat's head guard, who smeared frozen blood over the
shield's outer surface.

Amanda felt the air coming harder now, as if her own throat was
being clenched by an invisible hand. She accelerated a fraction more.
She could hear the others panting, but softly, three mouths open
wide and searching the tight confines for another shared breath.

They were almost at the outer perimeter of the debris field. Up
ahead drifted the freighter's only cannons. When the massive
structure blanketed them with shadow, Amanda accelerated a bit
more. She panted now as if she had run a hard race. She could
hear the others do likewise. The shield's interior was fogging
up, as they overcame the pump's ability to draw out their
moisture. When less than a hundred meters separated them from
the crevasse, she accelerated further.

The air grew pinched and stiflingly hot. When they entered the
cavern, it seemed as though the darkness made it even harder to
breathe. Amanda had to assume Hamoud remained stationary,
using the digging machines to mask him from the predators.

They went further and further; Amanda had no idea how deep
the cavern went. Her lungs burned with desperate need.

They found the yacht by landing on its bow.

Amanda heard the others gasping and knew she could not put
off the risk any longer. 'Princess, can you see the control baton?'

'It is pressed against my forehead.'

'Can you reach it?'

The entire confines were compressed further. An elbow jabbed
Amanda's throat, then, 'I have it.'

Amanda forced her head around, shoving her chin past Laila's
shoulder. 'OK, shift it up and . . . No, the other way. Left. Good.
I can see it now.' The comm-link was blinking red, which meant
it was turned on, yet the external connection was off, and she had
an incoming message. 'Grip the blinking light, it is part of a ring.'

'I feel it.'

'Turn it away from you until it clicks.'

'The light has gone green.'

Amanda did not recognize her own voice. 'Hamoud, if you can hear us, we've arrived, but we can't . . . You must bring us in.'

She had started to repeat the order when the bleak darkness was split by that most precious of sights, a rim of yellow and welcoming light as the airlock opened, silhouetting a figure that rushed out towards them.

FIFTY-TWO

Amanda showered and dressed and went back to work. There was no time for anything else. They were pressed on all sides by the urgent need to return the princess to safety, and do so before her absence was discovered and the opposition could claim her demise as a victory. Tired and bruised as she was, Ismat remained in the cockpit until she was certain Hamoud understood the urgency.

Amanda's suit was back on the destroyed ship, lost now to the debris field. So Hamoud left her on the yacht's controls as he suited up. He stood on the port bow, where she could watch his hand signals, and lifted the yacht slowly until he could see above the shadows' reach. Dust clouds and debris drifted overhead, blocking out stars in the same streaming way as a fast-moving storm. Which, Amanda supposed, this was.

At Hamoud's signal, Amanda halted about two meters below the cavern's ledge. The shadows were so precise they swallowed everything except the upper third of his body. Hamoud stayed there, motionless and hunting, then squatted down and started back towards the airlock.

Amanda was there when he cycled through. Hamoud nodded to the princess and said, 'They're gone.'

'What if they left a probe?'

He had clearly been considering the same risk. 'We will track across the surface, through the mining machines, until we are on the asteroid's opposite side. There we will do another scan. If the skies are clear, we leave.'

Moving among the mechanical diggers proved far easier than Amanda had feared. The crawlers were obviously rigged with sensors to keep them from colliding with each other. Hamoud remained so close to the surface that the yacht's shield was constantly pelted by rocks and debris moving as fast as bullets. The larger projectiles created a softer version of the same screech as when the blaster cannons had hit the freighter's defense.

Up close, the machines looked like huge metal caterpillars. They gripped the asteroid's surface with multiple claw-like appendages. The front loaders dipped and shoveled up massive hunks of rock, then lifted their mouths to the sky, just like an insect swallowing prey. Crawlers rushed from one digger to the next, retrieving refined blocks of mineral as they were deposited from the digger's back end. The machines moved with remarkable speed, a silent choreographed dance.

Then they were through, and the scan showed an empty sky. Hamoud accelerated away.

And kept accelerating.

They made an elliptical loop far beyond the Omani planetary orbit, out in the direction of the fourth planet. Hamoud pushed the yacht to its maximum acceleration velocity, just above twenty-four gravities. The engines roared with what seemed to Amanda to be a ferocious impatience.

Princess Ismat showed her age for the very first time. She showered and then collapsed on the master bed. Laila entered the galley and began preparing a meal. Amanda seated herself at the table opposite Ismat's bed, took pen and paper from a drawer, and began writing.

Half an hour later, Laila appeared with a plate of something. 'Should I awaken the princess?'

'Let her rest.' Amanda took bites and continued writing furiously. She had no idea what she ate and tasted nothing.

The longer she worked, the more the elements began coalescing. All the fragments she had been confronting since her arrival in the Lorian system now began to crystallize. Or so she hoped. A great deal of what she wrote was based upon pure conjecture; Amanda knew this, yet she could not say where the facts ended and her guesswork began. Which she took as a very good sign. The seamless nature of her analysis helped confirm that she was finally on the right track.

Hamoud's voice came over the comm-link. 'We are thirty minutes out and closing. The control tower has granted us a landing slot. How is the princess?'

'Awake,' Ismat replied from the bed. 'And sore. Come help me up, please.'

Amanda supported the princess as she moved to the fresher, waited until she was certain the older woman could support her own weight, and departed. Laila appeared with a tray just as Ismat emerged from the shower. The princess looked haggard, but alert and determined. She seated herself in the desk chair Amanda had vacated and sipped from her mug. Again. Then, 'I thought we were dead.'

'As did I,' Laila said. 'I wish to apologize . . .'

She stopped when Ismat raised the hand not holding her mug. 'I could not draw in enough air to screech with you. Say no more about it.'

Laila nodded. 'Thank you for saving us.'

'We are in your debt,' Ismat agreed.

Amanda took that as her sign. She pushed the five handwritten pages across the desk. 'I need you to send three n-space messages to Commander Rickets at GSA sector HQ.'

'What, all of this?'

'Yes. One relates to what has just happened. The second is about the situation on Random and the current status of our negotiations. And the third has to do with the Lorian system. I need Commander Rickets' help. Urgently.' She patted the pages. 'This explains why she must respond immediately.'

Amanda steeled herself. The cost of three n-space messages of this length would be astronomical. The princess would be well within her rights to demand that her own team edit and censor the outgoing information. Much of what Amanda had written was highly sensitive, potentially explosive.

Amanda watched as the princess folded the pages, handed them to Laila, and commanded, 'You will see that these go off immediately upon our arrival. And put them on my account.'

FIFTY-THREE

They landed on Oman's third and smallest moon. Domed enclaves rose from the lunar surface like illuminated dimples. Because they arrived in the dark phase, the domes' interiors shone through the transparent globes like a glimpse of Eden. Which was in fact their destination's name. Eden Spa was one of the system's most luxurious resorts, populated by flowering trees and animals drawn from every system in the protectorate.

As far as Amanda was concerned, Eden was just another place she did not get to explore.

She watched their descent from the co-pilot's chair. As they landed, she asked, 'Is it as nice as it appears?'

Hamoud read her sour expression correctly, for he replied, 'It is. As you will see for yourself. Someday very soon.'

'You better not just be saying that.'

Ismat had entered the cockpit unnoticed. 'Ah, Major. You do my heart a world of good.'

Hamoud smiled. 'Major, perhaps you would care to see off our guests.'

As they waited for the docking light to go green, Laila explained how the princess owned this resort and used it for numerous such clandestine events. Which was why Hamoud's claim to be just another transport making a delivery of fresh produce had not been challenged by the control tower. Laila and the princess both wore gowns from the admiral's collection. Amanda suspected the outfits were not currently in fashion. But combined with Ismat's customary haughty manner, their arrival would hopefully not arouse the suspicion of any passing guest.

Even so, she stood by the airlock's inner portal with a charged blaster in her right hand.

Ismat pointed to the weapon and said, 'There is no need for that.'

Amanda thought she was probably right. 'Just the same, Hamoud, tell them to approach unarmed. Guards included.'

'Roger that.'

The yacht rocked slightly as the tunnel sealed itself to the exterior airlock. Amanda checked the four approaching attendants for weapons, then stepped back. 'Princess, do you recognize them?'

'Yes.' Ismat tapped the monitor screen. 'My personal secretary, my senior adviser, and two guards I have known for years. They all have served me through numerous such absences. We have signals. Were there trouble, I would know.'

'Hamoud, release the outer lock.'

'Roger. Released.'

Amanda opened the inner portal and bowed. 'I hope we meet again very soon, Highness.'

Ismat stepped through, nodded to the attendants, waited for Laila to join her, then turned back and said, 'Your messages to GSA headquarters will go out immediately. Tell the admiral I accept all the terms as you have laid them out.'

Amanda was still standing there, gaping at the empty tunnel where the princess of Oman had been, when Hamoud came on line and said, 'Major, we are cleared for take-off.'

FIFTY-FOUR

Amanda waited while Hamoud set course for their return to the Lorian n-space portal. When he switched to autopilot and leaned back, she asked, 'How long does Commander Rickets need to do what we've asked?'

Hamoud's instant response said he had been working through the same issue. 'We should assume Barrat's n-space message was received and accepted.'

'Which means Rickets was prepped when the longer message from Princess Ismat arrived,' Amanda added. 'And the commander is not filing charges against us for going AWOL.'

Hamoud offered a weary smile. 'Not to mention how Nasim and I ignored a direct command from Barrat to journey back on *Invictus*.'

'Or how we've negotiated with a pirate king.'

'And then journeyed to yet another system in a ship taken as booty.' Hamoud nodded. 'Those prospects do not bear thinking about.'

'So . . . Timing.'

'Barrat was headed directly back to GSA sector HQ. He should have arrived . . .' Hamoud leaned forward and checked the chrono. 'A day and a half ago, at the very latest.'

'Which hopefully means my latest message arrived after Rickets read the full report, and started prepping.'

Hamoud nodded slowly. 'Knowing the commandant as I do, everything we require is already happening. Lightning does not strike fast enough to suit our commander.'

Amanda forced herself to say, 'Which leaves Nasim.' She offered Hamoud the tablet supplied by Laila and said, 'I need you to see something.'

While Hamoud read, she entered the owner's galley and started preparing a meal. The crew's quarters had a larger second galley, as clearly the staff had far outnumbered the clients. Amanda had no interest in eating in the formal dining hall, with its priceless works of art and gilded table and overly soft chairs. As Amanda set two places at the galley's narrow side-table, she spared a thought for the former owner and crew. Wondering where they were. If any survived. Hoping her tactics might save further assaults by space pirates.

She was loading their plates when Hamoud appeared in the doorway. His eyes were round with shock. 'Can this be true?'

'You saw it too. Good.' She set down his place. 'Come and eat.'

He slid into the bench opposite her, placed the tablet on the table between them, but made no move to begin his meal. 'I would have missed it entirely if you had not made those notes in the margin. The wording is nigh on impossible.'

'Please tell me you checked the original text to make sure Laila did not mistranslate.'

'It was my first action. There was no error.' He took a bite. 'This is delicious.'

She related what she had discovered further on. Hamoud was fully involved now and asked her to find the next passage for him. He read, looked up, and offered her a quietly intent gaze. Amanda loved how they were connected, how this strong and intelligent man was fully on her side. An ally she could trust with her life, and had, several times.

Hamoud said, 'This is truly amazing.'

'Check the original text,' she said. 'Just to be sure.'

He took another few bites as he read the flowery Arabic. She rose and cleared the table and set water on to make tea. Hamoud rose and helped her clean up. 'Laila's translation is exactly correct.'

She carried two steaming mugs back to the table, waited for Hamoud to join her, and said, 'I need to tell you what I hope is going to happen next.'

They continued planning until Amanda's exhaustion forced her to stop. Hamoud let her sleep until ten minutes before their arrival. When she asked how much rest he had taken, Hamoud did not respond.

The instant their yacht emerged from n-space, Amanda began her broadcast. 'This is Major Bostick in the admiral's vessel, calling the Random forces, requesting retrieval.'

She clicked off and glanced at Hamoud. He confirmed, 'Broadcasting on all channels.'

She repeated the alert, a third time, then Hamoud said, 'Vessel on fast approach. Surrus battlecruiser.'

Then a stranger's voice said, 'We have you in our sights. Stand down.'

The lack of proper address confirmed Amanda's worst fears. 'Who is hailing us, please?'

'I'll be the one asking questions. Power down your vessel.'

'I need to speak with the admiral.'

'That is not happening.'

'Admiral Leclerc issued us specific instructions. Upon our return—'

'The situation has changed. Stand down or be fired upon.'

Hamoud said softly, 'We have a second blip.'

Amanda felt a double electric thrill. First, for having gotten the situation very right. And second, for now holding the firepower to turn the tables on the pirate force.

'Negative,' she replied. '*You* will power down *your* vessel or *you* will be fired upon.'

She motioned to Hamoud, who opened his own comm-link and said, 'Brevetted Pilot Captain Hamoud hailing the GSA vessel on approach. Please identify yourself.'

Hamoud's alert went out on all channels, which meant the pirate skipper heard as well. The attackers came back with, 'Nice try. This is your last chance. Power down or die.'

Amanda would never have thought a time might come when she would be happy to hear the next voice. 'This is Captain Barrat of the GSA transport *Invictus*. Major Bostick, I have a message for you from Sector Commander Rickets.'

Hamoud said softly, 'Pirate vessel deploying fighters.'

Let them, she thought. 'Bostick here, Captain. Ready at this end.'

'From GSA Sector Commandant to Major Bostick. Agreed. Stop. *Invictus* and crew under your command for the duration. End message. How received?'

Amanda did not try to hold the melody of joy from her voice. 'Loud and clear, Skipper. Did you come armed as requested?'

'Affirmative. We carry a full squadron of fighters. They are powered up and awaiting orders.'

Amanda came very close to screaming, '*Deploy!* Repeat: *Deploy!*'

FIFTY-FIVE

Amanda did not bother to turn off her comm-link as she asked, 'Where is *Invictus*?'

In reply, Hamoud rose to his feet and pointed to a shadow growing steadily on their main screen, carving a dark silhouette from the stars. 'This is the pirate battlecruiser. There are five fighters deployed in close orbit. Now a sixth is being launched. See it?'

'No.'

'It doesn't matter.' He turned to the monitor showing the region directly behind their own vessel. 'This is *Invictus*.'

She was about to ask why they hadn't launched their own

fighters when the display shifted dramatically, and she realized they already had.

A full battle squadron flowed swiftly from the transport. The latest generation of GSA fighters were altogether a new species of warcraft. When the twenty-one vessels were fully deployed, their shields linked. The net appeared alive to her, an energy field like petals of a deadly silver-white bloom.

What was more, the outer perimeter sprouted six massive blaster cannons. Only these weapons were made from pure energy. And all of them were now aimed at the pirate ship.

Amanda found an exquisite pleasure in saying, 'Major Bostick here. You are ordered to withdraw your fighters and stand down.'

The voice had lost its cocky superiority, but none of its raw force. 'We'll go with the hard option. At least we'll have the honor of dying in battle.'

'It won't be a battle at all,' Amanda replied. 'You will be utterly destroyed, and there's nothing you can do about it.'

'Leclerc is on board. He'll die with us.'

'So he dies.' Amanda saw that her fingers were trembling and knew there was nothing she could do about it. 'What's one more dead pirate to us?'

The pirate skipper did not respond.

'Power down,' Amanda repeated. 'Release Leclerc, and we'll give you an unarmed transport and safe passage out of the empire.'

The man's sneer came through loud and clear. 'I'm expected to take the word of an empire officer on that?'

'Correct. You are. And you have ten seconds to accept.'

FIFTY-SIX

They were holding Leclerc in his own brig.

There were seventeen mutineers, less than a quarter of the total crew. But they had all held key positions, and they had also planned well. Amanda suspected the majority of Leclerc's opponents were still back on Random, awaiting word that the leader had been taken out. Only then would they move. Which meant every minute counted. Both for them and Leclerc.

The GSA fighter squadron was led by a hard-bitten colonel with a silver crewcut. His name was Chastain, and he wanted to keep the admiral caged. 'Give him and his troopers a dose of time behind bars, that's the ticket. Let them see the cold reality of refusing your offer. Which is far too generous, if you ask me.' He glared through the bars at Leclerc. 'Negotiate with a blaster in your hand and the man in chains, you'll see him come around soon enough.'

Once the revolt had been put down and the pirate ship had surrendered, Amanda had moved the yacht in close to the *Invictus* but did not dock. She ordered the pirate ship to be kept well away, with a skeleton crew from the *Invictus* at the controls, and a trio of fighters on constant alert. The would-be mutineers were held in the skipper's cabin under armed guard.

Amanda intended to shift Leclerc to the yacht. There he would hear her terms while in the shadow of GSA power. But he was not her prisoner. All this she had explained to the colonel and a gray-haired woman named Dower, adjutant to Commander Rickets. The adjutant observed everything and did not speak. Chastain did enough talking for the two of them.

Barrat, the *Invictus* skipper who had done his best to bring Amanda down, hovered in the background and sulked.

'I want a treaty that will stand the test of time and distance,' Amanda told the fighter squadron's leader. She turned to his number two, a hatchet-faced lieutenant, and said, 'Release the admiral.'

'You're making a mistake,' Chastain said, but he did not countermand her order.

'Your objections are noted.'

Chastain stepped back as the prison door swung open. His hand rested on his sidearm, but he did not unholster his weapon.

The admiral entered the corridor and held out his manacled wrists. Amanda released the cuffs herself. Up close, the admiral looked exhausted and severely battered. A bruise sprouted beneath his left eye, and there was blood on his collar from a cut to his jaw. The sleeve of his uniform was torn. She gave him a moment to rub his wrists and come to terms with the fact that she was now in charge, then asked, 'Do I have your word that you and your men will remain obedient to my command, until I see fit to release your ship?'

He refused to meet her gaze. 'You have it.'

'Order your crew to remain in their quarters, save for meals and exercise. Have your number two arrange details.' While Leclerc used the ship's comm-link, Amanda told Chastain's aide, 'You may free the others.'

'Aye, ma'am.'

Amanda asked Chastain, 'Can one of your fighters escort the admiral to his quarters on the yacht?'

Chastain looked ready to argue, but in the end merely turned to one of his pilots and said, 'See to it.'

'Aye, sir.'

When Leclerc cut off the comm-link, Amanda said, 'Admiral, I would respectfully ask that we meet again as soon as you are ready.'

Chastain glowered at the departing admiral and told Amanda, 'Waste of good air, talking to the likes of you. Comes with a first command, I suppose. A hint of power will drive some to distraction.'

'I like you, Colonel.'

'Terrible mistake, that. Just terrible.' He jerked his chin at the released crew. 'Thirty days in the brig, bread-and-water diet, a few screams off in the distance, that's my idea of keeping order. Does wonder for discipline. Ask my aide here. She'll tell you.'

The sharp-featured lieutenant spoke for the first time. 'Beneath Colonel Chastain's rough exterior beats no heart at all.'

'Leclerc is doing his best to take his world out of piracy. The mutineers want to keep to the old ways.'

Chastain showed surprise. 'You believe the word of a privateer?'

'They have found a mother lode of stardust on Random. They've brought in mining equipment from somewhere. He's filled a cavern with gold bullion. I've seen it. And beryllium. Titanium. Warehouses full of the rarest isotopes.'

He grunted. 'So this crew you've got locked away in that transport . . .'

'They're nothing. History.'

'They're mutineers and pirates both. They deserve death.'

'They'll get it. Here or later is less important than having Leclerc free and amenable to my terms.'

FIFTY-SEVEN

They traveled back from the pirate vessel on board the *Invictus* lighter. The term was a holdover from Earth's earlier days, when ocean-going vessels were both wooden and powered by sail. Back then, a lighter was a shallow-draft boat used in unloading – or lightening – ships that remained off-shore. While at the Officers' Academy, Amanda had loved spending her few free hours studying the heritage of mankind's quest for the stars. Back when crossing oceans was often the most harrowing of adventures.

Barrat's lighter was equipped with comfortable seats and a powerful comm-link, so that the skipper would never be out of touch with his ship. It was the sort of equipment required by a battle fleet commander, and said much about the transport captain and his ego.

Barrat traveled back in the co-pilot's seat, from which he scowled at the star-array surrounding his ship. Amanda leaned forward and said, 'Captain, I respectfully request you lend me a chef and several crew trained in the protocol of serving a formal meal.'

Barrat did not bother to turn around. 'And where do you intend to take them?'

'Leclerc's yacht.'

'Out of the question.' Barrat crossed his arms. 'You want my entire crew to miss a scheduled meal so you can entertain a pirate?'

'I need to make the admiral feel we are treating him with the respect a visiting diplomat deserves, sir.'

'Then bring him on board *my* vessel. *I* will serve as host.'

Amanda could feel the eyes tracking her conversation. 'Respectfully, sir, that will not work. Leclerc has spent a lifetime with the empire as his foe. To host him on board your vessel would suggest we are imposing our will on him by force.'

'Which is exactly what we should be doing.' Barrat scowled. 'This entire episode is one great heaping pile—'

Chastain broke in with, 'My squadron travels with its own cook. I suppose I could loan you him.'

'Thank you, Colonel. I gratefully accept.'

'And a few of my crew can handle dishes without breaking them. If I promise to break the heads of any fumble-fingered dolts.'

'In that case,' Amanda said, 'I invite you all to join us on the admiral's vessel. Shall we say two hours from now?'

Amanda had them drop her and Hamoud off at the yacht. The squadron's chef arrived minutes later, along with two assistant cooks and armloads of fresh provisions.

When the captain's lighter pulled up alongside the yacht two hours later, Barrat was the first to enter. He scowled at her greeting and did his best to ignore her entirely. Amanda dismissed the skipper and his foul mood. She had more important matters that required her immediate attention.

She asked Chastain, 'Would you lend me your aide, sir?' When he grunted assent, Amanda told the lieutenant, 'My compliments to the admiral. Tell him I hereby release his crew, but only on the provision that they travel to Random for my lieutenant and return immediately. Stress that last word, if you would. Without delay.'

'Aye, Major.'

'Once he's communicated with his ship, ask him to join us.'

When the lieutenant departed, Hamoud asked, 'You don't wish to speak with Leclerc directly about releasing Nasim?' When Amanda did not respond, Hamoud pressed, 'Why?'

Amanda still did not reply. The answer was that she could not spare time for any of Leclerc's arguments. Not with the larger quarrel looming just ahead.

The colonel's ire resurfaced. 'That scoundrel kept an officer of *my* service as *surety*?'

Dower, the gray-haired adjutant, stepped into the yacht and spoke for the first time in Amanda's hearing. 'It was the proper move.'

Chastain growled but said no more.

Amanda escorted the group into the sumptuous dining room. The craft's luxury was on full display here, from the ornately polished table to the original oils adorning three walls. The fourth

held a monitor as large as the cockpit's. Amanda assumed it was
an electronic array that displayed the starlit expanse. She had never
seen a shipboard window that large.

Amanda directed them into their seats. She was respectful but
firm, showing in deed as much as words that she was the one in
control. Hamoud took the chair at the table's opposite end, facing
her position at the head. Chastain was to her left, Leclerc's empty
chair to her right. The mysterious adjutant Amanda set to the other
side of Leclerc's empty chair. Chastain's aide arrived while they
were still taking their places and announced that the captain would
send off his vessel only when the treaty's terms were settled.
Amanda had expected nothing less and took the speed of this event
as a sign the admiral had already accepted the move long before
she asked. Amanda directed the aide into the seat next to her
colonel, then Hamoud, then Barrat between the pilot and Dower.
Their actions were stiffly uncertain, all save the squadron colonel,
who clearly was enjoying himself. 'I expect you've had your fill
of food packs, Major.'

'Enough to last a lifetime,' she assured him.

'My cook deserves to be boiled in his own sauce, but now and
then he comes up with something edible.'

'Our squadron's cook is the finest in this sector,' his aide assured
Amanda.

Chastain ignored the lieutenant. 'When was the last time you
had a decent meal?'

'On Random. The admiral considers himself an epicure.'

The colonel was not impressed. 'Sunless planet run by a pirate
gang. Fricassee of tunnel rat, more like.'

'The wines,' Amanda said, 'came all the way from Earth.'

Chastain's aide grinned at her as Chastain changed the subject.
'How did you know the pirate would be open to a change of
direction?'

'I didn't know,' Amanda replied. 'I hoped.'

'More than that,' Hamoud said. Like Amanda, he wore a simple
flight coverall drawn from the *Invictus* store. All the others seated
at the table wore formal dress uniforms, save Dower. Commander
Rickets' adjutant was dressed in a slate-gray pantsuit, as austere
and elegant as the woman herself. Amanda's uniform carried a
message. She and Hamoud were still on mission. She was held

by the commandant's orders. Resolving a planetary crisis. Nothing had changed, save for the fact that she was weeks late reporting in. But still.

Hamoud went on, 'The major has a remarkable ability to fit together components that I do not even notice until she announces a resolution.'

Amanda recounted the spy's report and their arrival on Loria and the search for a missing pirate ship. When she tried to swiftly gloss over her contact with the second pirate vessel, Hamoud slowed her down by describing the glyphs. Which stilled all motion around the table. Amanda was fairly certain the adjutant and perhaps also the colonel had studied the transcript of her messages to Rickets. But hearing Hamoud's account seized them just the same.

When Hamoud was done, Amanda related her analysis of Leclerc's position, the pressure he faced. 'The admiral attacked Loria because he had no choice. Those among his crew who wanted nothing more than the pirate's life were a constant threat. The cavern full of stardust was a ticking time bomb. Every day that he did not offer a real long-term alternative brought them one step closer to mutiny.'

Leclerc arrived then, resplendent in his dress uniform of midnight blue, severe and minus any gaudy trappings. Amanda rose with the others and said, 'Thank you for joining us, Admiral.'

The yacht's dining hall became filled with the fragrances of fresh food, overlaid by an atmosphere of power and money. A crystal-and-gold chandelier clung to the ceiling, illuminating the embossed china, the crystal goblets, the oiled paneling. The gilded table was inlaid with a design of some dark wood, possibly ebony. It formed a royal crest that Amanda did not recognize. She lifted her gaze from her plate and studied the group arrayed before her. Hamoud shared the exhaustion and strain that she felt, the fine-drawn look of living too close to the edge. Even so, she also sensed his strength and confidence, waiting patiently with the trust of a lifelong friend.

Her gaze shifted to Leclerc, who ate with the implacable grace of an aged hunting cat. Calm and resolute and ready for his next conflict.

Then Chastain. A human fireplug with the sardonic grin of a
man born to lead. He had the same far-seeing gaze as Hamoud.
Amanda liked the colonel. His gruff acerbic style was part of what
made him a great fighter pilot. His aide, the woman with a blade
for a face, caught Amanda's eye and smiled.

Amanda gave the dour transport captain a brief inspection.
Barrat was the only one seated here against his will. Despite his
best efforts to bring her down, he now served under Amanda's
command. She suspected he was aware of her gaze, and responded
with grim indifference.

Amanda then turned to the last person seated at the table.
Dower. The mystery woman. Gray in gaze and hair and civilian
dress. As if she wished to go unnoticed. Amanda suspected Dower
was actually the most powerful person present.

The food was excellent. After the second course, Amanda waved
away the serving staff and announced, 'It's time to lay out the
Omani princess's terms.'

Leclerc barely let her finish. 'This is an absolute scandal!'

Amanda had no experience with pirate kings. Or leaders of any
kind for that matter. She had to assume Leclerc's fury was real.
'With respect, Admiral, I disagree.'

'*Half!* You actually expect me to offer a would-be princess *half*
of all my riches?' The man's color had risen through a rainbow of
shades, from crimson to choleric to puce. 'She can't even offer
me a guarantee of being a ruler in anything but name!'

'Which is where your payment will come in,' Amanda replied.
She found herself growing increasingly calm. The admiral's
tempest seemed to strike some distant realm. She remained far
removed, able to study and analyze and act. 'She requires the
funds to finance a change in government. Help them now, and you
will become their ally for life.'

Amanda let the admiral storm for a while longer. In truth, she
did not mind the man's tirade. It granted her time to prepare.
Because the treaty between an Omani princess and the pirate king
was not the real reason for their being here at all.

Finally, she declared, 'All right, that's enough.'

The admiral was as taken aback by her calm demeanor as her
words. 'See here—'

'We all hereby accept that the deal being offered leaves you sorely put out. Nonetheless, you will accept it.' She held up her hand, stifling his objection. 'Admiral, that is all the time we have. Accept the deal.'

'How *dare* you—'

Amanda leaned forward and gave each word a soft verbal punch. 'Pay careful attention. It is time to move on.'

FIFTY-EIGHT

The next three days passed with brutal slowness. Amanda had never been busier, since much of what needed doing could not be entrusted to anyone else.

As soon as the admiral gave his grudging acceptance to the treaty, Amanda had him order the Surrus vessel back to Random. Their mission was both to inform the planet of the failed mutiny, confirm the treaty was in place, and, most importantly, bring back Nasim.

Before the battleship departed, Amanda requisitioned two of the Surrus vessel's fighters and a military transporter. By the time the ship returned two days later, the *Invictus* crew and the fighter squadron's own mechanics had completed their retrofit of the three pirate vessels. It was finicky and tedious work. The returning vessel brought both Nasim and news. The populace was tense, but accepting of the situation. By that point, Dower had completed the draft treaty, which Leclerc signed. Amanda ordered Barrat to forward the draft immediately to the Omani princess by n-space alert.

With Nasim safely back, Amanda launched the retrofitted vessels. The two fighters and the military transport were now all piloted long-distance from Barrat's lighter, which remained positioned outside the Lorian system.

The three former pirate vessels were heavily armed. With their controls handled from so far away, the vessels had to maintain some fragment of independence. But this meant overriding their entire built-in systems. They were going in weapons hot.

The wait grew ever more excruciating with every passing hour.

Chastain handled the delay most easily. His standard remit was to maintain a battle-ready squadron, even when there were months between actions. He and his crew swiftly resumed their normal shipboard routine.

Dower followed Amanda almost everywhere. Rickets' adjutant observed everything and remained silent except for the occasional question.

The skipper of the *Invictus* was another matter entirely.

Gradually, Barrat's impatience infected his entire crew. By the time Nasim arrived, Barrat's crew had begun calling their assignment nothing more than a storm in a planetary teacup. A pink one at that.

Amanda knew she risked losing control of the entire situation. Even so, she could not rush. Which was why she welcomed the adjutant's company. Amanda was fairly certain Dower was the only reason Barrat had not flown into a full-blown rage. So she fully answered every question Dower put to her, with the same care as she would an Academy examiner. If Dower could ignore Barrat's growing ire, so could she.

Nasim mostly rested. He insisted that he had not been mistreated. But the hostility that Amanda and Hamoud had briefly experienced had clearly been Nasim's constant companion. Some of his guards had apparently sought an excuse to override the admiral's orders and either kill or enslave him.

Twice Amanda tried to apologize for leaving him behind. Both times Nasim pretended not to hear her at all.

Towards the end of that long third day, everything changed.

Amanda marked the occasion by re-assembling the senior staff in the yacht's dining room. It was the first time she had set foot in there since confronting Leclerc. The same group was present, plus Barrat's number two. The admiral arrived still apparently angry over the treaty's terms, but Amanda suspected it was largely an act now. She had spent some time in his company, as they both remained on board the yacht with Nasim and Hamoud. Amanda had come to believe the admiral had always expected that something like the treaty's terms would be required. This was merely Leclerc's outsmarted-by-a-deal mask. And Amanda thought she knew why he maintained the act. He feared Dower intended to tack on an additional levy due to the empire. Leclerc was determined not to let this happen.

Barrat and his second were the last to arrive. Amanda and the others waited almost half an hour before his lighter docked with the yacht. Amanda knew Barrat showed up late to register his seething resentment. She knew the others were curious – all but Chastain, who could barely contain his excitement.

Barrat was too angry to notice. He pointed his number two to wait by the door, glared at Amanda, ignored Hamoud when the pilot pulled back a chair, and said, 'I wish to lodge a formal protest.'

Barrat was so caught up in his own ire that he failed to notice how none of the others sided with him. Instead, they studied him curiously. All but Chastain. Who clearly had trouble disguising his mirth.

'We've spent *three days* hovering above a *measly scientific outpost*. While you sent three unmanned vessels to orbit a *pink planet*.'

She decided there was no alternative but to let him vent. 'Weapons hot,' Amanda confirmed.

'Doesn't anybody else here find this a complete and utter waste of time and resources?' Barrat glanced around the table, noticed Chastain's smothered grin, and grew angrier still. 'I for one am *fed up*. This entire episode is nothing more than a *charade*. Why are we even here? I am *disgusted* by this utter disregard for proper—'

'That's quite enough.'

Dower silenced the captain as effectively as a gun to his head. She pointed to an empty chair. 'Sit.' Dower then turned to the skipper's aide hovering just inside the door. 'You too. Now.'

When the pair had taken their places, Dower turned to Amanda. 'Please carry on, Major.'

Amanda rose to her feet. 'What you are about to see was transmitted to us . . .'

Chastain's sharp-faced aide said, 'Ninety-seven minutes ago.'

Amanda nodded. 'Show them.'

Amanda's aim for sending off three armed unmanned vessels had been simple. Pose a real threat to Loria. And watch the system reveal its true nature.

The monitors were split in two, so that the view from the lighter and one of Chastain's fighters could be watched simultaneously. The pirates' fighters had been stationed directly above the island holding the scientific colony, while the military transport maintained a pole-to-pole orbit. They watched the transport complete a full orbit and arrive at its closest point to the unmanned fighters . . .

Then it happened.

It was one thing for Amanda and Hamoud to describe the planet's ability to tear apart a shielded battleship. And then for her to describe her vision of the suns becoming a solar cannon. She knew Chastain and Dower both wanted to believe her, though no such armament existed anywhere else in the empire. Amanda was determined that they witness for themselves Loria's true power.

Amanda watched once more as her dream or vision or whatever it was became real. The ribbons of light that flowed constantly between the two suns grew a myriad of tentacles. They writhed and expanded until they reached out across space, all the way to the orbiting planet.

The three vessels were entrapped, torn apart, and utterly destroyed.

Three bright flashes erupted from within the encasing tentacles, signs of the vessels' armaments exploding.

Then it was over. The tentacles retreated, the suns became linked by glowing ribbons. As if nothing had ever disturbed the system's proper calm. And nothing ever would.

Amanda needed a moment to still her heart and unlock her chest. When she was ready, she turned around. The table was rimmed by expressions of shock and utter disbelief, none more so than Barrat's.

She asked, 'Any questions?'

FIFTY-NINE

A manda held the group there for another hour and a half. She outlined precisely what she intended to do. As she had hoped, the sight of two stars becoming interplanetary weapons rendered the group completely pliable. Even Barrat was cowed, at least temporarily. So she hurried. Because as she spoke, she moved from hard facts into supposition. She knew she was right. But the only way to obtain evidence was to return to Loria. And in so doing, she was probably signing her own death warrant.

Her awareness of the planet's true nature meant there was no reason for the Lorians to let her live. Her value to them was lost. She became just another threat, to be torn apart as they had the glyphs.

It was only a matter of time before Dower or Chastain realized the same things. So Amanda hurried through her explanation and then announced her immediate departure. And her intention of traveling down alone. She gave them no chance to work out the flaws. Or the risk.

Her two pilots accompanied her to the shuttle, which had been brought back from Random with Nasim. As they stowed the items she had requested from the transport's stores, Nasim asked for a word.

He did not look well. Dark stains rimmed his eyes, and his cheekbones appeared scarred by permanent bruises. The dull light to his gaze made her chest ache. Amanda followed Nasim down the shuttle's ramp and around a fighter, over to a relatively isolated spot, where he launched straight in. 'When I was confined on Random, I listened to the arguments rage in the corridor outside my prison. I think they wanted me to hear. On and on they went, stopping only when they unlocked my door to pass in food.'

The man's calm monotone was painful to endure. But Amanda forced herself to stay silent. Anything she said at this point would merely add to the apologies he had refused to accept. As if they didn't matter. As if there was nothing to apologize for. Or, rather, nothing that could be made right with words.

'I tried to tell myself that the quarrels served a purpose. They mentioned several slaver worlds where they wanted to sell me. I'm fairly certain none of them are known to the empire.' Nasim made a fitful gesture, like waving off invisible vermin. 'Then I heard them speak of mutiny on the battleship, and Leclerc's capture, and a fight broke out in the corridor beyond my locked portal. I was helpless to do anything about my own fate. I knew I was going to die.'

She whispered, 'I was so wrong to have left you.'

'You had no choice.'

The flat toneless words impacted her far harder than rage. She knew the answer before she asked, just as she knew she could not refuse him. 'What can I do to make it right?'

'Let me come. Please.'

'Nasim, there's every chance this is a one-way trip.'

The look he gave her held a bottomless quality. As if he still gazed into his own grave. 'Were you to force me to stay, and if you did not return, my life would be over. I cannot give you the logic. But I know this to be true.'

She heard footsteps scrape across the steel deck, and Hamoud came into view. 'I for one fail to see how you could even think of leaving us behind.'

'We signed on for the mission,' Nasim said. 'Nothing has changed.'

Hamoud said, 'You think I became a fighter pilot to watch my fellow officers walk towards death alone?'

Her throat was so constricted she had trouble forcing out the words. 'I hate the idea of putting your lives at risk. Again. I just hate it.'

'It is not death that frightens us,' Nasim said. 'It is letting down a friend.'

Amanda swallowed hard. 'Hamoud, signal tower and request permission for us to depart.'

They both threw her parade-ground salutes. 'Aye, Major.'

SIXTY

Amanda gave herself a moment to recover. It was impossible to feel as great and as awful as she did just then. But as she cleared her face and started back, the commander's adjutant stepped into view. 'I need a word.'

Amanda assumed Dower had heard what had just transpired. Her presence could only mean one thing. Dower had figured out the unspoken and was here to order Amanda not to go. 'Ma'am, I have a very tight window of opportunity—'

'I am senior examiner for the empire's School of Diplomacy.'

Amanda had no idea what to say.

'Understand, Major, I am not speaking of admissions. I hold the key role in judging when our students are ready to be appointed as new Diplomats.' She closed the distance between them. Amanda could see tiny flecks of white in her gaze, like ice crystals floating in smoke. 'Commander Rickets and I have served together on a number of occasions. I had recently been seconded to her staff to advise on a particularly difficult issue. When your reports arrived, Rickets personally requested I come and observe you at work. I objected, saying my current role would not permit my absence, particularly on something so . . . well, "absurd" was the word I used. Rickets then gave me a direct order. I know now I was wrong to object.

'More than half of the Diplomatic Corps is made up of individuals observed in crisis situations of critical importance. Only there can we determine whether they possess the rare combination of qualities that a successful Diplomat must possess. Such qualities are either components of an individual's nature, or they are not. They can be honed through training, but never taught. These field appointments receive what amounts to a brevetted status as Diplomat, to be revoked if or when they fail in their duties. Understand, Major, such a brevetted promotion has never been granted to anyone as young and relatively untrained as you. So you will spend a year at the Academy. During this time you will be constantly monitored. Following this, Rickets has requested you be seconded to her staff. How do you respond?'

Amanda found herself incapable of speech. She nodded.

Dower did not seem to find anything amiss in Amanda's silence. 'You will, of course, continue to take courses at the Diplomacy School whenever time allows. This on-site training will continue for years. But you will be brevetted a full Diplomat at the end of that first year. Tell me you understand what I am saying.'

'Yes . . . I . . . Thank you.'

'You are most welcome.' Dower turned away. 'Major, do us and the empire a service. Come back alive.'

SIXTY-ONE

Hamoud landed the shuttle in the same position as before, just beyond the last of the scientists' buildings. At first glance, the island appeared completely normal, as quiet and calm as every other time they arrived. But Amanda thought she detected a charge to the place, strong as an odor. Which was impossible, since they remained sealed inside the lander.

Nasim muttered, 'Something is different.'

'They know,' Hamoud replied grimly.

'How can they know? We haven't spoken with anyone.'

'They're telepaths,' Hamoud replied.

'You heard the scientist the same as me. They cannot read thoughts.'

'So they say.' Hamoud cut the shuttle engines. 'Perhaps impressions are enough.'

Nasim pointed at the front monitor, toward the lab building. 'There. In the middle window. A face.'

'I saw it,' Hamoud said.

'It was Ying. The number two.'

Amanda did not speak. There was nothing to say. She thought the two men had it right. The island had undergone a drastic shift. 'Help me move the device into position.'

There was not enough room for the three of them to work, so

Amanda suited up while the two men shifted the massive machine onto the probe. She crossed to the airlock, cycled open the inner portal, then turned back and showed her friends the best smile she could manage. 'Just a walk in the park.'

When she opened the outer door and moved her scooter forward, the tension was much clearer. Like a predator lurking in the high grass. Another face flitted into view, then backed away. Through her comm set, she heard Hamoud say, 'Major, the device is powered up and in the green.'

'Pass it through. I'm moving onto the beach.'

She and the shuttle both had cameras and comm-links turned permanently on and linked to the *Invictus*. Amanda had thought it might feel strange, being monitored constantly, especially after having operated on her own for so long. But she found she did not mind. The *Invictus* could not effectively respond, not even in the case of urgent need. Once her shuttle had been released, Barrat had resumed station well beyond the planetary system. Radio communication required a ninety-three-minute delay. Amanda lifted the scooter as high as the lab's roof and scouted the island. 'I detect no movement.'

Nasim said, 'Heat signatures are all inside the lab.' A pause, then, 'Now this is very interesting.'

Hamoud asked, 'What?'

'All the scientists show a marked decrease in temperature. Seven, no, eight degrees off human-normal.'

Amanda silently amended, *If they are still human at all.*

Hamoud said, 'The probe and device are cycling out.'

'Hold them by the ramp's base,' Amanda said.

'Roger that.'

Amanda inspected the empty beach and thought, *Come on. I don't have all day.*

Twenty minutes later, the chief scientist and his deputy appeared in the lab building's doorway. The pair offered Amanda a cheery wave and started over. As if they had not kept her waiting. As if nothing had changed.

Hamoud said, 'It is as you predicted, Major. They both have become visibly altered.'

Amanda said, 'Nasim, begin the scan.'

'Roger that.' There was a pause, then, 'Scanning.'

Amanda glanced behind her. The probe hovered at the base of the shuttle's ramp, about a hand's breadth above the pink sand. Rising from the probe was a squat device encased in blue-gray plaststeel. A trio of arms rose at the ten, twelve, and two o'clock positions, all ending in glassy eyes. The device was a hospital-grade medical scanner, one designed for battlefield clinics. Which meant it possessed the capability to perform basically any preliminary health check and minor surgical procedure. And do so fast. The scanners could be ordered to perform a rough scan from a distance, such as swiftly checking an incoming platoon for poisons. The chief medic on the *Invictus* had repeatedly warned that doing what Amanda intended – checking for genetic changes from a distance of a dozen paces – was bound to result in errors. But Amanda was not after perfection. She merely wanted another page in the mission's final report. Just in case it had to be completed without her.

As the pair walked the shore towards her, Hamoud said, 'The pink pigmentation of their skin is definitely heightened. And it's spread to their hair and eyes.'

Amanda thought it looked like a combination of sunburn and a bleach job. Ying showed the most marked difference, contrasted against her black hair and eyes. Or, rather, they had previously been dark. Ying's hair was now ribbed in pink, bright as candy floss. Her eyes were tinted, and the irises had paled to an almost uniform rose.

Sayer smiled and said in greeting, 'So sorry to keep you waiting. We were completing a vital experiment.'

Amanda did not respond.

Ying demanded, 'What is the machine behind you?'

Amanda did not speak.

Sayer said, 'We have some good news, don't we, Doctor Ying?'

Ying asked, 'Is that a scanning device?'

Sayer said, 'We have managed to convince the Lorians that it is important for us to make a full off-planet presentation of our findings. The ban against leaving Loria has been lifted. All the issues you demanded answers to can now be discussed. At least, they can be once we arrive back.' He clapped his hands in theatrical glee. 'Isn't that wonderful?'

Ying asked, 'What is a hospital scanner doing here?'

Sayer seemed incapable of hearing his deputy. 'I can't tell you how delighted and excited Ying and I are. We can leave whenever you are ready—'

'You and all the other scientists must first submit to a full scan,' Amanda said. 'By full, I mean right down to the molecular level. We need to ensure that you carry no Lorian infections.'

Sayer's smile became even more forced. 'The planet has no bacteria, remember?'

'Or viruses,' Ling added. 'Or nanovirus.'

Sayer said, 'There hasn't been a single case of any infection in all the time—'

'We both know that's not what I'm talking about,' Amanda said.

As if to punctuate her remarks, the machine behind her gave off a loud ping.

Ying demanded, 'Are you scanning us now? Without our permission?'

'The scan is complete. That signal was to confirm the results have been processed and uploaded to the mothership.'

Both scientists lost their smile. 'That is *strictly* forbidden,' Ying said.

Amanda pointed at the pink clouds overhead. 'So we are perfectly clear, a full squadron of fighters are monitoring my life signs.'

Sayer's features flowed like wax. There was no anger. In fact, there was no emotion at all. Amanda found it almost refreshing to observe an honest expression. Sayer said, 'You don't think they will be destroyed as well?'

'They are holding position well outside the planetary system,' Amanda replied. 'But still close enough for their weapons to do serious damage. By serious, I mean erasing this planet's atmosphere and quite possibly evaporating the seas.'

'We will catch any incoming fire,' Ying snapped.

Amanda nodded. *We.* The word supplied the final confirmation that she had come for. 'You can certainly try. But these weapons are backed up by a military vessel further outside the system. Your planet's surface will most likely face total destruction.'

When they remained silent, Amanda said, 'Bring me the Diplomat.'

SIXTY-TWO

The suns crept upwards until they were directly overhead. Even so, Amanda had the sense of waiting through a twilight hour. An epoch was coming to an unexpected close, at least for Loria. The jarring note was so intense that not even the light of twin suns could erase the dark malevolence. Amanda thought she fully understood the hush now. The power to read her actual thoughts might elude them. Perhaps this was the core element behind the term 'Separate One.' But at some deep level, beyond human bone and sinew, they knew. The sense of being surrounded by a brooding rage denied all other possibilities.

Nasim said, 'The scientists are returning.'

The Lorian appeared through the underbrush, followed by Sayer and Ying. Amanda found it mildly curious how the scientists had taken on the Lorian's expressionless demeanor, while the Diplomat frowned as it approached.

Behind the trio, hundreds of Lorians slipped through the underbrush towards her. Thousands. Amanda started to ask why the island's entire population was necessary for this conversation, then decided it really didn't matter.

The Diplomat gave another of those distinctly human gestures, a subtle wave of one hand, halting the scientists. It continued to approach Amanda until it stood less than an arm's length away. 'How did you know?'

She liked that: the direct question, the removal of small, fragmented truths. 'Remember what I said about the Prime Directives of my species?'

The Diplomat nodded. 'The quest for answers.'

Amanda liked that too: the *quest*. 'We ask questions, we seek hidden truths, and we record our findings. Three hundred years ago, a survey vessel charted your world. Or, rather, it tried to. But there was no land mass on Loria. Not one island, not even at the poles. And the records described a planetary ocean full of dragons. Beasts as large as the survey vessel. Bigger.'

The Diplomat's slow nod was perhaps its most human-like gesture of all. 'We worried about that ship. We see now it was a mistake to let it leave.'

'If that ship had vanished, others would have followed,' Amanda replied. 'Is there really a "we" at all?'

The Lorian smiled. 'That question reminds us of the first leader of the human community.'

'Professor Darin,' Amanda said.

'He glimpsed portions of the truth. In his case, what he realized was why he had to be transitioned to the trees.' The Diplomat waved at the island's northern shore, where the gray mosslike growth hung from the tree limbs. 'We liked him. It was Darin who gave us hope that your species might be joined with us.'

Amanda kept talking, mostly because she wanted to ensure her analysis was part of the planetary records. 'The planet itself is alive, isn't it? You are merely appendages. And temporary ones at that.'

The Lorian shook its head. 'You humans with your millisecond existences, you dare call us temporary?'

'You did not realize there were other worlds to colonize until the Omani survey vessel arrived.'

'We suspected. So many suns, there had to be planets. The ship was merely confirmation.'

'So you set up islands and a land-based population as a lure,' Amanda went on.

'And it worked.'

'The Prime Directives didn't exist until the scientists arrived,' Amanda said.

'Of course they existed. They define the reality of every life form.'

'But they *weren't* defined,' Amanda insisted. 'They didn't need to be until you allowed the scientists to establish their colony. You spent years studying. Analyzing. Gradually you designed a structure that would draw them into the form required.'

The Lorian did not respond.

'You used these Prime Directives as a means of winnowing out the ones who could not be drawn into your fold. Who would not accept your invasion.'

The Lorian remained silent.

'The Gathering,' Amanda said. 'That is the culmination.'

The Lorian's face became as blank and wax-like as the scientists.

'For you, Gatherings are times of rejoining to your parent. For the humans, it was their time to be transformed into seed pods.'

The Lorian became not just still but featureless. No more separate from the island as the sand upon which it stood.

'You were going to send them out to populate other planets. Wake up other worlds. Turn them into living beings. Just like you.' Amanda leaned closer. 'I'm here to tell you this is not happening.'

The response, when it came, did not emerge from the Diplomat. At least, not in any singular fashion. Perhaps all the Lorians spoke. Or perhaps it was the island. 'You think you can imprison us? We are seven hundred million years old. We will outlive your race and its feeble memory. We have learned, and we will learn more. And the time will come when we transit out in all directions. And populate the universe with our kind.'

SIXTY-THREE

Amanda did not realize the toll it had taken until she started up the ramp. The slight incline almost defeated her.

As soon as the interior airlock door opened, Hamoud and Nasim were there to support her. Together they stripped off her suit and settled her into the co-pilot's chair. Hamoud retracted the ramp and lifted the shuttle from the planet, while Nasim fed her tea, then soup, then more tea. As they rose through the atmosphere, Amanda watched the island diminish below her. The change was not merely because of their acceleration into the sky.

The island was being dissolved.

It had served its purpose.

By the time they reached the lower clouds, the sea was empty. Placid. Blank.

Amanda held her breath as they passed through the pink froth. But the planet allowed them to depart.

They entered space, where the two suns remained bound together by ribbons of light.

As Hamoud accelerated away, Amanda said, 'I want to go home.'